P9-CMT-837

GUILTY PLEASURES

GUILTY PLEASURES

A Lina Townend Mystery

Judith Cutler

This first world edition published 2011
in Great Britain and in the USA by
SEVERN HOUSE PUBLISHERS LTD of
9–15 High Street, Sutton, Surrey, England, SM1 1DF.
Trade paperback edition first published
in Great Britain and the USA 2011 by
SEVERN HOUSE PUBLISHERS LTD

British Library Cataloguing in Publication Data

Cutler, Judith.
  Guilty pleasures. – (A Lina Townend mystery)
  1. Townend, Lina (Fictitious character)–Fiction.
  2. Antique dealers–Fiction. 3. Aristocracy (Social
  class)–Fiction. 4. Theft–Fiction. 5. Detective and
  mystery stories.
  I. Title II. Series
  823.9'2-dc22

ISBN-13: 978-0-7278-8048-2 (cased)
ISBN-13: 978-1-84751-362-5 (trade paper)

All Severn House titles are printed on acid-free paper.

Severn House Publishers support The Forest Stewardship Council [FSC],
the leading international forest certification organisation. All our
titles that are printed on Greenpeace-approved FSC-certified paper carry
the FSC logo.

MIX
Paper from
responsible sources
FSC
www.fsc.org   FSC® C018575

Typeset by Palimpsest Book Production Ltd.,
Falkirk, Stirlingshire, Scotland.
Printed and bound in Great Britain by
MPG Books Ltd., Bodmin, Cornwall.

For Vanya Cheney, with thanks for all her encouragement, not to mention the title. Thanks too to the real vicars, churchwardens and congregations in my life: may their fêtes always be profitable.

ONE

A hot and sticky afternoon toiling at another village's church fête is not my idea of pleasure. But when my old friend Robin Levitt, the vicar, phoned me to beg for my help, it was hard to say no.

'The couple who promised to take charge of the second-hand book stall both managed to pull muscles playing tennis yesterday afternoon.' He sighed down the phone. 'Fast and furious, they said. Oh dear, why aren't they keen on something dangerous, like white-water rafting?'

Why indeed? Except there wasn't too much opportunity for that in Kent.

'Sounds more furious than fast to me,' I said. 'What do I need to do?' I asked, admitting defeat without so much as a skirmish.

'Just stand behind ranks and ranks of tatty paperbacks and flog them to punters. You can do bulk discounts if you want – the former organist likes to buy a dozen crime at a time, preferably hard-boiled. Eighty-five and on a Zimmer. But she likes her blood and gore. And someone in the choir snaps up bodice-rippers quicker than you can unzip a . . . Sorry, Lina, not an appropriate image for a man of the cloth.'

His Adam's apple would be in mid-bobble.

'Don't mind me,' I said. 'Unzip whatever simile you want.' I was proud of that word. My education had been pretty well zero, in formal terms, but then Griff, my dear friend and better-than-a-grandfather, came into my life and rescued me from – well, everything that lies in wait for a young girl going wild on the streets. He not only gave me a roof over my head, he also taught me all he knew about antiques, and, most important of all, he loved me and let me love him. He also tried to make up what I'd missed when I'd skived off school. Similes and metaphors were just part of the latest stage of my education – simply because they existed, I suppose. Like onomatopoeia. I do love words like that, even if I can't always remember them, or, of course, what they mean.

God knows how I'd manage on a bookstall.

Robin embarked on a garbled apology. For one whose sermons were nice and short and clear – not that I heard many of them, most of my Sundays being taken up with antiques fairs – he was terribly prone to getting tangled up in everyday speech. 'The thing is, it's special – a matter of life and death, if you can say a building lives, though it can certainly be killed. And it might be a total waste of effort, but I have to try.'

'What time do you want me to turn up?' I asked, cutting across the knot, like some Greek hero Griff once told me about. I needed to know because Griff had a lunch date in London with an old friend and I would have to get cover in our shop. Mary Walker was always happy to work extra shifts, provided her shiny new fiancé could sit with her and tap away on his laptop. He was a retired accountant turned practising poet.

Robin was still apologetic. 'If I could get someone to set up the stall for you . . .'

'The best way for me to get to know what I've got is to lay everything out myself. Very well,' I mused as I jotted a note to myself, 'so it's pretty much an all-day affair.'

Perhaps I shouldn't have used that noun. Robin once had a bit of a thing for me. I might have had a bit of a thing for him as well, if it hadn't been for two other things: the damned Adam's apple, and, more important, his calling. Some of any antique dealer's life involves buying cheap and selling dear, and while Griff and I are proud of our reputation for absolute honesty about the provenance and integrity of our stock, there are one or two things I wouldn't want people to know about. People such as policemen and clergymen, who have to keep a closer eye than the average person on what Griff calls laws temporal and laws spiritual.

He swallowed. I heard the glug down the phone. 'We've got a Celebrity opening the fête at two,' he managed, 'so everything has to be set up by then. There are several hundred books in the vestry already, and people may bring more . . .'

'Excellent,' I said briskly. It was either that or swear in a way neither he nor Griff would approve of. 'I'd better be there by eleven, then. Oh, Robin – just one thing! Which church?'

Robin juggled at least five churches, maybe six, and it would never do to turn up at the wrong one. I knew St Mary's, and St Peter and St Paul's (yes, the two saints have to share the one building) because both churches were pretty well down the road from where my father lived, but he named one I'd never heard of, St Jude's, in Kenninge, an outpost right in the south of his benefice.

'Maybe you'd better bring a few sarnies because the tea ladies are very strict about not selling anything before the fête starts. And by then I hope you'll be too rushed off your feet to eat. The good news is there's a loo in what used to be the parson's stables,' he added. 'A bit basic, but a loo.'

You see what I mean about Robin being honest.

Since Griff was keener on Robin than on any of the other men I'd been linked with, he rubbed his hands with glee when I told him how I'd be spending my Saturday. 'The weather forecast's excellent. You should wear that delicious little straw hat that sets off your cheekbones so well. I'll bake a couple of cakes for those dragons of tea ladies – and you could take some of those books we got landed with at the last auction,' he added, with a bit more self-interest.

I could indeed. We'd wanted an immaculate calf-bound set of Fanny Burney for a collector friend of Griff's, and we'd had to buy eight cardboard boxes of tat to get it. I'd been meaning to take the rest of the books to my favourite charity shop, Oxfam, but maybe there'd be something the organist would fancy. Any leftovers could always go to Oxfam anyway.

When I turned up mid-morning on Saturday, I found that my stall was sheltered from any wind and most of the sun by a truly revolting Victorian family tomb, standing maybe ten foot high and draped with grumpy-looking angels. It blocked my view of what seemed to be a very old church indeed, the roof line sagging in the middle and one of the walls way out of true. There was no time to take a closer look now, however. I'd got to sort out all the boxes of books, both Griff's donation and those Robin had promised, which had been dumped beside the trestle tables. No one seemed particularly pleased to see me, and smiles only cracked faces when I produced Griff's gateaux for the cake team. Maybe it was something to do with the fact I'd used our van, with Tripp and Townend blazoned all over it. Perhaps they thought I was there to scavenge, not to give my most precious commodity, time.

On the other hand, there was an interesting-looking bric-a brac stall. And already a couple of familiar figures were sneaking up to it. Our instructions had been delivered with military clarity by a short woman clearly born to command, despite a mouthful of the worst teeth I'd ever seen. We were to sell nothing to anyone for any reason till we'd been Declared Open. The gentle-faced woman in charge of the bric-a-brac – far too much for one person to manage, spread over acres of tables – fluttered her beautifully manicured hands anxiously in a rather feeble protest. Minnie Fielding and Mel, who didn't, as far as I knew, have another name, were bottom-of-the-pond dealers who would make mincemeat of her and snaffle up anything worth having for no more than a couple of bob. And then they'd sidle up to people like Griff and me and try to flog it for as much as if it had impeccable provenance. Good luck to them – but not on my watch.

I sauntered over and simply slotted in behind the stallholder, folding my arms. Maybe I was born to command too – I might ask my disreputable father if we'd got any military glory in our genes. Mel and Minnie did a double take. Last time we'd met I'd told them where to put their identical fake Gallé vases, all four of them. And here I was guarding their prey. 'It's not two yet,' I said.

Mumbling that they had to be somewhere else by then, they hunched away from me and fixed my new companion with beseeching eyes. 'That little lady – I'll give you a quid,' Mel whispered, pointing at a filthy Worcester figure which, even with that damaged finger, might fetch £25 at a fair. Incidentally, if I restored her, she'd fetch a lot more.

'It's not two o'clock yet,' I said again, as much to my companion as to them. 'And the churchwarden will kill if we let anything go before then. If you want this lady – and she's worth twenty of anyone's money – you'll just have to be late for your next appointment, won't you?'

They agreed it would be better not to be, and sloped off.

'If they come back, get someone to call me,' I told the bemused stallholder. 'I'm Lina, by the way.'

'As in Lena Horne?'

'Yes, but spelt with an I.'

'And I'm Marjorie.'

We exchanged a friendly smile. She was probably in her sixties, but trim and with just enough colour in her hair.

'Those two,' I added, 'Minnie and Mel – I wouldn't trust them as far as I could throw them.'

'But not if no one else wants the stuff?'

I nearly said something foolish, like, 'I'll buy anything worth having myself and tell you what really ought to go to the tip, so it won't clog you up next year.' Nearly. Not quite. Griff would have killed me. *I* would have killed me. 'Look, how are you pricing this lot? It's mostly tat, and dirty tat too.' I picked up a plastic cruet set with mustard still encrusted on it. 'But some things are worth a bit. Why don't I put things on different tables: twenty pounds, fifteen, ten, five? Then the rest you can sell to anyone mug enough to offer you a quid – or even just take it off your hands.' That was by far the largest proportion. 'And if you're in any doubt, just ask me.'

Ten to two. Thanks to that precious loo, which turned out, though basic, to have a washbasin and plenty of floor space, I washed, brushed up and changed into a pretty retro dress with a fitted bodice and full skirt. I'd picked it up for a song, but it made me feel like a million dollars, and the blue went particularly well with the sun hat Griff had insisted I take. Actually, since I was in the shade, and I thought it made me look like someone from a nursery rhyme, I gave up on the hat and popped it safely in the van, remembering to set the alarm.

And here at last was our Celebrity, apparently a soap actor, but since soaps were one thing Griff would never let us watch I was none the wiser. There were a few tentative screams from a gaggle of girls who probably wouldn't buy anything, and a flutter of applause. His speech, delivered in a mockney accent, was well-nigh inaudible. More applause, and time to sell.

Not buy, of course. Well, to be frank I had already liberated a couple of the books from the cardboard boxes, not because they were valuable but because I wanted to read them. And I'd paid full whack, telling the garden-produce man what I was doing and making him witness the money I was putting into the tin. A tin! So naive! I should have brought a bumbag, so I could stow cash safely and keep an eye on roving hands. Actually, I needed an assistant. Who could I ask? I didn't know a soul, of course. There was no sign of Robin. Perhaps he was escorting the Celeb around. I was surprised I hadn't seen him earlier, to be honest, but then vicars had lots of things other than fêtes to worry about, especially when this fête was in the fierce hands of the woman I was thinking of as the Commandant. But they were capable hands, too. She'd spotted my difficulties and was over in an instant.

'Backup on its way!' she barked, trying to hide her jungle of teeth behind thin lips. Why had the NHS, so good at dental work, let her down so badly?

I nearly saluted, but limited myself to giving my friendliest smile and thanking her.

She was back in two minutes with two reliable-looking middle-aged men. Actually, Celeb and Robin apart, all the men ranged from middle-aged to what Griff insists is merely mature, as did the women. 'They can take over here. Marjorie's sending up distress flares! You're needed over on bric-a-brac.'

I really didn't want to be on bric-a-brac. It was too much of a busman's holiday. On the other hand, something was calling me from that direction. Quite loudly.

For some reason I'd been born what some of my mates call a divvy. Like a diviner finding water in a desert, I can scent from afar a precious item that no one else has noticed. It's a physical summons. You'd think it was a priceless gift, but in fact it's a two-edged sword. It never functions when I want it to. Just when it happens to call.

And it happened to call from a stall where I'd touched every single item without getting so much as a whisper.

Because a whole mass of people seethed round the tables, I managed to ignore the call for a good twenty minutes or so. I beat up the price on a couple of things that punters had probably picked up and then abandoned in the wrong section, and ruthlessly slashed a price I'd slapped on an item before I saw the crack that was now obvious to me, if not to the buyer. Seeing the mountain of rubbish still remaining, I grabbed a piece of card and a marker from Marjorie's basket and scrawled: *50P FOR ANY 2 ITEMS – THIS TABLE!* And yes, I did check there was nothing of value on the table before I put it in place. I even tried to move the table slightly to one side to avoid confusion. What was stopping the back legs? Stooping to have a look, I found some empty boxes and a couple of full ones.

'It's stuff I didn't have room for,' Marjorie explained. 'And Fiona says some of it's from Colonel Bridger, too,' she added in the reverent tone country people seem to keep for people who they think are their betters. I knew my father and never used it. Now wasn't the time to ask about this colonel, though, because she was off again. 'So I've got to put it out, although as far as I can see it's worse than the rest of your fifty pence table.'

My heart would have sunk, but for one thing. My divvy voice shouted, like on the old TV game-show, *open the boxes!*

'I can hold the fort while you sort it out,' Marjorie said.

So I had to.

As she'd said, there was nothing remotely promising to be seen. Some fellow dealers made a living out of kitchenalia, but even they'd have been hard put to wangle more than a quid from the first box I opened. The next box really should have gone to my original stall. It contained half a dozen really old Georgette Heyer paperbacks still in pristine condition, so I thought if no one else wanted them I'd buy them for Griff, who read Heyer in bed if he fancied he had the 'flu.

There was also a bigger book – folio size – pretty well falling apart, with the front cover and frontispiece missing. But surely it was more important than everything on the bric-a-brac tables put together, full of designs for chairs and so on, eighteenth century by the look of them. I didn't think they were by Adam, but they were that sort of period. A scholar would have pounced on the book, even though the back cover looked as if mice had been at it, and all the pages were badly foxed. Not knowing any scholars, I thought of English Heritage or the National Trust, or a couple of major libraries. So I had to buy it. No one else would, and it would be a sin to send it to landfill, the threat hanging over all the other unsold books in too poor a state to wish on Oxfam. But I'd no idea how much I should put into that tin. If only Robin was around.

I tried to explain the situation to Marjorie, but she only gave me half an ear. 'Just take the thing, do, my dear. Give me a pound if it would make you feel better. Is there anything else down there?'

If my instinct was anything to go by, there certainly was. Old hairbrushes and combs thick with hair and dandruff; chipped saucers, none matching; a tiny box, tarnished to within an inch of its life, with an embossed lid. It was too filthy for me to read the hallmark. Was that what was calling? Oh, yes. Though I'd no idea why. But there was something else too. My hand hovered. Over a screw of paper a couple of inches long. I opened it carefully, squeaked with delight, and turned it upside down. There! Crossed swords. Of course, other makers used crossed swords too, but this felt like quality Meissen. I knew where I was with this, at least.

'Look, Marjorie – isn't it lovely?'

'Pretty little thing – a parrot, is it?'

'Yup. Not just any parrot. A miniature Meissen parrot. Look, I could sell this for – let me think – about a hundred and twenty pounds, maybe more. And the box . . . Who knows? I'll pay you a hundred and fifty pounds for both. And if I make any more, which I may well, I promise to give it to Robin direct. Does that sound fair?'

'It sounds admirable to me, Lina,' said a voice. Robin at last.

'Let me write an IOU. And the same for this book of patterns.'

'Lina, you gave your word. That's enough for me. And I'm sure for Marjorie too.'

I shook my head. 'Griff's dinned it into me I must keep records – not just for your benefit but for mine.' I grabbed another of Marjorie's cards and wrote, signing and dating my bargain. 'Your signature too, please, Robin.'

He signed with a sudden flourish, laughing as he recounted Josephine Public's attempts to get the Celeb's autograph. For some reason he'd steadfastly refused to put pen to anything, even for money.

I didn't join in the general derision. Perhaps like me he was embarrassed by his handwriting; certainly, he hadn't had hours of patient help to improve it, as I had done.

As Robin put down the pen, a hand appeared from nowhere and grabbed the silver box.

TWO

R obin might look saintly, but he'd once been an amateur boxer. He'd also done time, as he put it, as a curate in a rough northern parish where the very few people who were in his congregation were more likely to take money off the collection plate than put it in. So his reflexes were good.

But the box disappeared before he could even cry out. The box, the hand, and, almost, the man attached to both. Younger than Mel, as far as I could see.

My reflexes weren't bad, although I'd learnt my skills at a far less orthodox school of fighting than Robin's. And I was pretty quick on my feet. So, vaulting over the table, I gave chase. Yelling 'Stop, thief!' might have been a good idea, if I'd had breath to spare, but at least Marjorie managed it – thin, squeaky, but a yell all the same. I was almost on the guy when someone got the wrong idea and shoved a foot under not the thief's legs but my mine. I went down. My skirt went up. And that was the end of my chase, not to mention my dignity.

'Don't worry about me! Get that bastard,' I shouted, forgetting where I was.

After a vital second's hesitation, Robin accelerated past me and had almost caught up with Lightfingers when a small object hurtled on to a gravestone. It took Robin's eye off his target for a vital second, and the thief was over the churchyard wall and into the adjoining woodland.

By now I was on my feet, hands and knees smarting with gravel-rash. All the same, I was mobile enough to make for whatever the thief had dropped. It was the poor box, now battered as well as tarnished. The impact had burst it open and strained the hinge holding the lid to the body. It came apart in my hands.

It seemed that first-aid to silver, in pieces or not, was not Robin's main concern. He didn't know whether to identify and rebuke whoever had tripped me, or to minister to my injuries. As for me, there was such a commotion amongst the stallholders and the visitors that I was afraid of more thefts, so I caught the Commandant's eye.

'First-aid box in loo,' she barked. Then, turning to the others, she declared, 'Nothing to worry about, good people. Plenty of tea in the pot. Loads of raffle tickets left. Let's do fête!'

A woman after my own heart.

The gravel rash was much less serious than that I'd had most weeks when I was a kid, but for some reason hurt much more. I must have forgotten how to fall. The main victim was the poor dress, and I spent more time swishing cold water on the bloodstains than on the whole of my own treatment.

There was a hammering on the door. My disappearance must have alarmed someone, or perhaps all those elderly bladders were panicking. Calling that I was fine and wouldn't be a minute, I tidied the place up a bit. And stowed the snuffbox where no one could get at it – thank goodness for the full skirt, which covered any giveaway bulge.

Sympathetic hands reached for me as I emerged, and I submitted to being guided to the refreshment tent, where I was loaded with tea and cakes. But I'm not really one to be coddled and fussed over by strangers, so I took the cup and plate back to the bric-a-brac stall, ready to return to work.

'Come on, folk,' I called. 'If it's worth nicking, it's worth buying. Let's see your money now! Roll up, roll up.' Sounded convincing.

Maybe it was my curiosity value that brought people flocking round. Whatever it was, we sold about five times as much as we had before, people pressing notes into our hands and not asking for change.

One person who I didn't see, however, was Robin. What had happened to him?

At last the surge died down. Nothing eluded the eye of the Commandant.

'Only another fifteen minutes to go before we can shut up shop. Did well there,' she said. 'Patched yourself up all right?'

I nodded, afraid she'd demand to see the dressings. 'Any idea where Robin might be?'

'Saw him at the apple-bobbing. Or maybe at the Chuck a Sponge. The far side of the church.'

Assuring her I could find him myself, I pottered off. There was a lot of splashing and laughter, but no Robin.

Before I could explore further, the Commandant called me over. 'Crisis on the bookstall!'

It was the organist, wanting to know whether Edward Marston and Amy Myers could be considered hard-boiled. I told her cheerily I'd no idea but that I liked the jackets, so she added them to her pile.

The funny thing about fêtes is you never get time to look at what should be the focus of the whole event, the church itself. At last, all the remaining bric-a-brac and books were repacked. Apart from those heading for Oxfam, some boxes were destined for the tip; others were going back in store in someone's barn so their contents could have another dreary outing next year. Why? If no one wanted the stuff now, why would they want it when it was a year older and smelt even mustier?

At last I could emerge from the shadow of the tomb – which, come to think of it, might have been the title of one of the books the organist had bought – and have a look round.

Whatever other skills the congregation had, flower arranging must have been up there with the best. The wooden-walled porch was so full of early sweet peas and roses that you could hardly smell the dry rot. Inside, other flowers glowed from the base of each squat pillar, each deeply recessed window sill. The font, huge and solid, quite out of proportion in the tiny nave, was surrounded by carnations. Exotic flowers I couldn't name cascaded from the altar. There was even a little posy on the end of each pew. The thought hit me quite uninvited: if ever I got married, I'd like it to be in a church like this.

I sat down on one of the choir stalls out of sight to ponder. Not so much about finding a man I might love enough to marry, but about leaving the man to whom I owed everything – Griff. It would be unbearable for us both. Worse than Emma trying to leave poor Mr Woodhouse, in that novel neither of us liked very much. At least there was no Mr Knightley to trouble Griff and me just at the moment, and although there'd

been a couple of Frank Churchills – far worse than Frank
Churchill, to be honest – my heart had been no more than
dented. Rather like that box, except I'd never been unhinged;
at least, not since Griff had taken me into his life. How about
that for a simile? – no, I mean a metaphor. When you get things
like that right, after all the things I've got wrong in my life,
you can't help smiling, so I gave God a thank you smile – I
was in His house after all, and liked to be polite, most of the
time, at least.

And I gave Him another smile when I discovered what
I'd been sitting on. Not just any old choir stall, but a
misericord, one of those seats that tips up to support the
chorister's bum if he has to sing during a long service.
Underneath the plain seat you'll often find carving, which
there was here. In turn, I found a fat man, a long-faced
woman who looked as if she'd got toothache, and what
looked like a Green Man. Maybe it was the evil-looking
imp next to him that made my retro necklace snap, the beads
cascading all over the floor, parts of which were so dark I
had to find them by touch. I hope I said nothing too offensive,
but I couldn't guarantee it.

'And what might you be doing, miss?' a voice demanded.

Scrabbling to my feet, I found myself eyeball to eyeball
with the Commandant and her teeth, set in snarling mode.
'Gathering up these,' I said, showing her a handful. 'What a
time and place for the string to give way.'

'Hmph,' she said, not pleasantly.

I almost asked when kneeling in a church had become a
crime. But she looked as tired as Griff after a busy fair, so I
simply smiled and fell into step with her as she headed for
the door. Actually, to be honest, I didn't fall into step. I was
herded, wasn't I? Anyway, someone called her, so I had another
dawdle, this time by some impressive memorials – not because
I could read the Latin, but because I wanted to make a point.

I was just leaving the church when Robin ran up the path.
To my amazement he was wearing his church gear – the white
nightie over the black skirt.

'Hoped I'd catch you,' he gasped, 'before you left.'

'Where've you been?' I asked stupidly.

'Nearly forgot a wedding at Brayham,' he said. 'Dear Lord, that was a close call. Anyway, what did the police say?' He collapsed into a handy pew.

I joined him. 'What police?'

'The police after the thief. I called them. That was when I remembered the wedding. Thank goodness the bride was even later than I was.'

I made a little rewinding gesture. 'Did you actually dial nine nine nine?'

'No. Someone with a mobile said he was doing it and why didn't I just scoot. What's the matter?'

I was twitching the end of my nose. Why had someone said he'd phone, which meant no one else would, and then obviously not done so?

'All these flowers giving you hay fever?'

'Just smelling a rat,' I said. 'But that's me. I smell them even when someone's gone to all this trouble to keep out the smell of damp. And isn't that dry rot in that funny little porch?'

'Our fault, not the original builder's,' he said quickly. 'Oak withstands most things, but not a blocked drain. As for damp, yes, we're missing some slates.'

'Will the money you raised today pay for everything?' I asked, just managing not to squeak in disbelief.

'Hardly. It's like the little Dutch boy and his thumb in the dyke, I suppose. We just stick in more thumbs.'

'Let's hope no one pulls his out, then – though he may get a plum, I suppose. OK, so how do we raise enough to do a proper job? I suppose you haven't got a handy millionaire or two in the congregation?'

'I wish. But then, would we want to accept tainted money?'

'Tainted?'

'Think of the rich man and the camel trying to get through the eye of a needle.'

'I thought you said that that was a reference to some narrow gate or other,' I said, referring to an explanation he'd given me months back.

He grinned. 'True. But think about it. How can anyone be a millionaire without exploiting someone?'

I could see him muscling up for a good philosophical

argument, so I nipped in with another question. 'OK, what about ordinary people?'

'There's a joke going round us clergy. The Archdeacon phones to say there's good news: there's plenty of money to repair the roof, or whatever. The bad news is it's still in people's pockets.'

'Ah. And are there enough pockets?'

'Not a chance. On a good day I get twenty souls, on a bad ten. Most are retired: the young aren't exactly leading a lemming rush to eight o'clock Communion. In terms of cash, it'd be cheaper to buy a minibus and ferry them to one of the other churches than to pay the heating and lighting. Not to mention the maintenance work.'

'But surely something as old as this must be listed?'

'Oh, yes. I think all churches may be, actually. And this one is special. So special I'm surprised – shocked – that English Heritage isn't prepared to help. Well, the cuts, Lina – everyone's having to tighten their belts, as they say.'

'Yours is on the tightest notch already. And those misericords are pretty important, aren't they?'

'Oh, yes.' He sighed, then buried his face in his hands. Although he wasn't on his knees, I thought he might be praying and didn't want to interrupt, so I sat quietly and looked about me. I was a sucker for lost causes. Was there anything I could do?

When he emerged from his silence, I asked bluntly, 'Have you any valuables to sell? The church, not you.'

'You'd have to talk to the churchwarden. Fiona. She'll know. She's wonderful – no parish priest should be without a Fiona, preferably a Fiona for each church.'

Fiona must be the Commandant. No need for him to know we hadn't entirely hit it off.

After a pale smile, he added, 'You know they've tacked another church on to the benefice? Eight altogether now.'

'All the extra services?' I squeaked. 'Not to mention extra parish work? You need a trade union,' I declared, getting to my feet. 'Come on, it's a lovely evening. Let's find a pub and I'll shout you a shandy and you can tell me who was supposed to have called the police. Hell! That's my van alarm!' Elbowing him aside, I sprinted out into the sun.

Whoever had tried to get into the van had presumably been put off by the noise, though not necessarily the one that the people restoring the churchyard to its usual state heard. We'd had our system tweaked, just a little, so in addition to the usual racket there was another, probably illegal noise, just out of the range of adult hearing. It came courtesy of one of Griff's shadowy friends, and I approved of it heartily – see, I'm *not* fit to be associated with an agent of whatever law you choose – and it was there to deter the odd enterprising youngster who thought he'd nick something to sell for his next fix, or just smash up anything handy. Until his ears started to hurt a very great deal. As mine were hurting now, though Griff's wouldn't even have picked up the evil sound.

When the alarm stopped and I could venture closer, I could see that there were a couple of marks on the back doors, from a jemmy by the look of it, but the defences were still intact. At this point I withdrew and covered my ears. I knew what was going to happen. Just when it seemed to have settled down, the alarm became very, very loud again. That was part of its charm. From a discreet distance I zapped the van and silenced the system. Presumably whoever had tried to break in had taken the same exit route as the guy who'd been after my silver box earlier, over the fence and into the woods. In jeans and trainers I'd have been in there chasing him. But not in this dress and these sandals.

I turned back. Robin had stripped down to civvies again, bundling his working gear over his arm. He still sported his dog collar, though, and it seemed wrong to let him go off to do my dirty work chasing after Crowbar Man dressed like that.

I managed a rueful smile. 'No harm done. That's what we have the alarm for, to put people off. And maybe the guy who promised to call the fuzz was just too busy.'

Shaking his head, he frowned. 'Two attempts at theft in one fête is two too many.'

'Do you remember who you asked?'

'I didn't ask. He offered. And I don't think I knew him. But the fête was well advertised – there was a really good piece on local radio – and I didn't know quite a number of the visitors.' The frown deepened. 'Does it mean we've not just got two attempted thefts, we've got two would-be thieves?'

There was no point in lying to Robin. 'Or maybe a thief and an accomplice?'

'You'd have thought one of us would have noticed someone trying to break into your van,' he mused. 'Why did no one say anything? Look, I'll have a word with Fiona.'

'She's as knackered as you are. Tell you what, do you have a parish mag that carries photos of events like this?'

'Yes. I think I saw Brian with his nice new digital jobbie.'

'When you've a moment, ask him to keep everything. He may have got a snap of the guy trying to lift that box. Or jemmy the van. Just by accident, when he was taking something else.'

He looked around. 'He's gone. But I'll email him.'

I put a hand on his arm and smiled. 'Can you hear that? It's the Rose and Crown calling, saying it's got a pint of best bitter with your name on it.'

He cocked his head: he could certainly hear something calling, but it turned out to be his phone. He took the call at once, his face changing from a nice bloke after a drink to a serious, concerned professional.

'That was the hospice. I'm afraid Mrs Garbett needs me. I'll see you soon, Lina – OK?' He managed a quick peck on my cheek and was gone.

THREE

Since Griff wouldn't be back till late, I called my father to say I'd drop in on the way home. With the impressive name of Lord Elham, he lived at the equally impressive address of Bossingham Hall. If you approached via the front it was *very* impressive indeed – a lovely Palladian house, perfectly symmetrical. However, my father had been relegated to just one wing, which he sometimes loudly resented. Since the trustees who now owned the place let him live rent free, I didn't think he had much to grumble about.

'I suppose you haven't brought any more bubbly?' he greeted me, flourishing a fresh bottle of champagne. He'd probably drunk his way through another during the course of the day.

It had taken me ages to realize I couldn't stop him being an alcoholic, but these days I supplemented his diet of Pot Noodles with home cooking and fresh fruit and vegetables and insisted he got through at least four cups of green tea a day. At least, he did when I was there to brew them, which wasn't as often as he thought it should be.

'I told you, I've been to a church fête.'

'But they have bottle stalls and tombola and raffles – you might have won something.'

I was quite taken aback. 'So they do. And I didn't buy a single ticket! Drat!'

'You'd probably have wasted your money anyway.'

'But that's the whole point of church fêtes – losing your money for a good cause.' He plainly didn't follow the concept, so I patted the bottle. 'I shall have to buy you some. Is there anything else you're short of?' I drifted us both into the kitchen to see what he needed.

The shopping list was getting quite long, which showed how much his diet had improved – who'd have thought of my father mentioning fruit, let alone eating it? – when he said,

'We'll need something to pay for all this with, won't we? Are you going to do your divvy act?'

'Tell you what, we'll have a cup of tea and I'll see what I can find. Divvy or no divvy.' Actually, I'd have killed for a glass of champagne, but I was driving. So green tea it was, on the grounds that it was good for him. He didn't like it, but didn't moan too much so long as it was jasmine-flavoured. Pity I hadn't managed to lay my hands on one of the fête's gorgeous cakes, or had the sense to keep back one of Griff's. Of course, he had donated them to the fête, not to my father.

Any other daughter might have asked her father what he'd been up to, but the answer would be either watching daytime TV, which I wasn't really qualified to talk about, or working for Titus Oates, which I certainly didn't want to discuss. Titus was a sort of mate of mine, though Griff disliked him intensely. But it's one thing having friends on the shady side of the law, and quite another to know your father is a master forger. So I told him about my day – not that he showed much interest in what I was up to until I mentioned Robin Levitt.

'That Bible-basher? Drops in to see me from time to time, but only brings bottom-end cava? Oh, he's a decent sort, but he's not good enough for my precious daughter, whatever that old queer of yours thinks. Griff. Sorry.'

I regarded him over the rim of the tea cup. How on earth did he think that the bastard daughter of a promiscuous lord – a lord, moreover, who'd been so careless in the matter of contraception that the *precious daughter* had thirty brothers and sisters out there, all equally illegitimate – might be a marital asset? But somewhere in that booze-dimmed brain was enough cunning to have got me out of at least one serious scrape.

To change the subject I told him about the attempted theft, which drew a tut of sympathy from him, as he appeared to notice my plasters and bandages for the first time. I even dug in my pocket where I'd transferred the little snuffbox and showed it to him.

What was my father doing looking knowledgeable? Snuffboxes weren't his line at all. Were they?

All he said, though, was, 'Pretty little thing. Will you be able to mend it?'

Good question. I'd made a bit of a name for Tripp and Townend with my restoration work, but that was china and occasionally glass. 'I've never tried fixing silver,' I admitted. 'And after that business with the Hungarian dish, I've not managed to get very fond of it.'

'Hmm. You've always struck me as being capable of doing anything you turned your mind to,' he said, surprising me. Then he returned to his priority. 'Anyway, I'm sure you'll find something to sell.' He removed the cup and saucer from my grasp. 'Come on. There's a new quiz show starting in twenty minutes, and I wouldn't want us to miss it.' Delete the *us* and you'll get his meaning. And perhaps *go on* would have been more accurate than *come on*.

Although my father had very little to do all day, illegal activities apart, he didn't think of filling the hours tidying or cleaning his wing of the house, though I have to admit that these days I no longer feared a visit to his kitchen might cause instant food-poisoning. Perhaps he was right to confine himself to polishing the sink and swabbing the tiles. All the other rooms were crammed with a weird assortment of objects. Some would have made a Sotheby's auctioneer reach sweaty-palmed for his gavel, some I'd have consigned to the tip as happily as I'd have disposed of this afternoon's leavings. It wasn't hard to tell one from another. In the rooms I hadn't already reorganized for him, it was more a question of reaching what I wanted without causing an avalanche of assorted plates, books and pictures, many, despite my efforts, still stacked willy-nilly on top of each other.

What I liked to do was stand in one of the corridors, or on a flight of stairs, and wait to be called. If my father was in a hurry, I'd just have to barge into a room at random and pick something. Then I'd clean whatever it was, sell it, taking ten per cent, and use the proceeds to buy him food, clothes or whatever. Champagne, mostly, though in the past I'd organized a fridge-freezer, a washing machine and tumble dryer. I kept a very strict account of what I'd taken and how much it had made. I even made him initial the transaction, just in case a half-brother or sister ever turned up claiming what they hoped was a fat inheritance and alleging I'd robbed him. Sometimes, like when

I held a rather poor oil painting of a family group like the one I was looking at now, I rather hoped a sibling would turn up. A sister would be nice, since there were plenty of assorted men in my life.

But enough of that.

The oil painting was far too primitive to attract a collector. I should imagine it was the result of one of my female ancestors finding some genteel occupation. Perhaps it ought to be back in the main part of the Hall, but it would give my father apoplexy if I suggested it. Maybe I could smuggle it in one day. I knew a couple of unauthorized entry-points and could easily slip through while my father was glued to the TV.

Meanwhile, I must hunt for something else. What about that pile of plates under a hideous split plastic planter? Four of them. Oh, ho! This might be my lucky day with birds. First the Meissen, and now what I was sure were Joseph Crawhall plates. Each had a bird with foliage on the front. And – yes – the reverse of each plate had a thumbnail head and shoulders self-portrait and was signed and dated. A set like that should keep my father in champagne for a while and would allow me to pop some in the emergency account we'd set up for him during one of our occasional forays together into Canterbury. I stowed them carefully in the planter, which I could bin at home.

By now he was well into his new programme, accusing it of being rubbish – who was I to argue? – and waving a casual hand in farewell. But then he actually got to his feet and zapped the TV. 'Nice evening. See you out,' he said. I was so surprised I nearly dropped the planter.

He made it as far as the top of his steps, which were nowhere near as grand as the approach to the house itself, but imposing enough in their way. Then he thought there might be some cricket on Five – not that he liked it, but he hated Griff to outscore him on sport, which was easy, seeing that we had Sky and there was nowhere to pop a dish on his part of this Grade One listed pile. Not officially. I was sure he'd find a place for one soon, however. We waved each other a casual goodbye, no more, and I set off.

It really was a nice evening, still warm with some low-flying birds scaring me half to death as they dived in front of the van. What if Robin had finished with his hospice call and fancied some company? I pulled over and reached for my mobile. But knowing him, even if his parishioner had died, he'd stay with the family until he thought he'd done all he could to ease their grief.

In any case, by now Griff would be waiting for me. I put the van into gear and set off.

'Sweet child, what on earth have you been up to?' On his return, much later than either of us had expected, Griff greeted me with horror.

I'd changed from the pretty dress – which had responded well to a gentle hand-washing and was now on the washing line – into shorts and T-shirt.

'Your legs! Your poor hands!'

'Not as bad as they look, I promise. I just took a bit of a tumble on some gravel. I'll tell you all about it when I've made you some tea. And when you've told me your news.'

'Not tea at this time of night. The caffeine . . . Something nice and cold and very alcoholic in the garden, so we can watch the swallows. My news,' he added dramatically, casting his panama hat on to the sofa, 'is that Miles has turned teetotal! Can you believe it? And he'd got it into the cotton-wool ball that passes in his case for a brain that we were to spend the afternoon shopping for a new outfit for him. It seems he's decided to make an honest woman of that vile Caro. And nothing more than tea to sustain us through a trawl of department stores, since he's too mean to go to Savile Row and Jermyn Street. Not too mean to buy a huge vulgar car, however, or to pay through the nose for parking. Not to mention the congestion charge. Remind me to send him something truly revolting for his wedding gift.'

'He and Caro must have everything by now, surely,' I said. 'So why not think out of the box, as they say, and buy him something quite different? A couple of goats, for instance. No. A loo! For somewhere in Africa, of course.'

His face changed from disbelief to amusement. 'A loo . . . A communal loo . . . Point me to the website, my sweet. But only when we've had our drink. A pitcher of Pimm's, I should think . . .' He caught my eye. 'Very well, just a glass. But make it nice and strong, loved one.'

We ate our supper in the garden, and at last I showed Griff my acquisitions. 'I need proper valuations so that I can put anything I owe into the church fund,' I said.

'Whatever happened to buy cheap, sell dear?'

I blinked. Griff had always dinned into me that one didn't diddle friends. I put the parrot into his hands first. On the other hand, he was always inclined be tetchy if he thought my father had seen something before he did.

He pulled a face. 'It's charming, but you'll need to find a collector to get back what you paid. Or a bird lover. Ah, this is what you suffered for, poor little thing.' He could have been referring to me or the snuffbox. A look at his face said he didn't think much of it, though he ran his finger carefully over the lid.

'Hard to tell – is this embossed work a hunting scene? But if you only paid a few pounds, even if you make a loss, it won't break us. And somehow I don't think, as your face suggests you fear, that you've mislaid your divvy gift. Both of these items will repay investigation, and I'm sure that Mrs Walker will know just the customer to take that parrot off your hands. A thirty-pound mark up would be fine. Yes, an extra thirty pounds for Robin, if you insist. As for this little box, let us go on the principle that if someone wants it enough to steal it, it must be worth having. A little homework is called for, isn't it?' He topped up my glass. 'You said you'd shown the snuffbox to your father. You didn't show him the folio? I thought not. And I think I can guess the reason. You're afraid it's one of his forgeries, aren't you?' He took my hand, shaking it gently. 'My dear one, your father specializes in single pages, or pamphlets at most.'

'Exactly. Just the sort of thing he'd copy!' I blurted. 'Tear pages out of a book like this and ruin it – not that there's much to ruin here, I admit – and then punt forgeries about the place via Titus.'

'Quite. I know you keep your ears resolutely shut when

there's gossip concerning the discovery of a rare item everyone assumed was lost, but that's what he does. He sees it as a little part-time job.' He added with a teasing smile, 'He's happy enough to talk about it to me when you go off on one of your divvying expeditions, leaving us alone to while away the hours.'

I nodded. My father would probably have filled me in on every last forged full-stop. It was just that I didn't want to know. I'm not sure why. 'He knew something about the snuffbox,' I whispered. 'He didn't say anything, though.'

'He was probably afraid you'd snap his head off. But there's no harm in your asking him, I'm sure. Any more than there is in asking him about this folio, though he's no expert on furniture.' He flicked through the smelly pages. 'Not Chippendale or Sheraton, I'd have thought – the lines aren't good enough, are they? Heavens, look at this strange Chinaman, with his moustache coming from the side of his nostrils. You know, I've a feeling I've seen some of this man's work . . . No, it's gone. As for the box, I'll pick a few brains and read a few books. I suspect the Internet is more your thing.'

It was. And to think I hadn't been able to switch on a computer, let alone use one, when I met Griff.

The last ray of sun left the garden. It would never do for Griff to catch cold, so I gathered the china and glasses on to the Victorian papier mâché tray.

'I only have one regret about giving up smoking,' he murmured, slapping his arm. 'A cigarette deals so efficiently with the little blighters who do so ruin a late evening garden. Come on, dear one, before they nibble your dear flesh into horrid red weals. The customers would be too worried about you to buy.'

'So they would,' I laughed, tucking my arm in his. 'Folkestone tomorrow, and I've not even packed our crates . . .'

FOUR

Titus Oates is one of the most invisible people I've ever met. He looks so ordinary that no one'd ever be able to do an e-fit of him, or pick him out at an ID parade. He's also so law-abiding – never drinks and drives, never passes a speed camera without smiling innocently at it, pays all his debts on time, would die on the spot if asked to fence stolen goods – that you'd never think that about a tenth of his dealings are on the iffy side of dodgy, as he puts it. The vast majority are squeaky clean, of course. Which is how he gets away with . . . whatever scam he happens to be involved in at the time, some of which involve my father's skills.

The Sunday fair at the Grand Hotel in Folkestone was one of his – and our – regular events. This particular Sunday the sunshine of the previous day had been replaced by lashing winds and driving rain.

'Anyone with any sense would have stayed in with the supplements,' Titus muttered as he slipped past clutching a paper cup of coffee, just like half the frozen punters, who no doubt assumed that June and warm sunny days were syn . . . synon . . . Drat. The word had gone. It meant *just the same thing*. Although there were some regulars – including a woman who'd got a wonderful deal from a rival stall on a piece of Staffordshire creamware I'd had my eye on – most of those trudging round wore holiday gear, showing more naked flesh than they'd have dreamed of doing in their own places. At least, I hoped so. All those men as old as Griff wearing their bellies over the top of half-mast knee-length trousers, hairy legs and huge trainers or flip-flops . . .

'Know anything about my father and the frontispiece to a volume of Georgian furniture patterns?' I asked. Titus preferred the direct approach.

'And would I tell you if I did? Old guy's entitled to a bit of privacy.'

'But?'

'Nothing I know about. And not very collectable, I'd have thought.'

'Unless you happen to be an expert on furniture.'

'I'll keep an ear open.' He drifted away. But half an hour later, when I was heading for the ladies' loo, he continued, as if without a break, 'Who's the cabinet maker?'

'No idea. No clues, not that I know of.'

I didn't tell Griff about either of the conversations – if that was what they were.

There was a guy in one corner, just past the stall selling postcards and travel memorabilia, who had a few bits and pieces of silver, so when I had a quiet moment I drifted over. There was a very pretty Edwardian tea caddy, coming in at £500, and a lot of spoons, none of which did anything for me at all, presumably because I hadn't been born with one in my mouth. Most of the other items were in the two to three hundred range – a couple of mugs and a few snuffboxes. Naturally, they were all in much better condition than the one I'd bought, which might of course be better off sold as scrap, the way precious metal prices were these days. But I hated to destroy anything someone had gone to a lot of trouble to make, and which someone had then used. I'd not managed to clean it, what with our late supper and early start for the fair.

I flicked a smile at the dealer, whom I'd not seen here before, or at any other fairs in the area, but he did not return it. The caddy was perfect, but I wasn't so sure about a sauce boat. The surface patina round a funny little engraved bird looked a tiny bit different from the rest. One thing I did know about silverware was that sometimes items were changed – not necessarily recently – to make them more saleable. So I picked it up and breathed hard on it. Oh, dear. There were the solder lines where the bird had been let in after something else, probably a crest, had been removed.

Maybe the dealer knew, but had gone ahead with the rather high price anyway. In that case, his wasn't a brain I wanted to pick. If he didn't know, there wasn't much point in trying to pick it, was there?

The next stall belonged to a dear old friend, Josie, who was

now as bent as a question mark. But her eyes were as bright
was ever, and her welcome as warm. She grabbed my wrists
so she could inspect my sore palms. 'Lucky you didn't break
anything, falling like that. And then where would you have
been? Couldn't have done your restoring then, my love.'

I had an idea that breaking your wrists in a fall was something more likely to happen when you were Josie's age, but
didn't want to upset her by arguing.

'How did you get on in Hastings yesterday?' she continued.
'Were you so busy you couldn't wave to an old duck like me?
Mind you, with a young fellow like that in tow, perhaps you
didn't even see me.'

'If I didn't wave, it was because I didn't see you. And it
wasn't a young fellow I was with – it was a whole churchyard
full of people, miles from Hastings.'

She looked sceptical, so I explained in a little more detail.

It was clear she still wasn't convinced. Perhaps her eyes
weren't as good as they once were. No point in arguing about
that, either. I admired a couple of pieces on her stand, only
to have her press them on me. 'Go on, chick. These earrings
would set off your eyes beautifully, and the necklace goes with
them like cream on a scone. And I'd rather give them to you
than have some other dealer flog them at twice their value.
Yes, this is absolutely my last fair, Lina. I'm selling up. Lock,
stock and barrel. You and Griff stay back after the others have
gone, will you? So you can pick out anything for your
business. I know you'll give me a fair price. But these
you must and shall have, just for yourself.' She reached up
and kissed me. 'So long as you remember to wave next time
you see me.'

Griff stared at me in horror. 'Josie's an institution! She can't
be retiring!'

I nodded. 'She's been threatening to ever since I've known
her. But I really think she means it. And I'm wondering – there
must be other folk here who'd like to give her a decent
send-off.'

'You make it sound like a funeral, sweet one. But you're
right. I believe the hotel could provide sandwiches and

champagne. If you organize that, I'll see to the guests. A discreet little promenade between stalls, of course . . .'

And not just between stalls either. I actually saw Griff speaking to Titus. I was so amazed that I almost gave the guy asking the price of a Chamberlain's Worcester plate the trade price, not the retail one. Neither Griff nor Titus would have been amused. I might have had difficulty seeing the funny side myself, come to think of it.

Soon after three, however, I was grinning like a Cheshire cat. We'd risked putting the Meissen parrot out, and had given it quite a high price to perch on, too. And someone swooped down and bought it, without a quibble. Seemed his daughter liked miniatures.

I smiled. 'Miniature vases too? Look at these gorgeous Worcester ones with bird paintings on the sides . . .'

Our card terminal had a few very happy moments.

It was, as Griff said, in his apparently spontaneous farewell speech to Josie, the end of an era. I knew how long it had taken him to write it, and how many backs of envelopes, but I wasn't about to snitch. Half of the room was in tears, the other half in tears of laughter. The champagne flowed, the dealers fell on the sandwiches and cupcakes – those had been my idea, but they looked a lot better than they tasted – as if they'd fasted for weeks. There were hugs all round.

Tripp and Townend had done Josie proud. The only thing that spoilt it for me was Josie's last plea to me: 'Next time you see me, just remember to wave. That's all I ask, lovie.'

The words niggled as I loaded the van, and niggled as I pulled on to the rectory forecourt – heavens, was the use of weed killer against the Ten Commandments? – to give Robin the cheque for the difference between what I'd paid for the Meissen and what I'd got for it. I'd expected Griff to argue about stopping off en route, but, as my father had observed, he had a soft spot for Robin . . . and was also keen on using the rectory loo.

Robin accepted the cheque with pleasure and offered us a cup of coffee. I accepted on Griff's behalf and drifted into the kitchen after him, only to have him try to shoo me out. No

wonder he was embarrassed to find me in such a tip. When
had he last washed up, for goodness' sake? And why would he
need to wash up when there was a dishwasher there?

'Because I haven't had time to empty the dishwasher, that's
why,' he said, his voice grainy with tiredness.

'OK. I'll empty it and pass all the stuff to you and you can
put it away without it ever having to touch – yuk – these work
surfaces. And then we'll load up and we'll wash anything that
we can't cram in. Heavens, Robin, you're as bad as my father.
Actually, that's an insult to my father. He keeps his kitchen
pretty clean these days.'

As we worked, I said, 'I thought young vicars were supposed
to be fighting off all the ladies in the parish; at least, they
were in those Barbara Pym novels that Griff read to me.'

'They were probably curates. And the ladies in my parish
don't ride bikes to eight o'clock Communion, remember,
they drive past the church – all the churches! – in four-by-
fours and drop the kids off at school early so they can whizz
off to their part-time but highly lucrative jobs.'

'I see. So they're not desperate to feed you and so on.'

'Especially the so on.'

'That's a great shame, if so on includes emptying the kitchen
bin and the sink tidy. It means you'll just have to do them
yourself.' I shooed him out and set to work refilling the
dishwasher.

'You treat him very cavalierly, angel heart,' Griff declared,
wandering in. 'Ah. I see why. Where does he keep his tea
towels?'

How I got talked into going with Robin to a concert in the
Cathedral the following evening, I've no idea. Griff's doing,
I suspect. Anyway, it was agreed we'd meet in Canterbury.

Griff would have preferred me to go in by train, since for
some unknown reason he didn't like the idea of my driving
round on my own after dusk, but I pointed out that the last
train left Canterbury for Bredeham at 9.35 p.m., and I'd be
properly stuck if the orchestra gave an encore. In fact, it was a
good job I had my own transport, because I found that we
were seated amongst some church dignitaries and their wives,

and that somehow Robin and I were absorbed into their after concert drink and nibbles do in the crypt.

Not my scene at all. But I wasn't the only nervous one. Seeing Robin's Adam's apple training for the Olympics, I couldn't back out and leave him to it.

Mostly people were talking about the concert, which left me in pretty scary territory. Griff and I often listened to music together, so I could tell my Verdi from my Vivaldi. But I was always bemused by the Cathedral's echo, not knowing which part of the orchestra to listen to first, and this was a piece I'd never heard before and couldn't make head or tail of. I really couldn't have said anything intelligent – except about the hardness of the seats. No wonder some people had brought their own cushions.

I stuck to Robin like glue, assuming he'd introduce me to people.

People swirled about us, everyone apparently knowing everyone else. Willy-nilly, a woman with a profile like a horse grabbed Robin by the arm and marched him off, leaving me eyeball to eyeball with a sleek middle-aged guy in a black roll-neck, probably cashmere. Clearly one of us ought to say something. I could have asked him what had brought him here, the opening gambit Griff said never failed. Since he was one of the few men there not sporting a dog collar, it might have worked. But he stared at me with something like horror, as if he really, really did not want to be anywhere near me, and turned so sharply that he jostled the canapés clean off a waiter's tray.

In less august company I might have yelled, 'Pardon me for living, I'm sure!' with a few extra words added, to make sure he knew I was offended. As it was, stranded, I felt a horrible wobble of the lower lip. What had I done to deserve that?

To cover my embarrassment, I bent to help the poor scrabbling waiter, but only made things worse, of course, so I surfaced sharply, almost colliding with an elderly guy with a rather well-filled lilac shirt.

I could try Griff's gambit on him, though he was clearly a clergyman. But he'd grasped some at least of the situation, and passed me a napkin to wipe my tapenade-covered fingers. And he spirited some more champagne from nowhere.

I ought to say something, apart, of course, from, 'Thank you,' which I gabbled several times.

Inspiration!

'It must be so hard,' I ventured, recalling that the crypt also housed the Treasury and its contents, 'to balance the vital maintenance of your lovely churches, and the need to preserve historical artefacts like those locked away down here.' That didn't sound too bad, did it?

Actually it did. It sounded as if I was preparing to interview him for the *Today* radio programme.

On the other hand, I got results. I might have fired a starting pistol. He poured out all the things I'd heard from Robin about small congregations and huge bills and the number of churches in benefices, plus a few more, including words like faculty and non-stipendiary. Finally, with an apologetic smile, he said, 'But I've talked enough shop—'

I really didn't want to talk about me, so I came in with a swift, 'And how does this affect you and your role?'

Bingo!

His eyebrow asked if I really wanted to know, but he responded, prompted, I think, by the fact that I threw in a question about poor St Jude's.

'Truly, absolutely enough shop!' he declared at last. 'Now, what's your connection with that wonderful old church?' he asked, with the sort of smile that made him seem really interested. Perhaps he was. And it was certainly something the first man was interested in. Very interested. Cashmere Roll-Neck had sidled up to us as if desperate to catch every last syllabub. Hell, that was a dessert Griff made. Very rich. I'd banned it. Syllabus? Syllable!

'None. Not really. I just helped with the fête on Saturday. And I thought – such a lovely building—'

'It's very good of you to be helping out, my dear, if you have no connection with the church.'

I was afraid an explanation might land Robin in some sort of ecclesiastical sh— But I probably shouldn't even think that word, not in the Cathedral.

'A friend asked me,' I said, not even looking in Robin's direction. Or in Cashmere Roll-Neck's. He was practically perched on Rev Lilac Shirt's arm. 'Just books and bric-a-brac.'

'Just two of the dirtiest jobs, bless you. Ah! I think His Grace is going to speak.'

'The Archbishop! Not the Archbishop of Canterbury! In person!' Miming a big beard, Griff, who'd stayed up to make sure I got home in one piece, sat down heavily and reached for his glass of whisky.

'Yes. Really nice guy. Twinkly eyes. He gave a short speech – very short, just a couple of sentences. Then he said hello to a load of us, no more than that – because he'd told us he had to get home. I couldn't work that bit out. Not a big deal, surely, a walk across the grass?'

'Ah, but the Archbishop of Canterbury lives in Lambeth Palace, sweet one. Lambeth as in London.'

'So why's he called the Archbishop of Canterbury, not the Archbishop of Lambeth?'

He embarked on a more detailed explanation than I needed right now. What I really needed was time to think about some questions I didn't actually want to ask myself. Josie said she'd waved to me in Hastings, when I wasn't there. This evening I'd given someone I didn't know the shock of his life. Did I have a double?

Or had one of my half-sisters surfaced?

If so, how did I feel about that?

FIVE

'Have you spoken to your father about the snuffbox – or indeed the pattern book – yet?' Griff asked over breakfast. The warm weather had returned, and we were in a sunny corner of the garden, the table covered with a jolly check cloth, just as if, Griff said, we were in France. We weren't in France, because there he'd have stuffed his face with croissants and apricot conserve, and his blood tests told him he shouldn't have much of either.

He knew I hadn't seen my father, of course, so I answered a question he hadn't asked. 'I'm worried about cleaning something so fragile.'

'So you've been putting it off. But that was yesterday, when your mind was full of what you should wear for the Cathedral concert. Now it's Tuesday, and you almost have the Archbishop's blessing on your work,' he said teasingly.

I put down my egg spoon with very great care. 'I did not spend yesterday worrying about clothes. You can't worry about clothes when you're trying to reunite a poor little Worcester shepherdess with her milk churn. The Archbishop didn't bless me, or my work. He said, "Good evening," and murmured something about the concert I didn't quite catch because someone else grabbed his attention by stepping between us, and I think he managed a kind smile for Robin. He didn't come out with any controversial comments about women bishops or Sharia law, either. OK?'

'So you're going to tackle it today?' He put down his spoon too, very quietly, in case a sudden movement would push me over into losing my temper good and proper. 'The snuffbox? You really are worried about it, aren't you, dear one? You don't doubt your skill, surely.'

'No, not my skill. I doubt my expertise. Hey, that sounded good, didn't it?' I added, rather taking away the effect.

He took my hand and squeezed it. I squeezed back. We were

friends again. 'Indeed it did. So tell me why. Are we back with your being a divvy? Is it something you sense about it?'

'I told you, it called me. That and the pattern book. Most times I can back up my divviness with nice hard information. Like when I pick out something at Bossingham Hall or at a fair. But not with either of these. I wouldn't ever try to clean the book. And yet I've a funny feeling that the box is even more precious. Not just because someone tried to nick it, either. Whoever it was could only have caught a glimpse of it – not enough to identify it. Just opp . . . opportunistic crime.'

'So one would think. But he must have known something about it to know it was silver.'

'Quite. To an inexperienced eye it would have been just some grubby black lump of metal. But he went for that, and nothing else. Weird, unless he either knew about little boxes in general or—' I pulled up short, because there was no way anyone could have known that box would be there. More slowly, I continued, 'I suppose he could just have wanted something because someone else did. Why didn't he try grabbing one of the items on the twenty pound table? There were things there that would have fetched a lot more if they'd been tarted up and taken to the right sale.'

'So you, who have made such a name for our humble firm as a restorer, don't feel you can restore this?'

'No,' I said flatly. 'I'm afraid of doing harm.'

'Would it hurt to clean just the area by the hallmark?'

'Probably not. Shall we have our coffee first?'

'There are times, my love, when procrastination is your middle name. The longer we leave it, the tenser you'll become – particularly if you're awash with caffeine. We'll have a cup to celebrate afterwards.'

Under the bright lights in the ordered calm of my workroom, we took it in turns to peer at the snuffbox's base through our eyepieces. All I could make out was what might be a very dim crowned leopard's head – London – and a strange shape, which didn't match anything in the table of hallmarks on the office wall.

'Old. Very old.' Griff removed his eyepiece and put it beside mine. 'I don't suppose you recall when the manufacturer's initials replaced identifying devices, do you, angel?' he asked casually.

'Sixteen ninety-seven,' I said promptly.

'For one who claims so little knowledge of silver—'

'I don't mean that sort of knowledge, not the sort you can get from books. I mean the sort of knowledge we both have of china. The feel. No, not just that. You know.'

'I do. Some sixth sense, but one born of knowledge and experience and love. I'm not surprised you're not in love with silver, but we shouldn't let that put you off. Now, as it happens, I think you're right to want to entrust this to a specialist. The only question is, to whom?'

We were silent.

'It might be important enough for a museum,' I said at last, in a small voice. We'd had a very bad experience last time we'd consulted a British Museum expert.

'It might. On the other hand, I have remembered someone in the trade who owes me a favour, quite a big one. Damian Winterbottom. We could ask when he gets back from the States. But I think we might need to go a bit higher in the food chain. You have two police contacts, Lina. And we might talk to either one of them.'

'Or neither,' I said. I meant to be blunt. I sounded rude.

Griff looked taken aback, even hurt.

'Sorry. I didn't mean to snap. Not Morris. Not unless I really, really have no other option.' I stared at the snuffbox. Morris might be in the Met's Fine Art Squad, and an obvious choice, but I didn't think it was wise to contact him out of the blue. He'd asked me never to contact him at home, and had plainly been uncomfortable when he'd met me in other circumstances.

'You still have feelings for him, loved one?'

'More to the point, I think he's still got feelings for me. And he's got a wife and baby and – no. I want you to promise me this, Griff – not to contact him either, not unless I'm in dire trouble and you can't think of another way out of it. For the baby's sake. Promise?'

'I promise. But what about handsome young Will Kinnersley? He's not spoken for.'

Will, Kent police's heritage officer, really was good-looking, and I'd fancied him at one time. He'd fancied me too, but we'd never quite got it together for some reason or another. On the other hand, if ever I was in a fix, he'd be a man I'd turn to. It wasn't just a matter of trusting him. I liked his offbeat approach to things.

'The police seem to have put him in purdah. He's off spreading best practice to all the police forces that don't have a heritage officer. And when he comes back to Maidstone he has his in-tray to deal with. And crimes. And court cases.'

'Which take up all his spare time?'

'What spare time? When he has a weekend free, you and I are off at some fair or other in the back of beyond.'

'You could skip some fairs, my love.'

I shook my head. 'It's my job, isn't it, selling? And I wouldn't expect him to give up the odd investigation just to spend time with me.'

'So you wouldn't. But it seems very sad that two lovely people who obviously like each other . . . On the other hand, you and Robin . . . Very well,' he said, pulling himself up short, probably because he'd seen my expression, 'what shall we do with the snuffbox?'

'Pop it into the safe. In fact, let's pop it into the extra-safe safe, the hidden one.'

His eyes rounded. 'Your vibes must be working overtime if you think it's as precious as that!'

I didn't argue. I just took it up to my bedroom and popped it in the place that only four people knew about: the man who'd installed it, Griff, me – and Morris. It wasn't quite alone. There was something of my father's too precious to lose in there too.

Which left the pattern book to worry about. But not today, because I had a pile of restoration work to do, everything needing a steady hand. So all thoughts of anything else had to be banished, until supper time at least.

'What I'd really like to do,' I told Griff as we finished our prawn risotto, with the last of the season's asparagus seared

and served on top, 'is find out how the snuffbox came to the
fête. Marjorie, the woman in charge of the stall—'

'Till you came along.'

'—mentioned a Colonel Bridger. He might be able to cast
some light on both that and the book.'

'Are you proposing to doorstep him?'

'*Please would you like your snuffbox back*? I don't think
so. But it'd be nice to know if he lives in a house old enough
to have furniture and fittings copied from the book.'

'Robin will know,' Griff said, deadpan.

So might Google. On the other hand, I'd been quite abrupt
with Griff, and it would be nice to make amends.

'I'd better contact him, hadn't I? At least I can trust him to
keep his mouth shut.'

'Indeed. The dear old C of E might not go in for confes-
sions, but its parsons must know not to blab. Why not make
the call now, my love, while I bring out our fruit salad. I
suppose I'm not allowed ice cream?'

'Half-fat crème fraiche,' I said.

I texted Robin that I planned to go and visit my father the
following day and wondered if we could meet up there. I'd
take something for lunch, I added. Using my father as a reason
for my journey might keep Robin where I wanted him – more
or less at arm's length. A nice friendly kiss in the car park
after a concert was one thing, sounding as if I was thinking
of seeing him regularly entirely another.

He agreed to meet me at Bossingham Hall at about noon.
So I texted my father – yes, he'd latched on to the idea pretty
quickly, largely because it didn't interrupt his TV-watching,
not to mention any less legal activities.

'We're on,' I told Griff as I filled the kettle for his peppermint
tea. 'And you know what, I might show my father that pattern
book too.'

SIX

At one time my father would rather have swallowed razor blades than anything except his beloved Pot Noodles. Now, however, he rubbed his hands with glee at the prospect of one of Griff's savoury flans. So too did Robin, who also registered the home-made bread and the fresh salad. Griff had thought of sending along a bottle of a very good rosé, which would suit the lovely weather, but we agreed that my father would much rather stick to his usual champagne, which Robin would regard as much more of a treat. I'd let Griff send a cake too, although I'd make sure Robin, thin as a lath, got the lion's share to take back to the rectory.

Robin was so good at conversational nothings that lunch went swimmingly. What a shame he hadn't been able to help me out on Monday evening. Funnily enough, I'd still not got round to asking the name of the guy I'd been talking to, but now wasn't the moment, and in any case, there had been several portly clerics there and I couldn't remember anything that might help identify him. I waited till our green tea, which my father drank more willingly than poor Robin, no doubt dying for a proper caffeine fix, to raise the subject of the fête's goodies.

My father weighed the snuffbox in his hand. 'I thought this looked familiar when you showed it me the other day,' he said slowly. 'And it still does. It used to be shinier here, where you use your thumb to flick it open. Dashed if I can remember whose thumb it was, though, if you get my meaning. Though I suppose there can't be all that many. Filthy habit, taking snuff. Though the stuff people sniff up their nostrils these days is more expensive. Is it true they do it in lavatories? Dear God!' He remembered his company. 'What about you, vicar? I mean, do you recognize it?'

'Absolutely not, sorry. Nor that book of yours, Lina.'

Bracing myself, I produced it. To my huge relief, my father

looked interested, but not cunning. Not immediately, anyway. Not until he'd held it and looked at several of the pages, especially the blank ones at the end. Just what he needed for his handiwork, a few authentically old pieces of paper. Well, he wasn't getting them from this, not if I had anything to do with it.

Seeing my face, he switched to looking interested again. 'I've not seen this before,' he said slowly. 'But I'd bet my last sixpence I know some of the things it illustrates. This design for a door frame and the door knobs and finger thingies and the whatsits – there's a word for everything.'

'Furniture?' I supplied.

'Right. I've seen them all.' Then his face fell. 'But I suppose they're pretty standard. Not exactly Woolworths, but off the shelf. I miss Woolies, you know. All those sweeties. Pick and mix. Not that Lina'd let me eat sweeties. And the funny thing is, I quite like that choc she brings me. Your line, I'd have thought, vicar.'

Robin looked puzzled.

'It's called Divine,' I explained. 'That lovely dark choc. Full of something with a long name that's good for the heart. Can't beat it.'

'Bit rich for me.' He touched the folio. 'So could this be what your father thinks, Lina – a sort of eighteenth-century IKEA catalogue?'

'If it had been, I'm sure Griff would have recognized the designs. Even though he's not a furniture man, he can pick out anything by Adam at a hundred paces. And Hepplewhite and Chippendale. But he doesn't know any of these.'

'Those are all upmarket,' Robin said. 'Even I've heard of them. But there must be some lower down the scale.' You could see him groping for a comparison.

I supplied it. 'The sort of thing the Bennet family would have, not Mr Darcy.'

'The man that went swimming in the lake with his clothes on?' my father asked. 'Stupid thing to do, if you ask me.'

'Actually, that wasn't in the original text,' Robin began.

'But I saw it. On TV.' As if that made it Holy Writ.

This was going nowhere fast.

'I wonder if Colonel Bridger would know anything about it,' I said to Robin. 'Is he the sort of person I could ask?'

'Bridger! You're not talking about old Bugger Bridger?' My father slapped his thigh.

'Are we?' I asked Robin. 'Talking about a man who might be one of my father's acquaintances, that is?'

'Colonel Bridger is the right age and – shall we say – from the right social milieu. He lives near Kenninge. Never comes to church. But he does know Fi Pargetter, of course.'

The Commandant.

'I bet he knows her in the Biblical sense, too, if it's old Bugger Bridger. Liked a bit of bum whether it was male or female,' my father added helpfully. He picked up the TV zapper. He must be getting bored.

'What sort of place does he have?' I asked quickly. 'Something splendid, like Bossingham Hall?'

Purple to the ears, Robin shook his head. 'A rather dark Edwardian pile. Detached, about an acre of ground. But nothing special.'

My phone rang. I'd have switched it to voicemail, but since it was Griff I took the call.

'Evelina,' he began, 'I've got an old friend here who'd like to meet you. I've asked him to supper, so you'd better tell young Will Kinnersley straightaway that you've had to cancel his invitation. I'm terribly sorry, but he'll have to come tomorrow instead.'

'I quite understand,' I said carefully. 'I'll be home as soon as I can be. Tell your guest to hang on.'

He cut the call without saying anything else.

'Someone's got Griff!' I yelled, grabbing my bag and haring out of the room.

My father flapped a hand. 'Aren't you going to hunt for goodies today, Lina?'

Robin twigged, at least. 'Police?'

Diving down the hall, I flung him my keys. 'Drive while I call them.'

He did.

I did what Griff had said. I called Will. He would trust my hunch; someone in a control room almost certainly wouldn't.

He picked up first ring.

'Get your mates out to Bredeham,' I said, just like that. 'Griff's just phoned – coded message. Trouble. I'm on my way there now, but it'll take half an hour.'

'I'm in bloody Abergavenny, Lina.'

'Your mates aren't. And they'll shift faster if you tell them than if someone like me dials nine nine nine.'

Robin drove well, better than I would have done. Faster. Probably more safely. And he might have been multitasking: his lips moved as if he was praying. Or he might just have been cursing the slow-joes who seemed to drop speed every time they approached a double white line, and to accelerate hard when the road was clear.

Griff didn't pick up when I tried to tell him I was coming. I left what I hoped was a careful message on his voicemail. Careful and cheery. Just as if nothing was wrong.

I'd expected to find half a dozen police cars crammed into the village street and the place bristling with armed police officers. Maybe a negotiator trying to get Griff away from a gunman.

'All very quiet here,' Robin observed, 'after your panic. Are you sure you called this one right?'

'I'd have heard from Will if I hadn't. Wouldn't I?' I called Will again as Robin looked for somewhere to park. Actually, there were far more vehicles around the place than there usually were, but all pretty ordinary.

'DCI Webb said she'd deal,' he said. 'So she may have gone for a different approach from blues and twos and razzmatazz. Try parking in your yard: see what happens.'

'Can't. Some bugger in a black Volvo's right across the gates.'

'Well then.'

'But it could be the guy who's got Griff.'

'Give me the registration number . . . One of ours, Lina,' he said, after a pause that seemed to last for ever. 'So approach with care but friendliness.'

Robin's eyebrows danced. 'Interesting turn of phrase, this policeman of yours. Do you want me to come with you? A dog collar works wonders.'

It certainly had an interesting effect on the surly driver playing FreeCell on his phone. 'I thought the old guy was going to be OK,' he gasped, switching off in mid-game.

Going to be? I choked back a sob.

Robin was calmer. 'I hope and pray he is. Can you tell us what's going on?'

'Better leave that to the DCI. There she is.' He pointed down the street.

DCI Freya Webb and I had met when one of her officers had turned out badly, though we'd had nothing to do with each other since. She greeted me with a cautious hug, her flame-coloured hair clashing something shocking with my fuchsia top, but to my amazement responded to Robin's outstretched hand and brilliant smile with a huge and unbecoming blush, with which of course her hair clashed even more.

'Seems Griff activated your alarm system the moment he had a chance. His assailant fled the scene.' It seemed to me she spoke more to Robin than to me; perhaps all police officers, even women, were somehow programmed to look up to men.

'So why didn't he phone to say he was OK?' I asked, scared, angry, resentful – all three and a few more.

'Because he isn't quite OK. He's in pain, but not desperate for death to put an end to it,' she said with a smile, waiting briefly for me to recognize the quotation, which I didn't. 'So I don't think he'll be needing you yet awhile, vicar,' she added, with a strange fluttery smile. Eventually, she tore her eyes from his and said to me, 'He got hit about the head, and there's quite nasty bruising to his arm and hands. He's in A and E in the William Harvey, Ashford. One of our officers is babysitting him until you go and collect him, Lina. Hang on! Before you gallop off, we'd like you to take just a few moments to walk through the property with Mandy Aitken, one of our SOCOs, to see if anything's missing.'

'The shop or the cottage?'

'Cottage. Seems he'd closed the shop for lunch – he insisted we put a little sign on the door apologizing for not opening it this afternoon. Said something about maybe calling Mrs Walker?'

It would take ages to explain to Mrs Walker why we needed her, because she'd ask endless questions. 'It's easier to leave the shop closed,' I said.

'Fair enough. Over here, Mandy! You'll have to dress up too, Lina,' she added, as Mandy produced an outfit like her own.

Last time I'd struggled into one of these suits Will and I had burst into the Snowman song. And I'd had a few very bad moments. Now I might be about to have even worse ones.

Mandy, the Scene of Crime expert, was a short blonde with killer spectacles – the sharply angled sort you see in optician's windows but can't imagine anyone wearing. With her protective suit, the effect was bizarre: a rectangular-eyed polar bear. She'd already put paper markers on the carpet. I didn't need one of her arrows to show me a patch of Griff's blood. Knowing him, his chief concern would be for the carpet itself, a lovely old Wilton, with muted colours and lovely sheen.

'Anything missing?'

'Not as far as I can see.' I pointed to the shards of a Moorcroft vase. 'But someone gave that a tidy whack.'

'Actually, someone used it to give someone else a tidy whack.' Mandy pointed with a gloved finger. 'Look – a bit of hair and skin, and some blood? I'd say Mr Tripp might have used it to repel the intruder. You see, he didn't have the sort of injury that would result in damage like that.'

So the blood wasn't Griff's. I sat down and swallowed hard. 'You'll be able to check our CCTV images,' I croaked at last, hoping Griff wouldn't be charged with assault. You never knew these days. 'Hidden camera.'

She pulled herself upright and stared. 'Where?'

'See that ornate picture frame?'

'Tucked in all those twiddly bits? Wow, that's neat.'

'I'll get you the movie.' Leaving her to it, I went through to the office. The safe gaped, half its contents on the floor. My voice strangled in my throat, just about I managed to call, 'Have you been in here yet?'

'Oh, dear.' She squatted on her haunches beside me. 'Can you tell if anything's missing? No, don't move anything, not unless you have to.'

'Griff wouldn't have opened this if he hadn't been forced to. I just hope he gave the man the combination and let him get on with it.'

'Another camera?'

I managed to smile at her. 'Spot on. Stills, this one. If you don't tell it not to, simply opening the door activates it.' I picked up some of the boxes which lay on the floor, spilling their expensive contents. 'He wasn't your normal thief if he didn't want pearls or diamonds, was he? They're not our usual line, which is Victorian china, but occasionally things come our way, and we keep them for a rainy day.'

'Like when the price of gold rockets?'

'Exactly. The trouble is, in our line, to get full value out of the gold, you have to melt it down. Destroy it completely, just so some bloated fat cat can stow another ingot into his safe deposit.'

'But this guy turned his nose up at your nest egg. Weird. You'd have thought he'd take a few free samples just on the off-chance.'

'Perhaps that was when Griff hit him.'

'No. The blood spatters show that definitely happened in the living room. Perhaps he was after one particular thing. Any idea what it might be?'

'Perhaps he gave up when Griff managed to activate the alarm,' I suggested.

'You're probably right.'

'As you can see, this lot would be safer if it was back in the safe. Can I put it back and lock it up? Then I'll give you the photos, if any. And the CCTV footage.'

'OK. I'd better let the DCI what'd been happening.' So although Mandy might be a very bright woman, she didn't seem to have noticed I'd dodged her question about what the intruder might have wanted.

The moment the last box was back in place and the combination reset, I pointed upwards. 'Shall I check that everything's OK up there? I need the loo, actually.'

I didn't, but I needed time to check that Griff hadn't had to betray the hiding place of an item I thought might have been the real target.

The snuffbox nestled cosily right at the back of the hidden safe.

'All seems fine,' I reported truthfully on my return. 'Now for the mugshot.' The release mechanism for the hidden camera was miniaturized too, and dead fiddly, but I managed it. 'Mind if I have a look, see if I recognize the bastard?' Not a word that Griff would have permitted that early in the day, but I needed to vent a little anger at least.

'Go ahead.'

I pressed Review and peered. 'Too small an image even for me, I'm afraid. But maybe when it's blown up a bit?'

'No problem. What about your security footage?'

'Easy-peasy.' I demonstrated.

'Very good images,' she said, pointing at Griff, cornered, reaching for the vase and then smashing it on the intruder's head.

'Hell – I hope your lot don't think they ought to prosecute him for assault or something!'

'I think the CPS take a more relaxed view of the Englishman trying to defend his castle these days,' she said. 'Was the vase valuable?'

'Valuable but ugly. Probably his subconscious made him choose it.' I watched a little longer. 'That guy – he looks really weird, doesn't he? His body language keeps changing. Actually, his body, more like. When he comes in, he looks ancient. But – here – he's lost his stoop and he looks quite strong and strapping. And his face no longer matches his body, does it?'

'Let's see what our geeks make of it, shall we?'

I handed over the DVD – but made sure I inserted a new one. Just in case. And put a new memory card in the safe camera.

Robin was still waiting patiently in the street when I emerged. 'Lina, I know I should stay with you, but I've got a funeral over at Kenninge in an hour.'

'I'm fine. Don't worry about me. But how are you going to get back? I need to go to Griff, and—'

'That's sorted. I'll take him back,' Freya said, blushing again. 'Blues and twos if necessary. One of my officers will take you over to Ashford, Lina, and—'

'No, thanks, I'd rather drive over myself. Then I can bring him home. Or it might be better to take him to his friend over in Tenterden, out of harm's way. I'll leave details with whoever's looking after him in Ashford, shall I?'

And they were gone, without so much as a backward glance.

So how did I feel about that? I was sure Freya would have a quotation to suit, however.

SEVEN

Griff's partner, Aidan, appears like a sympathetic Cheshire cat whenever Griff has a health crisis. I've learned to put up with it. After all, I have the better part of the bargain – I'm with Griff when he's well and wonderful fun; Aidan gets him when he's frail and tetchy.

So I didn't have too many reservations about phoning Aidan from A and E, and telling him about the assault.

'But your cottage has cameras where other people just have household dust,' he objected. 'However did the assailant gain access?'

'That's just what I'd like to know,' I said grimly, though pleased he'd referred to the cottage as ours, not just Griff's, as he used to do. 'As would the police. I've not had a chance to talk to him yet – he's still in the hands of the medics.'

'But he isn't in danger?' You could actually hear the anxiety in Aidan's voice. I might not like the man, but he's certainly devoted to Griff; he probably tolerated me for much the same reason.

'Absolutely not. At least, that's what they've told me. They're just stitching up a cut over his eyebrow. He's going to look pretty weird for the next few days.' I paused. I knew what was coming, largely because I'd just opened the door to the suggestion.

'Do you suppose a few days in Tenterden might be beneficial?'

Excellent. 'I can't think of anything better, Aidan. Followed by a couple of days with you in London. He deserves a treat. Last time he was there it was in the company of Miles Winterton, and he didn't enjoy it much. Apparently Miles has become teetotal.'

'Has he indeed!'

'And is marrying Caro.' I paused to allow that to sink in. 'He's giving them an African lavatory.'

'What a very appropriate comment, as it were!' He gave
the rich chuckle that I'd once absolutely hated, but which now
made me join in. 'And it was your idea? Of course it was!
My dear Lina, you are so good for him.'

'As you are. I know you won't let him eat or drink too
much, but you'll indulge him in other ways and he'll come
back full of energy to a nice clean cottage. I think it'll take a
specialist cleaner to tackle the carpet.'

'I'll get the firm I use to contact you.'

'Tell you what, Aidan – email me their details and I'll
contact them. You never know,' I added. 'After all, Chummie
knows there's literally blood on the carpet, and pretending to
be a cleaner could be a dodge he might use to try to get in.'

'You are such a credit to him, my dear. Now, you will tell
me how he goes on and when I can expect him?'

'He can tell you himself,' I said, joy at the sight of Griff
emerging into the waiting area making me generous. I passed
over the phone to Griff's more bandaged hand. After all, I
could hold the other.

The van wasn't exactly the sleek Mercedes Aidan would
have conveyed Griff in, but we always kept overnight bags
in the back, just in case we were ever trapped in bad weather
miles from anywhere, and it was, of course, already parked
in the William Harvey car park.

'I want the unedited version of events,' I said as I fastened
the seat belt for him. 'Chapter and verse. I know when you
have a chance to talk properly to Aidan, you'll fillet out all
the worst details so he doesn't worry too much, and I'm never
sure how much you trust the police—'

'A touch more than you do, my child. Particularly,' he added
dryly, 'as they have the benefit of all our security cameras to
check that I'm missing nothing out. But why mention Aidan?
And why are we taking the Tenterden road?'

'Because the chemicals they use to clean blood off carpets
might not be good for you, and because Aidan has invited you
to go up to London with him as soon as you're presentable.
Mind you,' I said, glancing sideways at him and wondering
how long it would take him to suggest I stayed over in

Tenterden too, 'that may be some time. Come on, Griff, what happened?'

He sighed. 'You know our friend X?'

'Yes. Well, of course, I know *of* him.' X was a drifter who irregularly turned up at our cottage first thing in the morning with items for Griff to buy. One glimpse of me and he'd stayed away six months at a stretch, so always I was stuck in my bedroom until he slipped away again, pocketing whatever cash Griff chose to give him. This was nowhere near what we'd sell for, but enough to keep him in cheap cider for a while. Any more and he'd drink himself to death within a week, Griff insisted. 'But it was never him, not in broad daylight, surely?'

'No. But a man who said he was a friend of his, with an urgent message.'

'Did he actually use X's name?'

'No. Now I come to think of it, he didn't. He just said, "Our friend." But you know I've always promised to be there for X if he ever needs me. I thought – if I thought at all, which I may not have done, having just been awoken from a little doze, if the truth be told – that he needed me to stand bail and had sent this man to fetch me.'

'Wouldn't the police have contacted you?'

'I'm sure you're right. I just wasn't thinking straight, as I said. Anyway, as soon as I stepped aside to let him in, I realized there was something wrong with his face.'

'Something wrong?' I had a weird thought of leprosy or something.

'I couldn't put my finger on it at first. By that time he'd hit me, and I'd retaliated with that over-the-top Moorcroft vase Aunt Bea left me. And then he persuaded me that I ought to open the safe. Well, I knew we were insured – I shall be able to replace that Moorcroft with something much more tasteful – and I knew about the camera. But I don't think even that will give us a true image of him. They'll see a poor aged man, balding, stooped.'

'I know. I looked. But then he seemed to get younger before my eyes. And then old again. Do you think the stoop was fake?'

'I think so. And I also suspect that he was wearing a very

good wig and particularly fine make-up. TV or film quality. That good. Might even have been wearing a latex mask or part-mask, I suppose.'

'And wearing gloves, no doubt.'

'Of course. But again, very fine, so I didn't see them through the peephole. And yes, I was alert enough to check, I'm sure of that.'

I slowed into a tail of traffic. There were often long queues on this route, which was far too narrow and winding to deserve to be called an A road. 'So what did you tell the police? Did you mention X? Because surely they'll ask why you let him in.'

'They already have. I said I thought he was an acquaintance from my long-ago theatre days. Cunning, don't you think? Because then I could introduce the idea of make-up, which you may be sure I did.'

'Did he say what he wanted?'

Griff pretended he was dozing.

'He did, didn't he? It was that damned snuffbox, wasn't it?'

'I'm afraid it was,' he said in a small voice.

'And what did you say?' I added, in an even smaller one. After all, it was my fault.

'That if it was valuable, you must have put it in the safe – I hoped that all the goodies in there would distract him. I said my hand was shaking too much to deal with the combination, and that he'd have to do it. Which is how he came to set off the alarm, because I forgot to tell him how to switch it off.' He was trying to divert me, I knew he was. 'So then he decided to make himself scarce. Do you think he'll come back, sweet one?'

If he was wearing make-up as clever as that, we might not recognize him if he did. 'Forewarned is forearmed,' I said brightly. 'And I'll find somewhere else to hide the snuffbox, just in case.'

'Such as where? Lina, my darling, I know what you're thinking – that you could conceal it at Bossingham Hall, and no one would ever find it. But consider the old man. You'd never forgive yourself if he got beaten up.'

It was a bit rich to refer to my father like that, when Griff was at least six years older. But he had a point.

'You're not suggesting I ought to keep it until that bastard comes back with another disguise and then just hand it over without an argument?'

'We don't need it, whatever it is. It's just a piece of metal.' When I said nothing, he sighed. 'Oh, my love, I know you divvied it, and I never doubt your instincts, never. But I just wonder if in this case the game isn't worth the candle. We're not experts or collectors.'

'There must be someone, not just this Damian of yours, who could help. We can't just sit around until he comes back.'

'But—'

'If someone wants it this badly it must have more than intrinsic value,' I said, with a bit of a jut to my jaw, not least because he'd taught me the expression in the first place.

'In that case, you know what we have to do, don't you? My angel, I know you don't want to get in touch with him yourself, but that doesn't stop me doing it. I want to entrust this to Morris.'

'Really, really, no. You promised me, remember! Morris's marriage has got to stick. Got to. Leda deserves a proper father, not an absentee one.' I scratched my head, desperately. 'More to the point, what if it turned out to have dodgy provenance? It'd be a police case before you could blink. That's why I wouldn't ask Will or Freya to help.'

'So you need someone strong with the morality of the police but not absolute subservience to the law—'

'Not Robin. Definitely not. If anyone asked him, he'd blush and give the game away. Besides,' I added, 'I need him to get me access to the guy who donated the book, remember?'

'My poor dim memory informs me that it was the same man who donated the snuffbox. Very well, you don't want to involve Robin as a guardian, but as your muscle. But if you have nothing to guard, what of all your enquiries then? I would click a dismissive thumb and finger if I could, sweet one. In fact, I'm going to put my foot down. That snuffbox has to leave the cottage. Preferably under the eye of the media, so our friend would know there was no point in coming back, but I suppose that's too much to hope.'

I allowed him to think I was too preoccupied with the traffic to respond. For some reason the pace had slowed to about five miles an hour.

'Bruce Farfrae,' Griff said at last. 'Thoroughly and lastingly married. You even chose his silver anniversary present, didn't you? No longer in the police. Fingers in every art pie going.'

'Not his thing, though. Impressionist painting, that's what he knows all about.'

'And other things, I should imagine, since before he went private he was Morris's superior officer at the Met. He's also kindly and avuncular.'

When Griff had taken me over as a young uneducated street urchin, I'd had no education to speak of. He'd dealt with that as best he could, but there were times when he used words I recognized but couldn't place. This one, however, was a stranger.

'*Avuncular?*'

'From the Latin. It originally meant *like a little grandfather,* which was how the Romans described maternal uncles.'

I smiled. 'Like your deputy? If I had an uncle.'

'If indeed I had the honour of being your true grandfather. Now it just means *like an uncle.* Kindly, dispassionate, supportive. And, in Farfrae's case, always happy if you can pick him out another print of the villages in his romantic past.'

'He didn't respond to my last emails,' I grumbled, 'and I really needed an uncle then.'

'He has explained, loved one. When a man is trying to sort out the provenance of middle-eastern art treasures that suddenly surfaced after the Iraq war and the looting of Baghdad's museums, then he can't always fly to your aid. Ah, I see the problem ahead. There's a tractor trying to turn into a field, and it's jammed in the gate. What fun.'

It was quite late in the day when I eventually delivered Griff to Aidan's. Overnight case apart, he kept a selection of clothes and other necessities there, even spare pills. I knew he'd be in good hands, even if he had to wait till he was able to go out before he could eat well. Aidan's eye-wateringly expensive kitchen was wasted on a man who could barely boil an egg. All the same, it was harder than usual to decline Aidan's invitation to stay. My excuse was that I wanted to get home in daylight, something that made no sense at all to me but always seemed to ring bells with them.

'But you could stay till morning,' Griff urged.

Aidan nodded, with courtesy, if not much enthusiasm.

'Tim the Bear would be so upset if I wasn't there at bedtime,' I said firmly, adding, when Griff opened his mouth for one more protest, 'and I haven't got Farfrae's contact details here.'

They couldn't argue with that. In any case, they had a diversion – a couple of plain clothes officers arrived clutching a laptop. Despite all our footage, they wanted to see if Griff could recognize anyone on their database. I left them to it.

EIGHT

Never having had a teddy bear when I was young, I was now the proud possessor of three. Two were very smart indeed, Steiff collectors' bears, complete with buttons in their ears. One looked smug enough to remind me of Aidan, who'd given him to me; the other always looked a bit furtive, possibly because Morris had used him as a sort of farewell and apology mixed.

The third bear, not collectable at all, was far more precious. He was Tim, a present from Griff. Tim had accompanied me on various travels and always gave me sound advice in the middle of the night if I couldn't sleep. It was he who, having suggested I shove our highly-illegal pepper spray in my pocket, joined me at the supper table – we'd got a new takeaway in the village, and although I was sure their speciality, chicken tikka with salad in a huge naan bread, was crammed with cholesterol and other things I wouldn't let Griff anywhere near, it was the best comfort food I knew. I hadn't had any lunch, after all.

Tim insisted I mustn't get any on his fur, but then made it quite clear I'd put off phoning Bruce Farfrae long enough. It was true. Since the Crime Scene team had finished with the cottage, I'd given it a spring-clean. I'd also changed all the towels and sheets, though I couldn't have given a single reason.

Making sure that the security system was active, not to mention having locked up very securely, I headed, with Tim in tow to supervise, to the office. I could have phoned Bruce, but thought an email might be better: it wouldn't disturb him if he had a rare evening with his wife, who apparently stayed at home when he was off on his adventures recovering stolen antiques, and I could sort out exactly what I wanted to say before I said it.

Hi, Bruce
I really need your help.

So far, so good. And then the front doorbell rang, I jumped out of my skin and Tim fell across the mouse and made me accidentally click the SEND button. So much for careful preparation.

Tim thought he'd better stay where he was, face down. Gripping the pepper spray, I headed for the security monitor and toggled it so I could see our guest. At first I didn't make sense of what I saw. Then I focused more clearly and realized I was eyeball to eyeball with a bedroll strapped to a rucksack. There was a tousle of blond hair beyond.

I might have summoned Bruce to the rescue, but I'd got Robin.

With a highly visible sign that he meant to protect, not comfort me. But then, I had Tim for that.

It's one thing sharing a takeaway curry last thing at night – Robin had turned up with that, too, and I found I could tuck in again – but quite another sharing breakfast with someone still crumpled from a night on the living-room floor, which he'd had to leave early not because I'd disturbed him but because the carpet-cleaning expert was ready for action. We caught whiffs of whatever he was using, although we closed the living room and kitchen doors.

Robin had had more of the wine I'd produced than was good for him and was silent to the point of miserable. Hung-over, probably, if I wanted to be less than charitable. I'd been up hours before him and had already sent a follow-up email to Bruce Farfrae, explaining the situation and apologizing for the note of panic in the tru . . . truc . . . truncated one I'd sent by mistake. Thank goodness for spellcheck.

'I want you to introduce me to Bugger Bridger, Robin,' I told him as I tipped grilled bacon, sausages and tomatoes on to his plate. 'Go on, a full English is supposed to be the best remedy for a bad head. Scrambled eggs? Fresh from the farmer who looks after our caravan. And Griff made the bread himself.'

He said nothing. Just tucked in, at first as delicately as if the food would bite him, then with increasing appetite.

When his plate was nothing but a smear of tomato ketchup

and a trace of golden yolk, I said, 'So when do we set out? I can leave the shop in Mrs Walker's hands.'

He shook his head. 'Look, I don't see how we can possibly go and knock at a guy's door and ask how he came into possession of two items and why he wanted to ditch them. Because that's what he did. He got rid of them. Didn't want them any more. Not our job to suggest he shouldn't.'

'You've got this wrong. It's not saying he should have kept them. It's finding the best place for them to go if he's really happy to be rid of them.'

'I still don't like it. It feels as if we're being nosy. Nannying him.'

'If I don't go with you I can always take my father,' I murmured, topping up his eighteenth-century coffee can.

Bugger Bridger's house was very disappointing. The Edwardian architect hadn't considered that the countryside usually had different houses from middle-class suburbs, and this had an air of simply being plonked on to the available space and having been embarrassed by its surroundings ever since. Lurking behind a high beech hedge, it turned up its nose at the farm buildings behind it, the other side of a straggle of privet and some chain link.

A large man with a brick-red face appeared in response to my tug on a long cast iron bell-pull. He looked over my shoulder, registering the van, Robin's poor old car and Robin himself. 'I was expecting you.' His salt and pepper moustache and eyebrows quivered, but not exactly with pleasure.

Whatever greeting I'd anticipated, it wasn't that. Then it dawned on me. 'My father's been round, has he, Colonel Bridger?'

'No idea why. Just said to expect a visit.'

Why had my father gone to the trouble of summoning a taxi – and the state of Bossingham Hall's approach track was such that some taxi firms had blacklisted him – and missing valuable viewing or forging time, just to visit a neighbour he'd ignored for years? And not say why I was coming? Perhaps he'd thought that Robin would chicken out of accompanying me, and that my virtue was in peril.

The more I proved I was a woman who could deal with most things, the more he appeared to think of me as his little girl. Since he'd scarcely seen me for more than a dozen hours when I was a child, I found this very strange. But I was also irritatingly touched that he might want to stop Bugger Bridger trying out his preferences on me.

'I suppose you'd better come in,' he said eventually, as if it was the last thing in the world he wanted.

'Thank you,' I said brightly, though I hung back for Robin.

Bridger opened the door a centimetre wider. 'You too, vicar, though I haven't a clue what you're here for – the fête was last week, and I gave Fi some stuff for you.'

Robin set his Adam's apple in motion. 'It was about the stuff you gave Fi that Ms Townend is here.'

'Townend? What sort of a name is that for Elham's daughter?' He glared first at Robin, then at me, as though we were equally to blame. But he stepped into the tiled hall – Minton, by the look of them, and all perfect. Perfectly clean, too, with a strong smell of beeswax polish battling it out with what was probably Flash. One of my foster mothers had been pretty well hooked on the stuff, so much so that I'd come across one of her other foster children scrubbing herself in the bath with it, in the belief – I shuddered to remember it – it would make her white. White as these walls, which had no pictures or anything else to mar their whiteness.

'I took my mother's name,' I said quietly, adding, because I didn't want to wash the dirty family linen in public, 'for business reasons. And it's because of my work as an antiques dealer that I'm here.'

'I'm not selling anything. If I'd known you were one of that crew I wouldn't even have opened the door to you, father or no father.'

'Quite right,' I countered. 'There are people out there you really must not trust. But I've come about two items you gave away – to Fi, to sell at the fête. A very old book, and a snuffbox.' I patted the bag they were travelling in.

'Old book? I like things to look the part. This is my idea of books.' He flung open a stained oak door, polished to the same degree of brilliance as all the other doors in the hall, and, I'm quite sure, in the whole house. 'That's my library.'

The floor, as immaculate as the doors, had a rectangle of what looked like an Afghan rug in the middle, a small oval table in the dead centre. Around the walls were perfectly matched shelves, interrupted in their flow only by the window and the deep-green velvet curtains. And on the perfectly matched shelves were perfectly matched books. All came in the livery of some upmarket book club – the Folio Society, perhaps. In its way, the effect was as bizarre as any slapdash room in my father's home.

'Been getting rid of all the rubbish, bit by bit. But there'll be a few boxes for you next year, vicar, and the year after that. All right and tight in the old stables. Watertight for the gee-gees, still watertight now.'

I thought of the rubbishy kitchen items and the old paper-backs. If other boxes contained items like them, there wouldn't be any point in opening them in a couple of years' time. On the other hand, he might have stowed a couple of other precious things without remembering them. 'Perhaps if I showed you the things that caught my eye, you might tell me something about them.' I touched the bag again.

'Dirty, are they? No, no! Step this way.'

We were in a quarry-tiled kitchen, the floor like glass, and the brand-new units – I'd seen some just like them in an upmarket showroom in Canterbury – all with their pristine doors tight shut. From somewhere the Colonel produced a copy of the *Sunday Telegraph*, spreading it carefully on the marble work-surface.

'There.'

I produced the folio first. I almost expected him to put on his Marigold rubber gloves to touch it, but he simply poked it with a fingertip.

'Rubbish. Only fit for the bin. But nothing to do with me. Never seen it before.'

'It was in one of the boxes you sent – along with a set of mint Georgette Heyers.'

'Who? What?'

'Regency romances.'

'Do I look the sort of person who'd read rubbishy stuff like that? For God's sake – sorry, padre. Why have you brought it here, anyway?'

'I just thought it was your book,' I said mildly. 'And I just thought . . .' Seeing his jaw harden into a stubborn line, I changed tack slightly. 'I want to give this to a museum, but it'll be far more use to them if they know a little about it. Such as which house all these lovely doorknobs were designed for.'

'Lovely? They're just doorknobs, woman. Strikes me it's not just your father that's cracked.'

Biting my lip, I closed the volume and tucked it away. But I couldn't resist fishing out the snuffbox and teasing it out of the wrap of tissue I'd swathed it in.

'What about this poor thing?'

'Never seen it before.' He stared. 'It's tat, woman. Junk.'

'One man's junk is another man's antique,' I said, with what I hoped was a charming smile. 'And this is a very old antique. Possibly very valuable.'

'So I thought you might want to have it back,' Robin said. 'An heirloom.'

'No point in heirlooms if you haven't got heirs.' He drew himself up, straightening his shoulders. 'If it ever was mine, which it wasn't, I must have given it to you. Yours to keep, vicar. Not hers.' He looked at me as if I was some sort of lowlife. Since I had been, I couldn't really argue.

'Lina bought it quite legitimately from the bric-a-brac stall, but says she wants to sell it on behalf of the church. To raise funds for us.'

'The more I know about it, the better chance I have of making an . . . an appropriate sale. As it is, someone might give me a tenner, if I'm lucky.' I took a risk. 'My father's sure he recognizes it. Remembers someone using it. But—'

'Surprised the old soak can remember his name. Though he had shaved before he came to see me. I'll give him that. And he hadn't pissed all down his trousers like he used to. I'll give this some thought, missy – how about that?'

I looked quickly at Robin, trying to cue him in. Someone ought to tell the old guy that someone wanted this very much indeed.

At last he got the message. 'The thing is, Colonel, that someone has already tried to steal this twice. One attempt ended in quite serious injury. I'd leave it here with you as an *aide-memoire*, but I wouldn't want to risk bringing a thief to your door. And risk to you.'

Bridger smiled grimly. 'Are you afraid of risk to me or risk to the snuffbox?'

Robin's smile was angelic. 'Both, actually.'

'Now what do we do with the wretched thing?' Robin asked as we stood beside our vehicles. 'You take it, you're in danger. I take it, I am. And the rectory, which doesn't actually belong to me, of course, but to the church, so I don't want any splintered doors or broken windows.'

I didn't quite follow his panicky logic. It wasn't as if the box had some tracking device attached to it. They knew it had reached our cottage because they knew I'd bought it and they'd seen my van. But since he'd put himself out for me, I'd better try and soothe him. 'Of course you don't. Robin, you did this for me once before – you got something really precious locked in a safe in the Cathedral—'

'No. Absolutely not. Mammon!' But his face softened. 'On the other hand, there's bound to be a safe somewhere in Kenninge church. It's about time I said Matins there. I'll lock it away when I go.' His grin might have been wiped from his face. 'But we're trying to save the church, aren't we, not have someone attack it with a JCB to fish the safe out wholesale.'

I blinked. Then I remembered a rash of raids on village post offices in the area, carried out by thieves who didn't bother with the finesse of guns and masks and whatnot. They simply nicked a JCB and scooped out the complete cash dispenser. 'Ah. I see what you mean.' I still didn't buy his reasoning.

'And in any case, don't you need it to show one of your expert friends?'

'The only one Griff would totally trust is in the States.'

My phone pinged. A text. And maybe the answer to our problem.

'Good news: it's Bruce Farfrae. Bad news: he's in the USA too.' And he wanted me to talk to Morris. So I was on my own, unless I could think of something quickly. 'Before you go off to Kenninge, could you come with me to Ashford? I need to hire a car, and there's a place there offers a good deal. If we drop off your car at the rectory, and we go together to Ashford and—'

'I get it: I follow you back to Bredeham, and you lock your nice visible van in the yard and potter round in something less obvious.'

'Got it in one. And while all this car shuffling is taking place, I may get some ideas about what to do next. Tell me, have you ever seen a house as neat and tidy, not to mention clean, as Bugger Bridger's? I mean,' I continued, recycling an expression I'd learned from Griff, 'talk about anal retentive!'

Robin started to laugh. And then became quite hysterical. And so, after a minute or two's brainwork, so did I.

NINE

There wasn't any need for us to drive from the hire-car firm in Ashford in convoy, so Robin set off in the van – I was only insuring the car for me – while I finished off the paperwork. I got a deal for three days. By the time I had to return it I should have worked out my next move. Should. Very big should. Maybe, more accurately, a might.

Once I'd got used to the new wheels – a silver Ka, pretty well invisible amongst all the other silver Kas, I thought – I drove briskly, taking the A20, not the M20, which the hire car guy told us was bunged up after a lorry had shed its load. Poor Robin would be stuck outside our yard until I arrived, unless Mrs Walker decided to risk letting him in.

It's a really nice route, once an art . . . artisanal . . . artesian? . . . road. It had been the main one to the coast till they built the M20, which was so often used as a giant car park during Operation Stack that I tended to use the old one as my regular route. *Arterial*, that's it! Mostly it's an ordinary single carriageway, without too many overtaking opportunities, as Robin had discovered yesterday. It had its share of rubber on the tarmac, where motorists had skidded back into their own lane, or been forced over by petrol-head overtakers coming towards them. Now, in a winding stretch between two picture-book villages, with woodland either side of the road, there was a brand new set of skid marks. They led straight into the grass verge, which had been chewed up by the car as it'd struggled free.

I felt very cold.

Telling myself that at least there was no wreck visible, so if it was him he must be safe, I pressed on.

Mrs Walker made a good mug of tea, and Robin was securely wrapped round one when I ran him to earth in the shop. The van, splattered with mud, but intact, was safe inside the yard, the gates locked and security activated. I decided I must discuss with Griff the possibility of giving her a rise.

'This guy tried to run me off the road,' Robin said. 'But then he backed off: something to do with a police car coming in the opposite direction, maybe. Why on earth didn't they book him? Anyway, knowing the roads round here I was able to dodge around a bit and shake him off. So here I am, safe and sound. But as soon as you've had a cuppa too, I must ask you to take me back to my car. I've got a benefice to run, Lina.'

This was the most firmly he'd ever spoken to me.

'No problem. And while I'm on the road, I'll pop on to see Freya Webb, or one of her minions. Unless you think you were the victim of straight bad driving, maybe you should come too. I doubt if we'll see her, since DCIs seem to spend their lives in budget meetings, but I'm sure she'll have a well-briefed underling.'

He nodded without comment, and soon, having called ahead to warn her, we were on the road.

To my amazement, ready to sign us in and give us our visitors' IDs, there was Freya in person, looking very spruce, with fresh make-up. Actually, I wasn't amazed at all. This time Freya's blush was matched by one from Robin. He must be seven or eight years younger than she, but who cared? I wasn't going to go down the cougar-toyboy route. Griff would rub his hands with glee when I told him, despite his not very secret hopes of Robin and me getting together.

Robin gave his story first, but I was almost as disappointed as Freya by the lack of detail. He didn't even recall the make of the car, just that it was large, black and mud-spattered. 'At first I thought it was bad driving,' he said. 'And then I thought of Lina and that accursed box.'

At which point, it was my turn. 'If Bugger Bridger really didn't recognize the snuffbox,' I concluded, 'then I wonder if someone put it in the box while it was in his old stable. Or at the fête itself, of course. And then they wanted it back.'

Robin blinked. 'So why didn't they simply ask for it? I'd have been happy to hand it over.'

Exactly. Chummie's mistake had been to grab it and run,

not ask politely. Robin would have asked a few questions first, but if he'd been satisfied, he'd have been reasonableness itself.

I might have been, too.

'Perhaps it wasn't really his to ask for,' I said. 'If it was stolen in the first place, he could hardly make a reasonable case for its return, could he?'

He looked troubled. 'It's a big assumption.'

Freya laughed kindly. I wondered how long she'd find his naï . . . nïa . . . his innocence funny. 'I think it's a justifiable one, given all the events since. I've had one of the team go through the missing property register, but I can't find an exact match. But we're not experts, of course. It's not really Will's period, is it, Lina?' If she expected a blush from me, she didn't get one. 'So I contacted Reg Morris, from the Met.'

I joggled my mug of coffee, as if to stir the milk in better. 'Fancy calling a kid Reg,' I said. 'No wonder he prefers just Morris. Anyway, what did he say?'

'You'll be able to ask him yourself later. He's working somewhere in Sussex and said he'd make a detour in on his way back to London.'

A casual look at my watch, as if I had other things to do with my day than hang around. 'Any idea what time he's expected?'

'Five-ish? Six-ish?'

She didn't seem particularly interested, and why should she? She probably had more than enough to do until then. Killing time was my problem. My first task was obviously to take Robin back to his car – except I had a shrewd suspicion he'd rather someone else offered. So when my phone announced an incoming text, I took it at once. It was from a client, happy with a restoration job and telling me to expect a call from a friend wanting me to tackle a broken statuette, but Freya and Robin weren't to know.

'Problem?' Robin asked, professionally concerned but not really ready to leap to his feet and abandon his coffee and the company.

'Not if Freya can organize a lift for you.' I maintained my serious expression.

Freya said easily, 'I'm sure we can manage that,' but couldn't suppress a tiny blush. 'I'll tell Reg Morris to call you to fix a meeting place, shall I? Before his journey's end?' she added with a little malice in her smile I didn't understand.

'It had better be here,' I said firmly, digging in the bag. 'Because this is where the snuffbox is staying. OK?' I plonked it on her desk, where it sat as pathetic and bedraggled as a wet sparrow. 'I'd like a tattoo on my forehead saying I haven't got it any more, but I don't suppose you can arrange that, can you?'

What she could arrange was someone to escort me out. Suddenly, the air felt fresher: I had an anonymous set of wheels, Robin might soon have another squeeze and I'd got rid of what had come to feel as heavy as an albatross. What else could a girl do but head for Maidstone M & S and buy some new undies?

Not to mention some Fairtrade T-shirts and, for the freezer, some of the flavoured chicken pieces Griff likes with the salad lunches I inflict on him. I was just wondering how else I could waste a little time when my foot was firmly trodden on by a heel attached to a well-upholstered body. As the guy turned, I placed him as the man I'd encountered in Canterbury Cathedral crypt. The one who'd stared at me with such hostility. He was cornered up against the olive oil.

'We've seen each other before,' I said. 'At the Cathedral. You looked at me like you're looking at me now, as if you'd rather I didn't exist.' I managed a smile, but one on the grim end of the scale. 'Could you tell me what the problem is?'

'I think you've got the wrong person, madam. So sorry about your foot.' He edged sideways.

'I've got another one,' I said lightly. 'Look, the other night you seemed to think we'd met before. At least, I presume you don't always go round glaring at strangers like that.'

'No, not at all, dear lady. Of course I remember our charming encounter.'

That wasn't how I'd have described it.

'They say everyone has a doppelgänger,' he said, edging away as if he thought I was a local loony.

Perhaps I was. But I couldn't quite let go. 'In what

circumstances did you meet this double of mine? I'd really like to know.'

An arm wove its way between us. 'Other people want to buy their extra virgin too, you know,' said an aggrieved voice.

By the time I'd apologized, he'd gone.

As I paid for my goodies, I pondered the thought of my double. I'd like to meet her, especially if she turned out to be one of my half-sisters, which wasn't impossible, given my father's generosity in spreading his favours about Kent. He knew of about thirty of us brothers and sisters – except there was a neat word for all of us, wasn't there? Possibly there were more he'd been too dozy to record. Since he'd promised me that whoever turned up, he'd still value me, I tried not to worry. From time to time, he still agonized about finding his mother's engagement ring for me. Given the state of his wing, it was more likely that I'd come across it in one of my periodic trawls for a really big find for him. As it was, on special occasions I wore the Cartier watch he'd insisted on giving me – a gift very far from being sneezed at.

So in theory I didn't find her a threat. She might have a share in my father, but she didn't have any share at all in Griff. And he was still by far the most important person in my life.

However, now the idea of a sin . . . a sid . . . a *sibling* – yes! – had wormed its way properly into my head, I thought I'd do something about the version of me that Josie had said she'd seen in Hastings. I'd have nipped down to see her, but this disruption of my working day had been long enough. I must get back to Bredeham. If a little voice suggested I might be thinking about spending time to make myself look nice for my forthcoming encounter with Morris, I shut it up abruptly. I had a queue as long as my arm of items waiting for me to restore them, and they needed the sort of steady hand you had when you weren't thinking of your private life.

TEN

For all my good intentions about devoting the next few hours to my job, I couldn't resist phoning Josie. She picked up first ring.

'It's killing me, all this rest,' she told me. 'Bored out of my skull I am, and I'll swear my back's worse without all the stretching and bending I was doing in the shop and at fairs. And quiet! It's so quiet round here. If you hear I've been dragged off kicking and screaming by the men in white coats – except they wear green dungarees, these days, don't they? – then you'll know why. Make sure you never let dear old Griff retire, won't you? I'd hate him to come to this. I can't even ask you to come down for a cuppa because I know you're always busy – have you fixed that crack in Elspeth's plate yet, by the way?'

'It's on my list. Towards the top,' I promised her. 'And I'll drop in for a cuppa and some of your cake when I take it back to her. But I want you to do something for me. No one else can, Josie, because no one else was there. That time you saw me and I didn't wave. Remember? I want you to jot down exactly where it was and what I was wearing. And if you can recall anything about the young man I was with, that would be a bonus, too.'

'You're thinking I made it all up, aren't you?'

'Absolutely not. The thing is, you're not the first person who says they saw me and I didn't acknowledge them,' I said, not quite accurately, but never mind. 'I'm just wondering if I've got a double. Well, not exactly a double. More a relative. And if I have, then I'd love to meet her.'

'Yes, you could do with some company your own age,' she said, surprising me. 'I mean, you and Griff were made for each other, but you need boyfriends and girlfriends too. That handsome man who fell head over heels with you, he was old enough to be your father,' she added with a sigh, though I wasn't sure why.

He was married, anyway. I hardly ever thought of him these days, except when he put high-class restoration work my way.

'Boyfriends might take me away from Griff,' I said. 'And he's done so much for me, it'd have to be someone really, really special to take me away from him.'

'I know that, lovey. But a few mates to giggle over new nail varnish with – that'd be lovely, wouldn't it, now? So I'll keep my eyes open for this other you. But I'll be a bit discreet, if you know what I mean.'

'In that case I'll pop Elspeth's plate right on top of my waiting list. So make sure you've made some cake.' Apart from anything else, a spot of baking might fill some of those suddenly empty hours for her.

'I'll go and buy some eggs this very afternoon,' she declared.

Five o'clock and no call from Morris.

I was so jumpy I could hardly have attached mud to velvet. I'd changed twice, and I'd spilt tea down the outfit I really wanted to wear. And I was so cross with myself that I'd snapped at Mrs Walker almost unnecessarily. I'd apologized afterwards and actually asked to see the photos of her and her fiancé Paul Banner at a ballroom-dancing weekend they'd spent at a nice hotel in Devon. So we parted friends again when she drove off back to Bossingham. I locked up as carefully as I always did and made sure all the security cameras responded to my cheery waves.

Still no call from Morris.

By six thirty, I'd watered the tubs and hanging baskets and was thinking about cleaning the van. In my nicest sandals, for heaven's sake. Maybe if I went and changed and got thoroughly soaked, he'd phone then.

I did, and he didn't. At least we had a nice clean van ready for when we could use it again.

What about supper? I'd sort of assumed we might all have supper together, once the business of the snuffbox had been dealt with, so I'd put off cooking anything. Of course I could eat two full meals without turning a hair, but I didn't want to do that too often, or those fifties dresses with their neat waists wouldn't fasten any more and I'd have to sell them again. Not a good thought.

It must have been about nine when the phone rang at last. Freya Webb.

'Just to let you know Morris has been and gone. There was a bad RTA on the A26, so he got held up. Anyway, he doesn't recognize the snuffbox either, not as such, but he was certainly excited and he's taken it away for safe keeping. I thought you'd be OK with that.'

'Absolutely fine. Thanks for letting me know. I take it he'll be in touch with you when he finds anything out?'

'Don't see why. Your property after all. Hang on.' There was a murmur her end. Was it Robin? Combining work with pleasure? With my solitary omelette almost forgotten, I had a tiny and very irritating pang, but not of hunger.

'Sorry about that. Now, when you're out and about, keep your eyes peeled just in case our friends haven't given up yet.'

I would indeed.

At ten o'clock, it was time to take my advice to Josie. I set to and baked. I couldn't eat the mound of scones I produced, but, as I told Griff in a nice long gossipy phone call, at least there'd be plenty of his favourites in the freezer when he got back.

It's hard to make a couple of days spent literally watching paint dry sound exciting. But in its own way it was satisfying, and eventually I was able to phone Josie and tell her I'd be ready to return her friend Elspeth's plate the next morning. I'd come back via Tenterden to catch up with Griff in person, too.

Elspeth lived in a very ordinary modern house not far from Josie's equally ordinary modern house on the outskirts of Hastings, so I shouldn't have been surprised when she declared she'd walk round to Josie's with me.

'She needs a bit of company, doesn't she?' she confided, looking for an umbrella though the sky was vividly blue. We strolled, very slowly, arm in arm, to be greeted with huge hugs and squawks of delight. For an instant I wondered what I was doing eating cake with two old ladies, however kind and generous they were, in a cluttered and airless little room, when I could have been down on the sea front, walking as fast as I

could and letting the wind take my hair. Or running along
hand in hand with . . .

But the cakes were brilliant, and the least I could do was
pay attention to Josie and conscientiously jot down everything
she could recall about the other me.

'In other words, you've got nowhere fast,' Griff sighed as I
finished my account of my morning's doings.

We were having lunch in the garden room – nothing as
vulgar as a conservatory for Aidan, but then, it would have
been a sin to tack anything like that on to his perfect Georgian
house. Aidan's idea of entertaining was to buy the best Waitrose
could offer. But Griff, despite his bruises, was rarely happier
than when he was cooking, and the perfect flan was definitely
home-made, full of double cream too, if I knew Griff. But he
was looking so much perkier, I didn't tell him off.

'Exactly. All she could remember was that she looked like
me, only with a harder face. And the bloke looked shifty. I
think she was inventing details – if you can call them that –
just to please me. But at least I've shortened the waiting list,
and she paid in cash. And I saw the sea in the distance, all
blue and sparkly. And now I'm here with you. So although
I've not made the best use of my time, I haven't wasted it.
And this is a perfect lunch.'

'I'm amazed you managed to eat any of it after dear Josie's
cakes. What a good job we only have fruit salad for dessert,'
he said wistfully.

'I have been trying to keep an eye on his diet,' Aidan said.
'But he has spoken highly of her confections.'

'What a good job she made me take away the rest of the
Victoria sponge she baked for me.'

So it was a nice easy time.

As we hugged goodbye, Griff whispered, 'And you really
are not unhappy at this development with Robin, sweet one?'

'Absolutely not. He's always been a friend, and I'm sure
we'll keep it that way.'

'It doesn't always happen when people embark on new
relationships, I fear. Maybe I should cancel this London trip
and come and keep an eye on you.'

'Don't even say the words. It's a long time since you had a nice break, and you both deserve it.'

But when I got back home it was very quiet, and Tim and I had to have a long conversation involving tissues before I settled down to tackle a really tricky bit of gilding on a Crown Derby vase.

One thing I really did not expect the following morning, horribly early, when I'd no more than thought about getting up and having a shower, was a phone call from Robin. All he said was he could do with some advice, and maybe we could meet for lunch at the Halfway House – a pub that just happened to be halfway between Bredeham and Bossingham.

'I'm sorry. I've absolutely got to finish an urgent job today, so . . . Look,' I relented, 'if you could make it over to Bredeham, I've got plenty of food here. Would that do?'

'It'll have to, I suppose.' That didn't sound like Robin at all.

'About one?' I suggested, equally offhand. But worried.

But it would never do to agonize over his love life when I was trying to be stoical about my lack of one, so, after a hasty shower and a piece of toast, I went to my workroom, where a particularly delicate piece of Chelsea waited for me. It was actually a good job he'd phoned so early – it was still shy of seven thirty. It meant I could get a really good run at the piece. In fact, I was so engrossed that I didn't hear the doorbell ring. When the noise finally penetrated my skull, I almost dropped my paintbrush.

Surely Robin had said lunchtime? And this was before breakfast for most people.

But it wasn't Robin I peered at through the peephole in the door. It was an old guy I'd never seen before. Not this close, at least.

ELEVEN

'**G**riff always puts a drop of whisky in,' X said, peering doubtfully at the mug of tea I'd made him.

I obliged.

'I never thought I'd get to meet you,' I said, passing the biscuits too. 'And at this time of day – you're usually such an early bird.'

'So long as you pass me message on to Griff,' he said, which didn't seem to be a reply to anything. He scoffed half the biscuits. With luck he'd finish the lot. I certainly wouldn't fancy eating anything he'd touched.

'I can get him on the phone for you if you like.' I picked up the handset and held it out to him.

I might have been offering a dead hedgehog.

'Word of mouth, that's how I deal. Got this little item for him. Tell him it's the usual terms.'

'Cash and say nothing to anyone,' I said. 'And a cheese sandwich?'

His eyes lit up. 'Don't usually get one of them.'

'And a drop of cider?'

'Now you're talking.'

I not only talked, I opened the kitchen door and propped it wide. X might be more forthcoming than I'd ever expected but his preparations for the visit hadn't included much in the way of personal hygiene.

'I could make you some ham sarnies to take with you too if you liked.'

'No mustard.'

'Right.'

'Titus said you were OK. Said you'd got spunk. True you're a divvy?'

My turn to hold back. That was one thing I didn't like spoken of, though I suppose most folk in our line of business must know. Then I smiled. 'Try me out.'

'Only meant to show Griff. Hang on.' He turned away from the table and dug in an inside pocket of his foul coat. Whatever he came up with was easily hidden under his hand as he laid it on the table.

This was the table Griff kneaded bread on, for goodness' sake. We'd need one of those surface sprays that kills ninety-nine per cent of all known germs.

'Don't do guessing games,' I said. 'I have to see whatever it is.'

'Not what I heard. Heard you could pick something out at fifty paces.'

'Maybe I did. That's why I let you in.' Probably, I'd picked out the smell and registered it certainly wasn't latex and cosmetics. I must have been off my head otherwise. But I wasn't getting anything in the way of vibes.

'Said you were pretty fly, Titus. OK, if I show you, means you got to buy it. And I won't take less than a tenner.'

My nod was meant to be offhand. Griff had dinned into me I mustn't worry that he never paid X anything like enough for the things he brought along to what were usually pre-breakfast meetings. If he gave the true value, Griff argued, then X would just go off and drink himself to death. Would ten pounds be dangerous? Was I meant to haggle? Was that part of X's game?

'Depends what I make of it,' I said coolly. 'Maybe just a fiver and an extra sarnie.'

It looked as if we had a deal. He removed his paw to reveal a poor battered piece of metal, which might have been the twin of the one everyone seemed to want. Bloody hell, it might well have been the twin. Forcing myself to be casual, I picked it up and looked at it, inside and out. 'I'd need my eyeglass.'

'As seen or no deal. And you got to divvy it for me.'

'A very old silver snuffbox. Probably late seventeenth century,' I said blithely, remembering the 1697 start date for hallmarks and not divvying at all. All I was doing was quoting an imaginary text book somewhere in my head.

Maybe I was befuddled by his fumes.

'Worth a tenner.' It was a statement, not a question.

'Eight and extra sarnies.' Making sure it was nowhere near any surface he could have touched, I fished out the loaf, one of Griff's best efforts, then the proper fresh-sliced ham the village deli prided itself on. 'No mustard, right, but a bit of Griff's chutney?' I waved the jar in the direction of his nose.

The poor bugger actually started to dribble.

Slicing as fast as I could, I made a mound of food. As he wolfed down the first round – cheese and chutney, this one – I said casually, 'Get this down Bossingham way?'

Mistake. Huge mistake. His hand covered it again.

'Griff never asks.'

I held up a hand. 'Sorry. No names, no pack drill. Right?' His jaw remained tight. 'And I'd better make it that tenner, hadn't I? More tea?'

His eyes went to the whisky.

I did the obvious. But it was the smallest splash.

The spare food wrapped in greaseproof paper, I dug for some cash in the old tea-caddy Griff kept specially – it was only tin, but in the shape of a bureau, with tiny gilded knobs and painted wood graining. Rust damage meant it was worth a big round zero, but it had belonged to Griff's grandmother and would never get thrown away. The fivers looked as battered as the poor caddy. But, eyes alight, he grabbed them, and the food parcel.

'Here, have these,' I said, giving him the remains of the packet of biscuits.

For the first time he smiled. 'Thought you were as tough as Griff. Now I can see you're a soft touch. I'll leave the back way, if it's all the same to you. Don't like front doors.' He paused. 'And don't forget to wipe them photos like Griff always does.'

Wipe photos? I knew I'd have to clean the kitchen from top to bottom, but that seemed a bit extreme even to me. And then, as I locked him out, it dawned on me what he meant: he wanted the footage of his arrival and departure deleted from our CCTV system.

The little snuffbox, washed carefully but very thoroughly in warm soapy water and then dried with a soft duster, was not the twin, but at least a close relative of the one now in Morris's hands. It was in much better condition, presumably because it hadn't been thrown across a churchyard. On its embossed lid, raised little figures, quite crude, and not as well finished as you'd expect, apparently shot birds. And it left me with a huge problem – not one I could discuss with Robin or with Morris, either. I wasn't even sure how much I could tell Griff, because although he bought a lot of stuff from X, he'd always told me he'd never, ever risked asking questions, simply because knowledge could be dangerous. If you thought something was stolen, for instance, you couldn't keep it or sell it, could you?

Or if . . . No, I didn't want to go there just yet. Except I did wish he hadn't said I was a soft touch. I thought he'd referred to my loading him with food.

Provenance or not, I tucked it into the hidden safe; at least I could bet that no one else knew where it was. And that was about all I could bet on. Except that it might have come from Bossingham, which set more alarm bells ringing in my head. If Bugger Bridger hadn't recognized the first snuffbox, which had definitely been tucked into one of his boxes, did it mean someone had put it in there – in the old stables, adjoining the farm – in order to keep it away from prying eyes? Only for it to be accidentally donated and then sold? And if that one had, did it mean that X had stolen this one from a similar hiding place? My thought processes were never good – now they tangled and knotted and I couldn't unpick them.

So what could I do to free them up? Obvious answer: clean the kitchen. Maybe if I didn't think, answers would just appear in my head.

Since we hadn't actually got one of those germ-killer sprays, it was time for bleach. I scrubbed the kitchen table, twice, and wiped all the other surfaces X might have accidentally touched. All my clothes into the machine. Another shower, involving particular attention to my hair. What if Griff came home to find I'd got nits? And then it dawned on me that I'd pretty well used up what I meant to give Robin for lunch. Even though the shops were only a five minute walk away, by the time everyone had asked after Griff and after me, and talked about Mrs Walker's forthcoming wedding, it was clear the Chelsea figure would have to wait.

*　　*　　*

If Robin noticed that the bread wasn't home-made, he didn't say anything. In fact, I might just as well have fed him some of my father's Pot Noodles instead of all the good fresh produce I'd organized for our lunch. Perhaps he was miffed with me for having brought him all the way out here. Certainly, he was preoccupied with something. I let him be: Griff always said it was a pre-something or other . . . prerequ . . . ah, the *prerogative* of a friend to be silent when he didn't want to talk.

Eventually, as I put a mug of coffee in front of him – forget the usual elegant little antique china cans! – he took a deep breath. 'Would you mind if we drank this in the garden? Only, I'm gasping for a fag.'

'You? Smoke? I've never heard you so much as mention cigarettes, except to moan when visitors leave nub ends in your church yards.' But I got up and fished out the nasty Bakelite ashtray with a deep burned scar in the middle we kept for emergencies like this and led the way into the garden.

What was up? Had he and Freya had a falling out? I wasn't sure I could deal with broken hearts except to suggest a friendly no strings bonk, and I was certainly wasn't going to offer that sort of consolation to Robin.

I knew from my therapist that when someone had problems you weren't supposed to jump in feet first and ask what the trouble was. Robin's couldn't have been anything like mine, but I presumed that the rules still held, so I sat and sipped and waited. He'd sucked hard through two cigarettes and a huge sigh before he said, 'Poor old St Jude's – living up to its name, I suppose.'

My education hadn't got that far, had it? But I knew about *Jude the Obscure*, because it was a novel that Griff and I had started reading together, until the scene where the children were hanged made me cry so much that Griff had closed the book and said he wouldn't open it again till I asked him to. And so far I hadn't.

'In what way?' That sounded better than plain old *how.* Less ignorant, at least.

'All that effort – and it seems to be a lost cause.'

St Jude. Patron saint of lost causes. Of course! I managed not to smile.

'We've had three estimates for the work we simply can't manage without, and they're eye-watering.'

'Which means?'

'If we can't raise the money, we can go to the diocese and negotiate handing over the building to the Churches Preservation Society. This means we can retain an option to worship there about four times a year but have no financial responsibility.'

'Sounds ideal.'

Wrong.

'Their priority isn't worship! It's purely the conservation of the building. Their idea is that the building should be used by the community. That's fine in a city, or even a suburb, where you could make it a homeless centre or something – but out here, Lina? A *community*? A few hens and a lot of middle-class ponies trapped behind electric fencing and never apparently ridden! I want it to be a living church; anything else is like shoving a dear aunt into a retirement home and abandoning her to strangers.'

'In that case, we have to raise the money to do the repairs, and you have to encourage more people on to the pews.'

'Interesting use of pronouns, Lina. *We* and *you*,' he explained, when I looked puzzled.

'Of course I know what pronouns are,' I said crossly. 'What's interesting about the way I used them?'

'The way you seemed to assume some responsibility for a building with which you haven't the remotest connection.'

That's what Griff had done for me, wasn't it? He'd taken me on without payment or official thanks. What a risk. If you're given a gift like that you have to pass it on. But it would have sounded a bit pompous to say it even to Robin, so I made a sort of sideways rock of the head, as if to say, *make what you like of it.*

He lit another cigarette. This way he wouldn't live to see what happened to St Jude's.

'The way people are chasing after that snuffbox means it's got to be worth something,' I mused. 'For something, read a lot. If it's not dodgy, and I hope Morris is checking even as we speak that it's kosher, then a specialist repair and an even more specialist sale should help.' I didn't mention X's snuffbox. Strictly speaking it wasn't mine but the firm's, which meant Griff had to decide what to do with it. With a bit of help from me.

'What about that IKEA catalogue? Any hopes of that?' I'd never heard Robin in scrounge-mode before.

'The only reason I bought it was to give it away,' I said flatly. I continued, hoping to sound more positive, 'You mentioned a safe in St Jude's as a possible hidey-hole for the snuffbox. Is there anything in there that could be sold?'

'We'd have to get a faculty. That's Anglican-ese for the culmination of a long consultation procedure to make sure no rogue vicar or churchwarden gets his fingers in the till.'

'Ah. That seems to sum up in a dozen words what a guy I was talking to at the drinkies thing took about ten minutes to explain—'

'Which guy?'

'One of the guests I turned to speak to snubbed me so hard that a nice clergyman had to rescue me. And then I really landed the poor vicar or whatever in it because I asked him about – well, I must have sounded like Sarah Montague on *Today* because I kept firing questions about the relative values of the church treasures down there in the museum and local churches' fabric needing repairs. The poor man couldn't get away. But he's not the interesting one, actually. The one who interested me was the rude guy.'

He ground his nub end into the paving. 'Have I missed something here? I thought we were talking about fund-raising and St Jude's.'

Wow. Not the time to raise all those worries about the other snuffbox, then. 'OK. Check out your safe and raise a faculty. It all starts with a form, that nice clergyman was saying. Get your form.'

Now it was his turn to go off at a tangent. 'Do you know who it was? The man you were talking to, of course.'

'The clergyman? One with a lilac shirt. Tubby, though he'd probably consider himself well-built. About fifty.'

'Sums up half a dozen churchmen I know.' Hunching away from me, he lit another cigarette. I had half a mind to bum one for myself, only I knew from bitter experience just how hard it was to give them up. He lit another from the stub. Any moment he'd have to nip down to the shop for some more.

When he said nothing, I said, 'I met him again, actually. Not the lilac clergyman, the man who had been so horrified to see me. He was in M and S in Maidstone. And he really did not seem pleased to see me. One scrap. Didn't even approach "charming" on the scale of "hostile to delighted". So I challenged him.' When he said nothing, I yakked on, 'I know I'm not everyone's cup of tea, but such loathing . . .'

As if he hadn't heard a word, he searched for another cigarette, took it, and crumpled the packet, dropping it on the table, as if some underpaid waitress would suddenly appear to tidy it away. 'Shall we go and look at what's in the safe?'

I thought of my workroom and the queue of silent, broken antiques, and said, 'I really don't know anything about silver. Especially eccles . . . excel . . . especially church silver. Anything at all.'

'But you might know someone who does?'

'There are specialist firms – I'm sure Lilac Shirt would know, since he talked so knowledgeably about the whole thing. Actually,' I continued, hesitantly, 'he mentioned it being the churchwardens' responsibility. Maybe you should talk to them first?'

'St Jude's has only got one. Fi.'

'She'll know someone!'

'I really thought I could depend on you.'

'The other day you said you had a benefice to run. I've got a business to run.'

As if to prove the point, the office phone rang. Without looking back, I got up to take the call.

'I thought you were never coming back,' Robin grumbled.

I didn't sit beside him, but gathered up the coffee things and his fag packet. I'd seen Griff ease visitors away like this without them even knowing they'd had the old heave-ho. 'There's some museum with a bit of a panic on. In the cuts they had to shed their expert conservation staff, and now something important needs a repair. So they've asked me. They're couriering the item down tomorrow, so I have to shift

the rest of today's work as fast as I can. Look, if you really
need me, I could see you at St Jude's about eight?'

He went bright scarlet. 'I'm afraid I'm booked this evening.'

Was he indeed?

'At least phone Fi. And see if you can identify Lilac Shirt.
Actually, he might be able to identify my Mr Nasty. I'd be
really grateful if he could.' I turned as if to head back into
the house.

He didn't move.

Picking up his fag end, I walked away anyway.

Despite the intense lights and the almost clinical state of my
workroom, it was hard to concentrate on the Chelsea figure.
Robin clearly thought I'd let him down big time, but as I'd
told him for the nth time, waving him off, I really knew
absolutely zero about ecclesiastical plate. At least the word
had come back. But he was really huffy, and I wasn't sure how
to repair the rift, bar phoning up and offering to see the stuff
later in the afternoon, which I really couldn't afford the time
for.

At last I got into the right rhythm, and the hand began to
look like a hand again. Yes.

When the phone rang, I was surprised to see how dark the
outside world was. And to find how stiff my back and legs
were. I'd obviously broken my own rule, which was to get up
and walk round every half hour or so.

Eight thirty. Well, at least I was ready for tomorrow's
delivery.

And the phone was still ringing.

TWELVE

'Watch your back, girl, that's all I say,' a familiar voice growled.

'Titus?'

'Nod's as good as a wink, that's what I always say.'

'It would be if I knew what you're talking about,' I said.

'Listen, have you come across someone who looks like me but seems to have annoyed people?'

'Like I said, watch your back.' The wretched man cut the call.

How cheering was that?

I sat on the stairs. For Titus to phone was dead serious. Especially on our landline – he'd had this idea that mobile calls were less traceable, and, though he'd now discovered he was mistaken, he still preferred . . . Well, he'd have preferred carrier pigeons with tiny scraps of paper that could be chewed and swallowed.

So it wasn't very surprising that I actually screamed when the front doorbell rang. A long heavy ring, not one to take no for an answer. It had to for a while, at least – I checked on the security system to see if I should open the door or scarper. Actually, of course, that wasn't an option, but dialling 999 and maybe ruining Robin's evening with Freya might be.

One glance and I flew to the door. I shouldn't have. I should have been cool and dignified, and certainly not ready to fling my arms round the neck of a married man.

'Hi, Morris.' I think I sounded friendly but cautious. That was what he seemed to need. That and whisky so stiff he'd not be able to drive legally for a few hours. What a good job I'd kept my arms firmly under control.

He took a couple of sips and then left the tumbler on the kitchen table. I've no idea how we'd fetched up in the kitchen, not the living room. He didn't seem to know either, but he pulled out his usual chair and sat down.

'How much do you know about snuffboxes, Lina?'

I clicked my fingers. 'That much. Less, actually.'

'But you knew your find was precious?'

'My *purchase*. I bought it legitimately. With a promise to pay any more to the church fund when I sold it for what it was worth.' I sat too.

'Your *purchase*. How much do you know about history?'

I pulled a face. 'I can do periods – like the Normans and their vile castles. But not dates. Well, 1066 I suppose.'

He raised his eyes to heaven. 'Vile castles! They include some of our finest pieces of architecture. And are the precursors of even finer ones.'

'They all say this to me.' I put my thumb down on the table top and made a squashing movement. 'Down with the natives.'

'But you're probably descended from a Norman aristocrat!'

'You can look at my father and think I should be proud to know that?' Then I remembered that Morris was inclined to be respectful to him, and even drop out the occasional 'My lord'. 'Anyway, why this sudden interest in castles?'

'Not castles, Lina. History. Do you know anything about the Commonwealth?'

I gaped. 'You mean the Games in India and Rwanda joining and—'

'The other Commonwealth.'

'You really have lost me.'

'You've heard of the Restoration?'

'Ah! King Charles and spaniels and Nell Gwyn and oranges and Lely portraits.'

'Excellent. Well, we know they had snuffboxes in the Restoration period. And – since Shakespeare makes one of his characters taking snuff from what he calls a pouncet box—'

I was sure the books I'd read called them something else, but I couldn't remember what. I stayed mum.

'—we suspect that Elizabethans had the equivalent of snuffboxes. But no one's ever found one from the intervening period. Not the right size and design and shape. You couldn't go into a museum and point to one and guarantee it was a snuffbox. Until now. Until you found – bought it – and I got it authenticated. You've picked up the Holy Grail of snuffbox collectors.'

From being tidily sitting down, we suddenly found ourselves in each other's arms. It was a hug. No more. A big, solid hug. And then I pushed away.

'There's just one problem, Morris,' I said, wishing I didn't have to. 'I think I've got another one.'

We were sitting down again, this time in my workroom, with all the lights focused on my tenner's worth from X.

'And you still won't tell me where you got it? Oh, come off it, Lina; it came via that stinking old scoundrel from whom Griff gets a few bits and bobs from time to time. I've met him, remember! I can't remember who was more surprised, him or me.' He chuckled at the memory, a really nice treacly laugh with a smile that lit up his whole face.

It was a bit more than a few bits and bobs, but I wasn't going to point that out. Or to confirm his theory. We owed X far too much for me to dob him in; friend Morris might be, but he was still a policeman.

'Suppose you just tell me about it,' I said.

'I could tell you my theory. The first is that both this and the other one have come from the same collection, presumably not by fair means. Oh, you might have paid good money for the first one, but that doesn't mean it should ever have been offered for sale.'

I pulled a face. 'I actually went and talked to the guy in whose cardboard box of rubbish it had turned up. Bugger Bridger, as my father called him. They're neighbours, but not close, in any sense.' I paused to let Morris's next gust of laughter subside. 'Colonel Bridger said he'd never seen it. On the other hand, my father said he dimly recognized it: he'd seen someone in the neighbourhood take snuff from it – even recalled a worn bit by the catch where the owner's thumb would have rubbed it. And though at one time he did most things dimly, these days he does seem to have a bit more functioning between the ears. So he might be telling the truth.'

'And Bugger Bridger might be lying?'

'I wouldn't bet on it. One theory, for what it's worth, is that someone slipped it into the box either by mistake or for safe keeping. And either in his stable, where he kept the box, or at the fête, when I found it and someone tried to nick it.'

'That bit's news to me. Any CCTV footage?'

'Morris, this is deepest, most rural Kent! I did suggest that Robin ask the guy who'd been taking snaps of the event for the parish mag for all his photos, on the off-chance they showed anything, anything at all, but he's been a bit busy and I'm afraid I forgot to remind him.'

He fished out a notepad and jotted. 'And X said?'

'You've met X. He's not given to gossip, is he?'

'But I'd trust you to slide in a salient question.' His smile made the room feel a lot warmer.

'I did fish a bit – mentioned Bossingham. Which made him try to cancel the deal – cost me an extra couple of quid. Shit, Morris! You bastard! I didn't want to involve X, not at all!' I'd done the unforgivable – I'd betrayed a friend's trust. 'Just take the fucking thing and go. Now. And I hope it's a sodding fake!'

He tore the page from his pad and, tearing it into confetti, pressed it into my palm. I dropped the shreds in the kitchen waste bin, destined for the compost heap.

'All off the record, Lina. And I promise not to run X to earth unless I really have to. And I shall keep your name out of it.'

'You? *You* might. But *you* won't be talking to him. Not with your rank. It'll be some shiny underling keen to please and to get a promotion who does that. Someone who doesn't know the meaning of discretion. Don't you understand? He trusted me. And I've grassed him up!' I bunched my fists, ready to do violence.

He grabbed my wrists. 'No, you are not going to hit yourself. For God's sake, what would Griff say if he came home and found you with a pair of black eyes? Stop it. Sit down. Please.'

I stared. How did he know about my self-harming? I thought that was between me and Griff.

As I shuddered into quiet, he moved his hands up my arms, across my shoulders, and to my face. 'Don't you understand, Lina, I would never, ever do anything to harm you?'

And I believed him. Until he kissed me.

THIRTEEN

We'd got as far as my bed before I truly realized what was happening. Not that I wasn't willing. I was more than willing. Heavens, I was tearing his clothes off.

It was the sight of the three bears on my bed that brought me to my senses, in particular the one he'd once given me as a farewell present. Farewell as in 'I'm going to be the father of someone else's baby'.

'Stop. We have to stop,' I gasped, pulling away from him. 'We mustn't. You're married.' He'd actually bought a belated engagement ring for Penny from our shop, which I felt at the time was a weird thing to do. And Griff and I had sent a pretty coral and silver rattle cum teething ring for their baby's christening. 'You're Leda's father, remember.' I grabbed Tim as a shield, before realizing it might have been a stronger statement to hold the one he'd given me. I'd never cared for it enough to give it a name until Griff had pointed out what a swell it was, as superior as the bear Aidan had given me. They'd become Nash and Brummell.

'Leda's father, am I? Not according to my dear wife.' He grabbed Tim and hurled him at the wall.

Retrieving him and hugging him better, I put him back on the pillow. Turning to Morris, I took a deep breath. 'Come downstairs. I'll get some coffee and you can tell me all about it.'

I think he sank at least as much whisky as coffee, but I didn't blame him.

'A DNA test on a baby? It sounds a bit extreme,' I said. I knew it was only a gob-swab, because I'd been resisting someone's demands for me to have one, but I was old enough to make my own decisions, and obviously Leda wasn't.

'That's what the other guy wants. A horn player in the same orchestra,' he said, staring at the empty glass.

'And Penny agrees?'

'She thinks it's highly likely – always did, apparently. To think I only went back to her because she was pregnant.'

There was a very long silence. I didn't think I should break it – to be honest, I wasn't sure I could, given the effect that Penny's pregnancy had had on me.

'I love her. Utterly and completely. I'd die for her. I knew the first moment I saw her, the moment I first held her in my arms. I love comforting her in the middle of the night. I didn't know love could be like this. It hurts, Lina. She's part of me. And now some scientist's going to come along and say she's not. She's part of someone else.'

For a time I'd thought he was saying all those things about Penny, and I was ready to scream. Now I realized who he meant, I understood completely. 'Only biologically. Like me and my father. I may have his genes, but it's Griff I love. Much the same way as you love Leda.'

'So what do I do?'

I knew he didn't really want an answer, but he got one all the same, even if it was a question. 'Where's Leda now?'

'With her parents.' I didn't know a voice could sound so bitter. 'I've been turfed out of my own house.'

'Bloody hell. And what does your lawyer say?'

'What's the point of involving the law?'

'You're a policeman and you have to ask that?' I squeaked. 'No, no more whisky. You can sleep here, but you've got to be on the road first thing, banging on the door of the best family law solicitor there is.'

'Why?' he asked dully.

'Because if you love Leda that much, you can bet she loves you. OK? And it'd be more than a crime to drop out of her life – it'd be a sin!'

'Where are you going?'

'To switch on the computer. Surf the Internet. Find you that lawyer.'

Breakfast was a very strange meal. It was highly nutritious, because breakfasts at our cottage always were, but equally full of things not said.

The second snuffbox sat on the table between us.

'And your theory is?' Morris asked, prodding it.

'That the first is genuine. Well, who am I to argue with your experts? I bet when they'd cleaned it up they found the area of wear my father remembers. This one? When it's cleaned up, I bet you'll find a brilliant copy, artificially aged. Only it may not be worn thin by generations of thumbs. All the same, I'd like you to take it with you – right? And you leave me a receipt. And a receipt for the other one, come to think of it.'

'I left one with Freya Webb.'

'Who hasn't got round to passing it on to me yet. And I want it not because I don't trust either of you, but because I really want to have a bit of paper to wave at anyone who turns up here demanding the box.'

'You really think you're at risk as long as anyone thinks it's here?'

'Didn't Freya make that clear? Someone breaks in here and beats Griff up in his own home, which is why he's with Aidan in Tenterden.' I didn't so much as flick a glance at him under my eyelashes. 'Sure, we've got lots of photos of him, currently in police hands, but Griff's sure the intruder was wearing really brilliant make-up. And with his stage background, he should know. So all the computer matching in the world may not come up with the right mugshot. It's not just us, either, of course. Mrs Walker is very careful about shop security, and her fiancé's with her a lot of the time, but she's vulnerable. Someone even tried to run Robin off the road when he was driving our van,' I added, 'so I've got myself nice anonymous hired wheels. Actually, what I really need is not so much a receipt as a tattoo on my forehead: *I haven't got the damned snuffbox any more!*'

He smiled slowly. 'You know, it's a bit of a risk, but I might be able to improve on that. It'll take a couple of hours to set it up, but it might protect you and even flush out the rightful owner. Can't think why I didn't think of it before.'

'You've had a lot on your plate,' I said. 'And you've still got to get that lawyer sorted. Though,' I continued thoughtfully, 'in the cold light of day I wonder if ordinary conversation might be better. If they're in the same orchestra, they'll both be playing at the same time. What'll happen to poor Leda then? They can't just pop her quietly into a cello case.'

'Relegate myself to being a free babysitter?'

'Isn't that what a lot of fathers opt to do? Quality time, Morris: she could be all yours most evenings. How about that?' Even as I said the words, I could see drawbacks. An officer as senior as Morris couldn't guarantee having acres of empty hours. 'I do think you need your house back, though,' I conceded.

'Bloody right I do. I think Penny sees that. It's all bloody Oliver's fault.'

'Split his lip for him: then he wouldn't be able to play.'

'Don't tempt me.' Actually, it was all too clear that I did – tempt him, I mean. 'Can I use your office?' he asked quickly. 'Make a few calls, send a few emails?'

'Feel free.'

Suddenly everything seemed to have two meanings. Blushing painfully, I cleared the table, stowing what I could in the dishwasher, stacking the rest for hand-washing. Manual work was supposed to help you think clearly – that was what I always said. But it didn't seem to be working this morning.

I agreed to Morris's weird plan because I thought it might help St Jude's church. So it wasn't just me standing beside the ancient church door, but Robin and Fi too. The reporter was a friendly woman about my age whom I recognized from *South East Today*.

'So it's St Jude's that will benefit from the sale of this historic box?' she summed up.

'Unless the rightful owner comes forward,' I said clearly. 'Meanwhile, it's in safe hands. Because the police think it might have been stolen, it's locked away safely at Scotland Yard.'

There. It was what I think is called a wrap. Robin and I hugged. So did Robin and Fi, who managed to clasp me very loosely indeed for appearance' sake, but didn't put her heart into it, not by any means. I'd no idea what I'd done to get up her nose, but something had clearly offended her.

While the cameraman stowed his gear, the reporter and I

nattered a bit about my work, which I'd carefully not mentioned at all during the interview. Morris's idea had been that I should simply appear as someone helping out at the fête, not as an antiques dealer. He wanted me to radiate innocence, some righteous indignation that someone had tried to nick anything from a church, and a noble generosity to wrap the whole thing up. He'd watched some of the interview, but had had to nip off to his car to take a phone call.

He was still on the phone when the interview finished, so I was happy to talk to the reporter as long as she wanted. Only then did I admit I had anything to do with antiques, though I played it down, as if really I was just a restorer. She seemed to think that this was a weird job for a young woman. When she mentioned the possibility of a little piece on the evening news, I smiled even more and passed her my card. But I said I'd rather wait till the snuffbox problem had been resolved; I reasoned that the more publicity for Tripp and Townend the better, but not if it cast in doubt all my nobility.

Robin grabbed me. 'I'm not happy about not telling all the truth. You know, about your job, and about your getting tripped up and injured and—'

'This is for a two minute piece, Robin. May be edited down further, the reporter said. The police press people only organized it to get people off my back and to do what you and I tried the other day – to find who really owns it. Didn't someone say that less is more?'

Morris closed his phone so I let myself into his car.

'Well done. It all looked highly professional,' he said, with a smile. 'Lunch?'

'Why not?'

'I've been texting Penny, like you suggested.'

Had I?

'I said all those things I said to you. I said I didn't care whose biological child Leda was. I wanted to be part of her life. One way or another.'

'And she said?'

'She'd think about it. Which may not sound much but is an improvement, believe me. Thank you.' He kissed my cheek.

Chastely. Only when we were miles from a camera did he kiss me again. On the mouth. Far less chastely.

I waved him off from the cottage, now mercifully free of snuffboxes. All the same, I locked up carefully, only opening the door to take in the couriered parcel containing what turned out to be an exquisite piece of Meissen. So that was the rest of my day filled, apart from a couple of phone calls to and from Griff.

He was over the moon at the piece on the TV and talked of my going across to Tenterden for a celebration supper.

'No booze till I've finished this group,' I said. 'One little shake of the hand and there goes five thousand pounds' worth of porcelain. We'll have a proper party when you and Aidan get back from London. Did you manage to get tickets for that opera . . .?'

On a roll, and without Griff to hassle me about beauty sleep, I worked on. It wasn't until nearly one that I went back to my bedroom.

Tim, Nash and Brummell regarded me wide-eyed. But at least I could guarantee they wouldn't tell a soul what they'd seen in the last twenty-four hours.

FOURTEEN

'd only just cleared my breakfast things when the phone rang. Robin was on his way and thought he'd better let me know in advance.

It was hard to work out his tone, but I said he would be welcome. After all, I had to stay in for another parcel delivery. A piece of early twentieth century Worcester, it was important enough to come by special courier, not just lumped in a van with a lot of other parcels. I knew the driver quite well by now, since the repair was one of several sent by a fellow antiques dealer, Harvey Sanditon. Harvey and I seemed to have something going at one time, only it didn't work out. He still put work my way, usually in a highly flirtatious tone that I tried to match. I was over the whole thing, but happy to take his money, and happier still to work on the high class china and porcelain he specialized in.

When she let herself into the shop, Mrs Walker was in a chatty mood, full of my TV appearance. She was really peeved I'd not plugged Tripp and Townend, and it was only the sound of the house doorbell that allowed me to escape.

I checked. Yes, it was Robin.

'I managed to get the photos you wanted,' he said, sounding something between sulky and apologetic. 'Of the fête. Quite a lot. Brian emailed them to me. I put them on this memory stick,' he added, now triumphant.

Making coffee, I didn't point out he could have forwarded everything to our computer. For a bright man with an Oxbridge degree, Robin could sometimes be as dim as me.

It was a lovely morning, the sun warming the corner where Griff and I sometimes have breakfast, so, having set the locks and activated the security system, I led the way outside. Just in case, I took the old ashtray too.

Robin glared at it. 'It's nearly as bad as taking snuff, isn't it? I've just been reading up on James I. Not keen on tobacco in any form. It was very much an illicit pleasure.' He lit up, all the same. 'Didn't stop people, I'll bet. How's Griff, by the way?'

'Pleased as Punch. Aidan's managed to get tickets for *Magic Flute*,' I said, 'with that Russian soprano.'

Wrong.

'Do you realize how much subsidy something like the Royal Opera House gets? Whereas wonderful local theatre groups, those that spend their lives touring cold, miserable village halls with no facilities to speak of, can't squeeze a penny out of the Arts Council?'

I did, but thought I'd better let him talk his talk and finish a second fag before saying anything.

Time ticked by.

'Let's go and look at those photos,' I risked suggesting, not just to change the subject and diffuse some of the general anger buzzing round him this morning, but also to speed things on. Even without the delivery, I had enough restoration work for three weeks, but I also had to think about an antiques fair coming up in Devon. Griff had promised to be back with me in time, thank goodness; all that preparation and setting up aren't much fun on your own. I stood up. Robin took the hint and followed me inside to the office.

We peered at the screen. Dozens and dozens of photos.

'Brian had a new camera,' Robin explained. As if he needed to.

At least everything was properly focused – my guess was that the camera did that all by itself. But as for framing and composing . . . Well, I didn't take many snaps myself, but Aidan did, and he had a strict rule that he never let anyone see what he'd done until he'd run them through a computer program that would straighten verticals, crop rubbish from the edges and improve colour saturation. That was just for starters. Maybe someone should introduce this guy to the program.

So here were upwards of sixty photos of people I'd never seen before. I clicked through them quite quickly, which I could tell irritated Robin, who wanted me to deal with them with due decorum. But I'd only caught glimpses of the would-be thief – from behind at that – and of the guy who'd tripped me, and thought that if I gave myself the same conditions it would help me to recognize them. It didn't. I went and fetched my magnifying glass, which I wielded with a flourish. Time to concentrate. Capital C. Not just on the foreground either. Now would Robin realize I was taking it seriously?

'No luck?' he prompted me.

'Not on the thief. Nor on the guy who tripped me. Or have I missed someone?'

'No. But I think that's the guy who promised to call the police.' He pointed. 'He's not one of my parishioners, however, so I don't suppose it helps much.'

I followed the line of his finger, already showing signs of nicotine staining. Time to perk things up a bit, so I went into the Crop part of Photosmart, our photo program, clipping away everything I didn't want. The result was very fuzzy, however. 'Doesn't ring any bells. But that guy there – the one next to the guy in the stocks – I know him all right. He was the man at the reception and in M and S – the one who looked at me as if I were something you'd brought in on your shoe. This one.' I clicked away. 'Do you know him?'

'Not from Adam. Just a guy.'

'But a guy who gets to go to the Cathedral drinkies. So someone must know him,' I added helpfully.

'If you think I'm going to phone the Archbishop's office and ask for the guest list, forget it. All he did was grump at you. You challenged him later. He denied it. End of.'

Something had really got to him, hadn't it?

Something about a soft answer turning away wrath came into my brain. 'How about you? Any familiar faces apart from phone man? You know, people who've dropped into church once and then popped up again?'

'People do that all the time. You don't sign an attendance contract, you know. I mean, how often do you go to your parish church, let alone any of mine?'

'Point taken. People work on Sundays these days, don't they? But you're the sort of person to pick up vibes, Robin.'

'Spotting a would-be thief while I'm giving him Communion? Don't think so.'

We were spared any more squabbling by the arrival of the

courier bringing my next repair. Trev, a wiry man in his fifties who loved antiques in a quiet and undemonstrative way, always insisted on carrying the parcel into what he called my operating theatre. Then he would unpack it himself, getting me to sign for the damage I'd been asked to deal with and noting anything else. Robin wandered in.

'This is Trev, who's brought this for me to work on,' I said. 'And this is Robin. Look, Trev's just driven up from Devon. You don't suppose you could rustle up a cuppa for him while I check over my patient?'

A few minutes later he came in with a mug and a fistful of papers. 'Pressed the wrong button on the computer,' he muttered. 'I can't stop it. It's just spewing them out.'

I dashed down to find more cascading on to the floor. He'd only started to print all the photos. Fine. Except they were A4.

'Never mind,' I said brightly, as I returned. 'Only ordinary office paper, after all.' And I'd got backup supplies of all the colour cartridges he'd almost certainly emptied.

Trev watched me straighten them up into a tidy sheaf. 'What's this – the ugly bugs' ball? Sorry, vicar,' he added hurriedly.

Robin looked bemused rather than affronted. 'You've come all the way from Devon with just this vase?'

'It's one of a pair,' I said. 'Together they're worth something in the eight thousand pounds range. Separately or with one broken—' I shook my head.

'But they're just vases.'

'They're by Harry Davies,' Trev said, as if that would make everything clear. He stroked the gilded plinth.

Robin shook his head. Any moment we could have a rerun of his attack on the opera.

'Tell you what,' I said, 'the guy who sent this knows everyone in the antiques world. Right?'

Trev nodded. 'At the top end, at least,' he said.

'And you know a lot more,' I added, with a grin, which he returned.

The first snuffbox would almost certainly qualify, if Morris was to be believed. But I mustn't think of Morris now. 'Would

you mind if Trev looked at these photos? And then took them
back to show Harvey? They might just place someone.'

'What about the Data Protection Act? People's privacy?' he
squeaked.

'What about Griff getting beaten up? And you getting run
off the road? If I were you,' I added airily, 'I'd take the memory
stick along to Freya and see if any faces match any of her
records. Help her to steal a march on Scotland Yard.'

I might have flicked the Happy switch.

'Really? Do you think she'd mind?'

'She might find it extremely useful. As might Morris, of
course. I'll email these to him,' I said. 'See who comes up
with something first.'

Leafing through the photos, shaking his head from time to
time, Trev listened, sipping tea with which there was clearly
something wrong, though he was too polite to say so. At last,
with the air of someone who'd made a major sacrifice, he said,
'Mind if I use—'

'You know where it is,' I smiled.

'You're sure you can trust him?' Robin hissed. 'In your
house?'

'I always have.' But on those occasions Griff had been with
me. On impulse I reached for the phone.

Harvey answered first ring.

'Lovely vase,' I greeted him.

'Arrived safely?'

'Would you expect anything else of Trev?'

'Nothing.'

'I was going to send you a load of photos, just in case
there's anyone there you might know. Anyone, and however
you know them.'

'Sounds very mysterious.'

'I don't want to put ideas into your head: now we've spoken,
I'll email them instead, but I warn you they'll take forever to
send and receive – they're unedited.'

'Why not just the hard copies then? Via Trev?'

'Because I want you to look at figures in the background.
I know you've got a programme that can enhance
everything.'

'I have indeed. I never needed it to enhance you, however.' He paused while we shared a flirtatious giggle before asking, 'I suppose I can't come to collect the vase in person?'

'Of course you can.' Another game we always played. If he ever did turn up in person, I'd be so surprised that I'd probably drop whatever I'd repaired. 'Or you could drop into Matford next week and collect it then,' I added.

'Angel. Will Griff be there? I'll shout you both dinner at a little place I've just discovered. A gem to match you. Can you put me on to Trev?'

'Here he is now.'

Trev took the handset, but spoke to me. 'There's this really old guy still hanging around. He drifted away when I came to the door, but he's still at the end of the street. Just checked.'

Harvey must have picked something up. I heard him squawk: 'Keep an eye on her, Trevor.' I wish he hadn't added, 'Can't risk any damage to those hands of hers.'

It was probably just X, I told myself, with more goodies. He certainly wouldn't want to appear at the same time as anyone else. On the other hand, it was late in the day for a man who liked to arrive before breakfast, so I nipped down to check on the security system. It didn't take long for the men to join me. The three of us peered at the current view from our cameras. The street was empty as far as the cameras could scan. So I rewound to about five minutes before Trev arrived. Sure enough, an old guy wandered past, and then back again. Trev's anonymous Ford van arrived. The old man drifted away. Actually, a pretty fast drift. But then he came back again, and, staying the far side of the van, bent as if he was looking under a wheel arch. Somehow I didn't think he was checking the tyretread. I rewound to the time Robin arrived. His car got the same treatment, again from the side further from the pavement. But where was the old guy now?

Trev was ready to dash out and start hunting. I held him back. 'We don't know what he's put there and what will activate it.' Pressing the phone into Robin's hand I said, 'We need the police. Call Freya. Speed dial! It'll be quicker than nine nine nine. Now!'

FIFTEEN

'He was just attaching tracker devices,' Freya said. I was amazed she'd come out in person, since she was really a number-cruncher these days, as she was the first to point out. However, perhaps she liked to escape into the real world from time to time, especially when it was Robin who put in the call. 'Cheap and cheerful makes, easy to get hold of on the Internet. Plus he's scraped something off both sets of tyres, for some reason. Just cleared out a bit of the tread. I'd like you to get them changed before you think of driving off – you're both members of a car-rescue service, yes? And our forensic people will have a look.'

The village street was quiet again. It hadn't been very noisy before, apart from a few indrawn breaths and the sigh of curtains being twitched as our neighbours watched a guy operate a robot from the safety of an armoured car. He might have been working in Afghanistan. At least he didn't find anything nasty enough to warrant blowing anything up. Any moment an AA van might turn up for Trev, but Robin was going to have to change his wheel himself, since it seemed letting his membership lapse had been one of his recent economies.

Not replacing a highly illegal spare might have come under the same heading, too. He stared at it glumly, clearly unable to put it on the car under the gaze of a senior policewoman with whom he shared what Griff would discreetly call a mutual attraction – goodness knows what he'd call this episode with Morris – and a couple of lingering male helpers.

Looking at the poor car leaning on an unsteady jack, I heard myself say, 'I'll run you over to Maidstone when we're finished here.' It wasn't pure kindness. There were certain items from the bottom of my make-up drawer, well below the level of my cosmetics, that needed replacing. I might have inherited my lust from my father, but I certainly wasn't going to be as careless as he. Ever. But to save Griff's blushes as much as my own, I didn't feel I could buy them from the village pharmacy or from the mini-supermarket.

Once again I copied everything from our security system for the police, and then waved them off. Next it was Trev's turn.

'Mind you,' he said, fastening his seat belt, 'I really don't like leaving you on your own. A slip of a girl like you. You know Harvey'd come up if you said the word. Never known him so smitten, Lina.'

'Oh, we always flirt like that on the phone,' I said. 'Doesn't mean anything, Trev.'

'It might not to you. You want to meet Mrs Sanditon. Estelle. Then you'd see why he's sweet on you. Plus you're pretty enough in your own right. And as for those clever hands of yours . . . Well, like I say, you'd only have to pick up the phone. Tell you what, I could drive him – chaperone you.'

He would too, wouldn't he? 'Thanks, Trev, I appreciate that. See you next time,' I said, patting the roof of his van. 'Look after yourself.'

'Nice to know whoever that guy was can't track me, anyway,' he said. His face fell. 'Unless he left another one anywhere . . . No, he didn't have time to, did he? Goodbye, luvvy – God bless!' He waved, ready to pull out.

I stopped him. 'Tell you what, you keep an eye on that rear view mirror. And I'll get the fuzz to do an extra check on Robin's. If there's a problem, I promise to call you as soon as I know.'

By the time Robin and I got back, a familiar Saab was sitting in the White Hart car park. Morris strolled up to the cottage while we were wrestling with the new tyre, and, leaning against our front door, offered helpful suggestions.

'Haven't you got some masterpiece you ought to go and ransom?' I asked, pushing a lock of hair off my face with the back of my hand. Robin might be bright and generally strong, but he really was clueless about cars. All the more reason for AA membership, I'd have thought.

'There's one in Sweden, but Interpol are on to that. Are you sure that's not a bit overinflated? Or maybe it's the others that are soft. He embarked on the classic manly *see, I know the right pressures just by kicking the tyre walls* routine, with Robin soon joining in. I let myself into the house to find soap and water and have a conversation with Tim the Bear, before sending Robin off with a suggestion that the fuzz forensic team might like to give the whole car another once-over.

'The TV ploy didn't work, then,' I said later as Morris passed me a mug of tea. It was too hot, so I put it on the bedside cupboard. 'Because if it had, whoever planted the tracking devices would have known he didn't need to bother tailing my contacts.'

'So we're looking for someone in the south-east who doesn't watch TV or read the local press – we got a lot of newspaper coverage too,' he said ironically. 'There, you didn't even see it yourself, did you?'

'I've not had a lot of time, with the succession of visitors I've had this morning. You included, of course. Why did you come down?'

'I'd have thought the last hour made that abundantly clear. Plus I was out Folkestone way – someone trying to spirit something they shouldn't have through the Tunnel – when Freya Webb called to say there was further activity here. I wanted to make sure you were all right. Being guarded by teddy bears is one thing; I thought you might need a police presence. And I'd say you were expecting me.' He patted my morning's purchase. 'Maybe hoping?' It might have sounded smug, but he looked almost anxious.

I peered into my mug. Josie would have wanted to read the tea leaves. Even thinking about her made me twitch with guilt – I'd never phoned to ask about my double, or to pass on Griff's thanks for the cake, in whichever order. I'd never – the list was quite long.

'Post-coital *tristesse*?' he asked, touching my hair.

'Might be, if I knew the words,' I grumbled, trying hard to work out the meaning. Morris was one of the few people I'd ever told about my poor vocabulary (I'd learnt that word very early on!), and as far as I knew was the only one who'd ever betrayed my trust. He'd meant if for the best, of course, but a lot of things go wrong when people do that. 'The thing is, Morris, I've let all this snuffbox business bury me. I've got work to do, contracts to fulfil, a big fair next week. All without Griff, of course.'

'I can't say I'm sorry Griff's not here at the moment.'

'I know. He really needs a change after that break-in.'

'I wasn't quite thinking of Griff's well-being, Lina.'

'Neither was I, to tell you the truth,' I admitted. 'But every minute I listen to Robin's miseries, for instance, and he's got so much to bear at the moment, is a minute I can't be doing something else. A something that keeps our business afloat.'

'No, the economic climate's not good, is it? Any moment I expect a call saying our squad's been abolished or merged and that I've been transferred to Traffic.'

'Now who's got post-coital *tristesse*?' He didn't correct me so I must have used the term properly. 'Seriously, what if they do close you down?'

'I go private. Bruce Farfrae's always on at me to go in with him. Crime never stops, even when police officers are being made redundant. He'd like me to run his New York office. But obviously, I wouldn't want to move to the US.' He kissed my lips. 'Obviously. But we were talking about you, Lina. Your problems. Which I'm about to make worse, actually, as far as invading your time is concerned. I want to chew this business over with you officially.'

'Which means we'd better get dressed and go into the office,' I said, swinging my legs on to the floor.'

'Absolutely. But not just yet.'

'So when you went to see Colonel Bridger, he denied all knowledge of the snuffbox and this poor thing.' He patted the poor tatty folio.

'Never seen either of them ever before. My father recognized the box, don't forget.' *And would love to get his sticky mitts on the folio*, I added, but silently. To the best of my knowledge, Morris still thought my father was a boozy old idiot.

'I think we should talk to your father.' He got to his feet – we were off now, it seemed.

'And while we're in Bossingham, maybe we should look at

Bugger Bridger's neighbours. The ones sharing a boundary
with him. They could have popped it into his box of rubbish,
hoping someone would pick it up at the fête?'

'Why? It sounds a dead risky move. *Was* a dead risky move.
After all, you got there first. The whole point of covert
operations like that is that they're successful and that no one
else knows about them. But we can at least look at their
property. Now what?'

'Just texting my father to say we're on our way.'

'Texting? That's a bit twenty-first century!'

'So is Sky, and he's still hoping to find a hidden site for a
dish.' I didn't like not telling Morris that sending a text was
simply warning my father not to be doing any illicit forging
when we arrived. I preferred Morris to think of him as a
doddery old soak, rather than as a master forger.

'The locks you installed for me are still working very well,
as you can see,' my father told Morris. 'Had a bit of a scare
then – nice quiet life since. Until some other bastard turns up
claiming to be one of the family.'

As always, I tried not to flinch at the word. What was I if
not a bastard?

'It's surprising none has,' Morris ventured. After all, he'd
seen my father's list of sexual partners and their offspring.

'Nothing for them if they did. Everything belongs to the bloody
trust. Even that damn apology for a track, though they won't
admit it. Hope your suspension's still in one piece? The sump?'

Morris blinked. 'I think so.'

'Actually, there's a few quid in a trust fund Lina insisted I
set up. Sold some book to the nation – wouldn't take a penny
profit for herself. Maybe I've already told you. Sorry. Have
some more fizz.' He topped up Morris's glass before he could
put his hand over it. 'Any chance of your finding a few goodies
to sell, Lina? And bringing in a few cases next time you come?'

'In a minute,' I said. 'Morris is really here to talk about
that snuffbox I showed you. You said you remembered someone
round here using it. Colonel Bridger didn't. In fact, he didn't
even recognize it.'

'Johnnie Come Lately, isn't he? They say he's tidying up

his place because he's importing a mail order bride. Certainly didn't want to let me in to clutter the place up.'

'Nor Robin the Vicar and me when we went to talk to him. And no, he didn't so much as pinch my bum, thanks to you.'

My father leant confidingly towards me. 'It's not so much pinching, Lina, as—'

Morris rescued me. 'Is he normally a hospitable man? Or is this reluctance to admit people a recent development?'

'Always been a few pence short of a shilling – but then, the army, you see,' my father explained. I think.

'But you knew the snuffbox?' Morris fished in a pocket and put it into my father's hand.

'Yes, indeed. And it isn't this one, young man. The one I knew was worn, where the owner flicked it open. I told you, Lina. This is some copy. Not sure they've got the pattern the right way round either.'

Silently, I passed over my eyeglass. After a bit of a fuss about fitting it, as if he didn't use one regularly for his work, he peered at the snuffbox. 'Saw something on the box the other day. I know Lina thinks I'm wasting my time, but I learn some things you'd never dream of.'

He did.

'They can forge almost anything, you know.'

I looked away.

'And if someone thinks there's a market – bingo! Some nasty folk living in Kent, you know. A lot of so-called businessmen get shot – turns out their posh houses and great carts of cars are paid for by drugs money. Someone kidnapped in Ashford. A man gunned down outside Sainsbury's. Kenneth Noye gets road rage. People nick JCBs and dig cash machines out of post offices. It all happens here.'

Morris nodded, as if the information was new to him. 'So you think this is a forgery?' He looked at me. I'd said the same thing, hadn't I? And asked him to get it tested.

There was no stopping my father. 'Man in the news the other day selling fake furniture to people with more money than sense. He was Kent, too, come to think of it. And Lina tells me there's a man at these fairs she goes to sells nothing but dodgy bookshelves and dressers.'

I nodded. It was true. I was so impressed by all this righteous indignation that I almost believed my father had never forged an Elizabethan document in his life. With luck the idea would never even cross Morris's mind. When he spoke, I wasn't sure, however.

'So why do you think this is a fake?'

My father sighed, as if Morris was a dim child. 'You wouldn't get two of these boxes, not cropping up in the same place. The one I knew has been knocking around fifty years or so to my knowledge. Worn. This one – good as new, apart from this tarnish. None of the stuff Lina sells for me is dodgy, is it, my girl?' Before I could answer, he continued, 'And before you ask, she keeps a record of everything she takes – which she makes me sign, as if she's some Betterware salesman – and then she tells me how much she makes, keeps back her ten per cent and then makes me give her a receipt.'

'I'm just anxious in case any of the rest of your family turn up and accuse me of diddling you,' I said with a blush.

'Well, go and find me a pot of gold at the end of the corridor and sell it for me, there's a good girl. I'll just open another bottle of bubbly for Morris here.'

Leaving them alone had not been on my agenda. But I could hardly insist I stay and mind him.

'Before we drink any more, just tell me who was using this snuffbox. I mean, the original, of course,' Morris began as I left the room.

I didn't let myself stay and eavesdrop, much as I'd have liked to. All I heard was my father saying, 'I could be mistaken, probably am, but I've an idea it was old . . .'

For some time I'd had my eye on a pair of filthy Meissen lambs with cute little pink bows round their necks. I found them sickly sentimental, but a client had mentioned he'd started collecting sheep. Each to their own – and if it brought in cash I was happy to oblige. Once I'd cleaned these up, provided they were as perfect as they looked, they'd buy a few weeks' booze. So I grabbed them and headed back to the others.

My father stared. 'You know, I came across a few more of those the other day. Come with me.'

I managed not to gape. But he was right. In the far corner

of a filthy and broken corner cupboard on a half landing were three others – not with bows, but possibly earlier and more valuable. I gathered them carefully up, putting two in Morris's surprised hands. 'Nearly a flock now,' I said. 'Any more?'

'Any more, *Pa*,' he corrected me. 'Father's a bit pompous. Don't hold with this fashion of kids calling their parents by their Christian names, either.'

I made my mouth work. 'Any more, Pa?'

'As it happens, there may be one in the old nursery. I had it when I was a nipper.'

'That's in the trustees' half,' I objected. 'So you're not entitled.'

'Not even if I played with it with my nanny?'

'Probably not,' Morris said, still staring at his burden.

I tell you, it was nothing to mine.

'So your father – your *pa* – actually recalls seeing the snuffbox when he was young. Shame his memory stops there.'

'You're lucky to get any recollections from him. They're what Griff calls intermittent.'

'But why has the box surfaced now?' He braced himself as I, who'd held back on the champagne and was just within the alcohol limit, drove very slowly down the disputed track. 'And he's a lot better than when I last met him, Lina – what have you done to him? Hey, why are you crying? No, stop. Pull over and tell me all about it.'

It took several sobs and a lot of false starts before I could say it. 'All the time I've known him I've never called him anything. Not to his face. I mean, not a name. And now he wants me to.' I might have turned on a tap. And then I choked. 'Griff – he'll be so upset!'

'Why?'

'Because he's afraid I'll come to love my father best and leave the cottage and go and live at the Hall.'

'And will you?'

'Not a chance.'

He took my hand, and asked more quietly, 'Will you *ever* leave Griff and the cottage?'

SIXTEEN

Before I could get halfway to framing an answer to that, my phone rang. Pulling a face, I took the call. 'Robin?'

'Seems there's another tracker device on my car. So there's probably one on that guy Trev's too. Which means he's leading whoever down to your friend Harvey.'

'So it does. I'll call them.' With a word to Morris, I did just that – Trev first, since he was presumably most at risk. 'Just drive straight to your nearest police station,' I suggested.

'They're called phone boxes down here. But I take your point. Thanks for the warning. Will you tell Harvey or will I?'

'What is there to tell him? Unless you're outside his place now?'

'About a mile away as it happens. I'll do a nice big circle and fetch up in Exeter. God bless, luvvy!'

I phoned Harvey anyway, just to put him in the picture, and then started the engine again. 'Bugger Bridger's,' I said.

'Couldn't have put it better myself. OK. But we'll talk later – right?' He squeezed my hand.

I returned the pressure. 'The honest truth is I don't know. I really don't. It's more than just leaving a family home would be. He's my best friend and my business partner. And without him, I'd be less than nothing – some skeletal drug addict tart sleeping with strangers to bum enough for my next fix. He's given me everything – even my birth father, my pa, in a way. Hell's bells!' I'd been nosing out into the single track lane, but nearly lost my bonnet to a 4x4. I fell in behind it, at a pace that would have made Griff squeak in protest.

Unlike the 4x4, I dropped down to thirty to drive through the handful of houses that made up Bossingham and didn't speed up much to cross the Minnis.

'This used to be open land,' I said, gesturing. 'A common. But then it seemed that the wrong sort of undergrowth was taking over, so they got the best means of keeping it in check. Animals.'

'Hence the fences? Seems a shame.'

'Apparently, once they've done their job, they round up the animals, pull down and re-erect the fences, and put the animals in their new fields. All very scientific.'

'And all completely irrelevant to your present – well, crisis doesn't seem too strong a word for it. You're doing what I've seen people in bad accidents do – rabbit on about things with their mouths to stop their brains having to deal with more important issues.'

'Gee, thanks, Dr Morris.' I drove in silence for a while, but had an idea he was watching me. At last I said, 'The colonel's place is over there. There's a lay-by about fifty metres further on: I'll pull in there so he doesn't think I'm hassling him again.'

'He won't see you at all, Lina. He'll see me, and if he challenges me, I've got my ID to protect me. Why don't you phone Griff and tell him what's been happening?'

'And spoil his holiday? He's off to Covent Garden with Aidan – a boys' night out with bells on.'

With a squeeze of the hand, he was gone. I poked the sound system and came up with Classic FM. Not sure I wanted to be soothed, I hunted round for some other stations. Nope. Nothing I fancied. Once I was deep into pop culture; somehow Griff had weaned me off it, though I drew the line at his idea of pop, the Bee Gees. News? Another outrage in Afghanistan, with kids my age blown to bits. Even the weather forecast was bad, especially in the south-west, where Griff and I were heading at the weekend.

'You're right,' Morris declared as he let himself in and fastened his seat belt. 'Anyone could get into the colonel's outbuildings, and not just from the farmyard the other side either. There's only one window on the side of the house you'd have to pass if you came from the road. I made it there and back without having baying hounds set on me.'

'And you saw?'

'Boxes of what looked liked books and tat, in equal measure. I should arrange to be away for next year's church fête, if I

were you – you don't want to have to push crap like that to
unsuspecting punters.'

'Poor St Jude's needs more than the odd fête, poor thing.
It's a lovely place – feels right inside, though the churchyard's
dominated by a pretty nasty Victorian family tomb, all marble
angels and terracotta curlicues.'

'Is it far? It'd be nice to see the source of all this
business.'

'Five minutes down the road.'

Someone had left the wrought iron gates open, despite the
little notice suggesting they close it. Another asked people to
clear up after their dogs.

'Why exercise animals here when there's a perfectly good
wood next door?' Morris demanded. 'I see what you mean
about that tomb: wouldn't be out of place in Highgate cemetery,
maybe, but in a backwater like this!' He stopped, frowning.

Naturally, I did too, trying to work out why he looked so
troubled. There was a sweet smell I'd not noticed before,
but then, the countryside was full of weird smells, most of
them a bit off. And flies. They'd not bothered us during the
fête. As one, we headed where they seemed to be gathering,
the porch, but Morris beat me to it.

In one strange move he stopped, turned and, scooping me
to him for a moment, turned me round and pushed me towards
the car. 'Go and call Robin, but make him stay with you. I'll
do the rest. When I can get sodding network coverage, that
is!' he added, almost shaking his mobile.

He paced with me, still making sure I didn't turn back. Did
he think I'd turn in to a pillar of salt or something? At last he
got through, hunching so I didn't hear everything he said. But
I didn't need to, did I? For all his professionalism, even a
policeman couldn't disguise his shock at finding a body. IC1
male.

Who? Not Robin, obviously, or I wouldn't be calling his
number now. The colonel? No. Suddenly I felt very sick, and
not the nausea that came with the smell of death. More
closed down inside. Like a divvying attack, only worse. I knew
who the flies were after. Just like that. Morris didn't need to

come over to break the news gently, though he did. And I think the fact I told him before he could speak that it was X scared him as much as it scared me.

Robin arrived a very few minutes after a whole fleet of police vehicles. 'Any idea who—?'

I nodded, unable to stop tears from dripping off my nose. I don't think I was actually crying for X, to be honest. Not as such. Griff had always dinned into me that one extra drink could kill him, that the stuff he usually consumed would have rotted the liver of most other men years back. But I could hardly embark on a detailed account of my own personal events, even though I felt deeply dishonest when Robin assumed I was grief-stricken for someone I knew well.

With Morris, later, much later, in the safety of our kitchen, I was more honest. 'I only met him once. Met, as in had a conversation, as opposed to seeing him sliding away from the cottage. Same as you, really. Just the once. But I'd fed him, which makes everything seem more personal.'

He nodded as if he'd understood. 'It would have been a hard enough day for you even without this,' he said.

'You're sure it was natural causes?'

'That's the third time you've asked that. And my answer's the same. We'll have to wait for the post-mortem. To be honest, I'd be surprised if it was anything else: hell, Lina, when I saw – met – him he looked dreadfully ill.' He stared somewhere I couldn't see. 'It might not have been only the lack of personal hygiene that made him smell like that, you know.' He stopped, looking pretty choked himself. 'Now, about phoning Griff. He'd want to be here, you know. Looking after you.'

'And mourning X himself. Shit, Morris, I don't even know the poor guy's name!'

'Which is another reason for calling Griff.'

As if agreeing, I checked my watch. Nearly eight. Griff would be in the opera house by now, mobile firmly off. 'Too late. I'll have to wait till – what time will the opera finish? Eleven? And he needs his sleep, Morris – he's not been well,' I pleaded.

He held my face so I couldn't turn away from him. 'You've

got this all wrong, Lina. He'd want to look after you, not be nannied himself. He's a grown man – can make his own decisions about coming back overnight. OK, we'll have to leave phoning till after the opera's over, though believe me I have been known to have a call put out at the Festival Hall when I needed to. And by the way, don't think I don't know you weren't buying him time.' The warmth of his eyes belied his stern voice. 'And maybe buying us time too? Maybe you didn't want me scooting off to a Travelodge or something and leaving you with only Tim the Bear and his smart but uncuddled friends for company?'

I didn't argue. I poured us both another glass of wine, but found I didn't want mine.

'Did I see an Indian takeaway down in the village?' he asked. 'Nothing like too much cholesterol, excess salt and meat from a dubious supplier when you feel a bit down. Shall we walk down together and set all the neighbours gossiping?'

In the event, I didn't reach Griff till the following morning. He'd forgotten to switch his mobile back on again, and in the end I had to call the more efficient Aidan's. Aidan didn't see any reason why Griff should abandon the timed tickets for the latest National Gallery exhibition, not to come and mourn someone who merely dredged car-boot sales and came up with the occasional find. However, Griff did, immediately. But only to come and comfort me.

Morris took over. There was something very intimate about having him take the handset from my hand and continue my conversation.

'She's all right, Griff, I promise you. No, of course I didn't let her – I ID'd him myself, of course. So there's no reason why you should come down before you've looked your look – the Kent police will want to know everything you know about him, but since it looks as if his liver finally gave up the ghost, I can't imagine it'll be anything more than that. Nothing urgent till after the PM anyway . . . No, I don't like the word *autopsy* either. Of course I will. And I'm sure young Robin will be round to offer a spot of spiritual consolation.'

*   *   *

'The press'll love this, won't they? The church gets featured because of its fête. Twenty-four hours later a wino breathes his last in the porch the fête was raising money for.' Robin paused to reflect on what he'd said. He didn't appear to think it was inappropriate, which shocked me. 'The worst of it is, it's an unexplained death, so St Jude's being treated as a possible crime scene – which means I can't even get in to pray for him.'

He was sitting in the garden again; actually, puffing away like Thomas the Tank Engine, he was pacing round, glaring from time to time as if to rebuke the garden for being so tiny. Comforter he was not, although the only reason Morris had headed back to London was because he thought Robin could do a better professional job. He'd promised to be back as soon as he humanly could, but like me, he had work to do, and X's death was naturally being investigated by Kent police.

Eventually, I asked, 'How has Fi taken the news? I mean, right on her patch – even more hers than yours because you've got all those other churches to worry about and that one's very much her baby.'

He flushed. 'I couldn't get through to her last night or this morning. She must be away. You can't just leave a message with someone's answering service saying someone's died, can you? So I thought I'd write a proper note and drop it round, which I did. And I'll make a follow-up visit when I head back.'

'She'll have heard if she was anywhere near the local news,' I pointed out. 'Funny she hasn't phoned you.' Funny, and though I didn't say it, a bit worrying, for one reason or another. Perhaps, on the other hand, she was on the razzle with Colonel Bridger and not worrying about mundane things like unexplained deaths.

As soon as I could, I shooed him off, saying I must work despite everything. Which I tried. Nothing as complicated as Harvey's Edwardian vase. Another wretched Victorian Toby jug from our collector client. Even when new and perfect, this would never have been attractive, let alone beautiful.

I'd just finished the first bit of gluing, when the phone went. Lovely Morris, saying he'd arrived safely and one or two other things of no interest to anyone but me, to which I responded

with equally private things. Suddenly, however, I heard myself
saying, 'Did I ever tell you I have a doppelgänger?' and pouring
out the whole story of Cashmere Roll-Neck and Josie.

He didn't laugh. He didn't say anything for a bit. At last
he said, 'I think we should make every effort to find her.' And
it didn't sound as if he wanted us to invite her to tea.

I made him promise not to go knocking on Josie's door – or,
indeed, let anyone else disturb her. As for Cashmere Roll-Neck,
Morris would have no compunction in asking the people in
charge of the Cathedral party for a guest list.

'But why the interest?' I pressed him.

'I don't know, really. Just policeman's nose. Like your divvy
instinct. But I've got word someone's trying to nick a Monet
from someone with more money than security, and I'm afraid
your double will have to go on the back-burner.'

'Sounds pretty uncomfortable for her. Anyway, I owe Josie
a phone call, and I'll raise it with her then.'

'Will you tell Robin I'm on to Cashmere Roll-Neck? Is
he all right, by the way? He seems really edgy.'

'Edgy doesn't begin to describe it. I'm really worried about
him, but he's so offhand, it's hard to ask all the sympathetic
questions a friend should put. I know he's overworked, and
domestic things seem to be getting on top of him. He's really
worried about the future of St Jude's – and now X's death, of
course.'

'Sounds to me as if he's not been the shoulder to cry on I
hoped he'd be.'

'His poor shoulders are so hunched, it'd be hard to find
anywhere to lean. Ah!' I added with a grin, 'Griff's back – I
just heard him call.'

'And what will you tell him about us?'

'The way he is, he'll probably tell me.'

SEVENTEEN

G riff, however, barely had time to do more than drop a bunch of exciting-looking bags in the kitchen and sink into his favourite chair with a cup of green tea before the Kent police arrived, in the form of a tough-looking officer I'd met before, Steve – never Chalky – White. Then he'd been in uniform. Now he was in CID, he said with a grin that removed most of the Neanderthal from his features. He was here to talk about X. You could see him put quotation marks round the letter.

'Trouble is, we've no idea who he is, and we hoped you could fill us in a little, Mr Tripp. We gather that you were at least acquainted with him.'

'I've never used his real name, ever. Even to Lina he was always X. Because I promised I wouldn't. I'm not even sure the name he gave me is his real name, because he didn't trust many people. He scavenged car-boot sales and skips, and despite his perpetual fug of alcohol he had an eye for a bargain. He bought dirt cheap and sold for not very much more. Lina was shocked at how little I paid him, but that was part of the deal. He told me if I gave him twenty pounds, it would become twenty pounds' worth of alcohol. He didn't need to tell me that such an amount could be fatal. He made regular trips here and, I should imagine, to other dealers. I never asked, though, Mr White, because I was sure he wouldn't tell me. Once he came to find DI Morris of the Met Fine Arts Squad having breakfast here. I should be very surprised if he told him any more about himself. And very recently he came across Lina, I hear – who fed him well and gave him a couple of pounds more than he'd have got out of me.' He flashed me a loving smile.

'Did he always bring good quality items, sir?'

'Sometimes he brought absolute pups. I still paid him. Once he brought an item I sold for thousands. I still gave him no more than a tenner. But he wanted me to know if anything happened to him. If he died, of course,' he corrected himself angrily. 'I don't think he expected it to be in a comfortable bed. He said he always carried a slip of paper telling whoever found him to contact me.' Griff's voice was very bleak. 'Always,' he added.

Steve's head jerked back. 'I don't think – I'd better check on that, sir.'

'Please do. It may have significance. You know that someone forced his way into our cottage recently – I've only just returned from a touch of convalescence. The intruder gained admittance by claiming he had news of X for me.'

Steve had done his homework. 'You didn't say that in your statement, sir.'

'So I didn't. Because X wouldn't have thanked me for bringing him to your attention. But now he's dead, I can.'

'You still refer to him as X, sir.'

'My apologies. Graham Parker. I believe he was in what they now call the military, which is surely an adjective, not a noun. Another Americanism, I fear. The SAS. So he was a tough man. I only dared mention his family once. I believe the expression is "being blanked out". As for his daily doings, I know nothing. It wasn't that I didn't care, Officer. I took the view that as long as he came here for regular amounts of money – and yes, I fed him too, Lina, when he would accept it – I was keeping together what little was left of his self-esteem. In fact, I was always surprised to see him again – constantly afraid that one of your colleagues would bring the sad news of his death, brought by that slip of paper which I deduce has not been found. Or acted on?' Griff shot him a suddenly sharp look.

Steve took the hint. Producing his mobile, he asked Griff if he could make a call.

'You'll find the best coverage over by the door.'

We watched Steve's face. We knew the answer before he gave it.

'So what happened to it?' he wondered aloud, sitting down hard. He produced that grin again, but an ironic version, making him look very sinister. 'Your visitor might know. And I've some news, sir. Normally in a case like this, the PM is low priority. It's suddenly jumped up the list.'

Griff nodded. 'Are you ex-army yourself?'

'I look as if I should have been, you mean? Actually, my degree was in Divinity.'

I tried not to goggle and even harder not to squeak when I piped up, 'He sold me a snuffbox. Pretty well the twin of the priceless one I talked about on TV. It was a fake,' I said bluntly. 'I didn't say anything so I don't know if he knew it was. But he was ready to grab it back when I asked him if he'd got it from near Bossingham. Does this mean he knew something or that he just didn't like being questioned?' I asked, meaning the question for Griff.

'More likely just the latter,' he said.

If I hadn't been to London, Griff reasoned, London should come to me. The bags he'd had to leave in the kitchen were full of things he hoped would please me. The plunder this time included the latest phone, with every app in the world: I'd have to ask Morris to talk me through using it, since Griff handed it over as if it had dropped from a spaceship. There were prettier undies than I'd ever have bought for myself, unguents to keep me eternally youthful and sweet smelling, a palette of eye make-up, and so many titbits from Harrods Food Hall we might never have to cook again. Actually, these were really for Griff, but I accepted them as part of the whole coney . . . corny . . . the whole overflowing horn thing they had on statues with flowers and fruit tumbling out. I'd have to look it up. There was even another bear from Aidan, another limited-edition button-eared Steiff. They really had started to attach themselves to me, like the beginning of an expensive collection, but I relegated them to my bookshelves so that Tim, who cost comparatively little but who was worth more than rubies, wouldn't feel threatened.

Cornucopia!

Griff's face had healed nicely, and he tried desperately to bubble with enthusiasm about his trip.

'There's no need,' I said, pouring him a more generous pre-supper drink than usual. 'I hardly knew X, but I feel sort of sore, here.' I pressed my heart. 'Did you really tell Steve White everything about him?'

'Everything I knew. Which was nothing. Family? Friends? There must be people out there wondering what happened to dear old Graham, or to that strange Mr Parker. And now they may find out the most horrible way.'

While I put out a selection of the Harrods' delights, Griff checked the messages I'd taken for him and his personal, as opposed to our business, emails. The phone rang. I was ready to dive for it, but of course he was in the office already, so I was jumping up and down by the time Griff returned.

'Josie,' he said. 'Apparently, your double is alive and kicking in St Leonard's. She's seen her twice on the bus. But, of course, poor Josie isn't up to tailing anyone, not unobtrusively at least, poor darling.' He looked at me. 'Do I gather that dear Josie wasn't the person you hoped was phoning?'

'It's the news I didn't want. I've a nasty feeling it's not going to turn out well, this double.'

He hugged me, but then held me so he could look at my face. 'Could she be a half-sister? Would this worry you? You've pretty well got your father house-trained at last. Are you afraid this newcomer will upset the tenor of your existence?'

I let him see that I was trying hard to work things out. 'I think my father and I are gradually managing a working relationship, not really father and daughter for all he wants me to call him Pa. Yes!' He'd know my smile wasn't altogether wholehearted. 'Quite a breakthrough. And in the past, when he thought other people might have some claim on him, he went out of his way – for him! – to reassure me that they'd have to work their passage, same as I'd done. So that's not really a problem. It's just the fact that this other Lina's obviously really upset someone else very badly. The guy at the Cathedral,' I reminded him. 'I met him again in M and S and he recurled—'

'Recoiled, loved one.'

'He recoiled as if he'd come across a viper among the olive oil bottles.'

'As one would. So what do you propose to do?'

'Lie low for a bit. With witnesses, preferably! Oh, Griff,

I've spent so much time with Robin, who's going through some sort of personal crisis, and with Morris, whose got a bit of a crisis of his own, I'm so behind in my work, and we've got Matford looming and—'

'Morris? A crisis? Not that I want you to break confidences, loved one.'

'The cuts and his job, for one thing. And there's a problem with Penny.'

'Ah.' To my surprise he hugged me again.

I had a sudden panic. Would he smell Morris's aftershave on my hair? And what would he say – or worse, not say – if he did?

'We could skip Matford? It's only one day.'

'I've got a repair for Harvey I told him I'd return to him when we were down. Oh, Griff, that nice man Trev had a tracking device planted on his van – two, actually, same as Robin did – when he brought the vase down. Everything's so bloody complicated – hiding in my workroom doing nothing but make things better seems such a lovely idea.'

'One that can easily be put into operation, I trust. But your work needs a steady hand, dear child. With all that's been afflicting you, are you sure you can manage it?'

I think my jaw jutted a bit. 'I've never let anyone down yet.'

With Griff pottering around the cottage and taking over the Internet part of our business again, I settled down into a steady routine of work. Weekday and weekend blended into one when I shut the workroom door.

At least, that was the theory.

Griff set himself the task of dealing with Robin: he prepared a pile of meals for his freezer and, against my advice, set off in our van to deliver them. He also made me take time out to return the hire car. Talk about bravado. I just hoped the villain who was so keen on getting his hands on the box had seen the TV programme and knew I didn't have it any more.

Steve dropped by again, but he needed to speak to Griff, not me, so I only had an edited version of the interviews, which, Griff told me, only consisted of news that there was nothing definite from the PM, but further tests were needed and would take time.

'By the way, I said we'd pay for his funeral, as and when,' he added sadly.

Morris, deep into the Monet plot, texted me from time to time and sent a couple of longer emails. It seemed he had half his house back, but that he and Penny lived in different parts of it (was it some mansion?). He spent as much time with Leda as he could, for which Penny seemed grateful. I don't know whether this was meant to cheer me or not; I don't know whether it did or not.

EIGHTEEN

No one seeing Matford would imagine what a haven of safety it seemed to me. I even greeted the smell like an old friend.

I've never been sure what the smell was. A lot of industrial-strength disinfectant for starters. That isn't surprising, since Matford isn't an upmarket girls' school supplementing the fees to maintain a Victorian pile or a purpose-built hall like those in the NEC. Matford lurks in an industrial estate on the outskirts of Exeter and is really a cattle market. If you have any doubts, look behind the stalls and their displays: you'll see large signs directing you to the Dairy Cattle Sale Ring and Sheep Pennage and giving you advice on how to keep flies and midges from your stock. There's a firm of charted accountants, presumably specializing in farmers' money, and, something Griff always points out, no matter how many times I've seen them, the premises of Townsend, Chartered Surveyors. I always manage a giggle for him when he offers to cross out the 's' to make the surname like mine.

It wasn't so much a giggle as an ironic snort that we both gave when we saw where our stand had been located this time. Right outside the offices of Devon County Council Trading Standards Service.

'Just in case we try to palm off a dud and get caught out,' Griff said.

As if.

Once we had set up, adjusting the lighting as carefully as if we were in the salon of a stately home, I set out for my usual prowl. Often dealers came across items that didn't sit well with their usual stock and would give fellow dealers a discount on them. Griff had a partial Clarice Cliff tea set he really didn't like and was well out of our core period, but even as I headed off, I could see a Cliff specialist heading his way.

On a mostly treen stand, I was offered a shagreen spectacle case that was ideal for one of our regulars back in Kent. What I really hoped was that I would be summoned to something by my divvy instinct, as I often was – though preferably nothing as controversial as the snuffbox.

Not a single inviting vibe. I was just about to drift back when I saw a familiar face. What was Titus Oates doing so far from home? There was no point in making a beeline for him: that wasn't how you approached Titus. But he caught my eye and gave the tiniest of nods.

I was just passing the Prime Cattle sign when he drifted over to me.

'A lot of murky stuff going on,' he said. 'Griff OK now?'

'Over there. Shame about X.'

His face tightened, no doubt about it. And Titus never, ever allowed himself to show emotion. 'Told you to watch your back, didn't I?' He added, 'Never drank himself to death before, did he?'

I stared. So he thought the death was suspicious – I think.

Another tiny nod. 'Your old man's very busy. Wouldn't do to drop by without due warning. Specially with that cop of yours in tow.'

'I texted Pa the other day. He said it wasn't a good time. And I've been busy since. Well, this for one thing.' Why did I always end up talking like him?

'Pa? Hmm. Might welcome your thoughts on something. Not now.' He was gone.

What an honour! The great Titus wanting my advice! It wasn't usually like that. What on earth was he puzzled by? I did another turn of the area, in the opposite direction from the one he'd taken, but still had no vibes. Not good ones, at least.

'Are you well, my love?' Griff greeted me, still stowing cash in his wallet.

'Just the smell making me queasy, probably.'

'It's enough to turn one vegetarian, isn't it? Ah! Here comes Joe Public. And in good numbers too.'

When I saw it, I knew what Titus had wanted me to check. A snuffbox. Not just any snuffbox – I knew next to nothing about the things in general, after all. Another copy of the precious original. I didn't even reach out to touch it. I knew the stallholder by sight; I knew nothing bad of him. But in the middle of an interesting – and dead expensive, given the fair's location – collection of silver and pewter was this fake.

Titus caught my eye across the hall. This time I shook my head. He turned away. Trying to keep my face as expressionless as Titus', I headed back to our stall. What should I do? Griff was flirting with what sounded like an old flame, a man who looked so seedy and second-hand that I could only presume Griff felt he needed to keep in practice. I did the obvious thing. I took the money for a pretty pair of Swansea pearlware plates from a waiting and talkative customer and, mobile – the old one – in hand, went outside.

'Morris – I've found another one.'

'Shit. What sort of price?' He whistled when I told him. 'Going on the assumption it's kosher, then?'

'Not high enough for the real deal, surely? But too high even for what Griff sometimes calls an *homage*. Are you still there?'

'Just thinking. I'm due for a conference call with Interpol in three minutes. So I can't help.'

'Bit of a step from London to Exeter anyway.'

'Not necessarily. It depends who's down there.' He gave a lovely rude laugh. Then he was quiet. 'Sorry, I'm still thinking. And I'm not sure that you're the one to do this, because of your reputation as a divvie. I need someone to go and buy it. And pay full whack. And get every piece of documentation going. Provenance on the receipt, that sort of thing. But not you. I wonder if I know someone in Devon CID well enough . . . Shit, I'll have to call you back on this. Maybe an hour – maybe two . . .'

'I think I've solved the problem,' I said. 'Someone's turned up, and he's just the guy to help.' Sadly, I cut the call.

Two someones, actually. Harvey, who got a formal air kiss, and Trev, who got a proper hug. 'No, don't go in yet,' I said. 'This is what one of you has got to do . . .'

Harvey's face grew more serious by the second. 'And if I won't?'

'The vase gets it,' I said.

'Not the Harry Davies!' He sounded genuinely shocked, as if he believed me.

I played along. 'The Harry Davies I've spent fifteen hours repairing and regilding. That one.'

Knackered and feeling dirty, although we probably weren't, since our caravan had all mod cons, we had to put on our best bibs and tuckers, whatever they were, to dine out with Harvey and, most disconcertingly, his wife, whom I'd never met. I'd have preferred Trev's company, particularly in view of what he'd said about her.

We met near the restaurant he'd suggested, one specializing in seafood down in the Quayside area. As you'd expect on a Saturday evening, the whole scene was buzzing; I was almost disappointed when he led us to a small, quiet place, with only a dozen or so well-spaced tables. I had to admit, however, it was better for Griff's hearing. Even though I'd persuaded him to admit there was a problem and he now sported a pair of hearing aids no one dared notice or mention, he still found loud trattorias trying. And the carpets and table linen were definitely his sort of thing. And, presumably, Harvey's.

Harvey looked as chic as he always did; Griff assured me that good tailoring always did that to a man, a point he himself proved in a suit he'd bought on his London break.

Estelle, who shook hands as if I was a wet fish, was a few years older than Harvey, I thought, despite the work on her face, which left her looking not so much young as desperately sad. However, she wasn't just smart and elegant. She was intimidatingly well turned out, from her beautifully cut and coloured hair to her manicured feet. *Pedicured* feet. I recognized the dress from a Sunday supplement, but didn't know the designer – probably one with a capital D. The wow-factor heavy silver jewellery was modern Danish at a guess. 'Georg Jensen,' Griff mouthed.

I always found summer difficult to dress for, unless I went for the vintage look Griff preferred, which sometimes made me look like Little Bo Peep. A sudden flutter of the brain made me wonder if Pa had liberated the sheep illicitly from his old nursery. He was quite capable of it, especially when he'd warned me off. I'd plumped for a silk dress Griff had picked out last time we'd been to London together. It hadn't been expensive to start with, and had been further reduced, but he insisted the empire line suited me. It did until I sat down opposite Estelle. Provincial, that was what I felt.

And tonight I felt provincial in my conversation too. Griff was full of London news, not just the opera but a couple of actors – household-name actors – he'd lunched with and the exhibitions he'd been to. Estelle mentioned her box at the ENO; Harvey talked about his friends at Sotheby's. I did what Griff said always pleased people. I let them get on with it and fired occasional questions to show I'd been listening. Since I didn't know what the ENO was, I was a little stuck, especially as I thought to ask might be a question too far.

Then I let a disgraceful thing happen. I let my phone ring. I wasn't sure my blush was because it was so not done or because the caller I switched to voicemail was Morris. At least I had the decency to wait till the main course was over before slipping to the loo.

I was glad the call was over by the time Estelle joined me in there.

I knew I ought to say something. I looked around me at the chic decor – those interesting glass washbasins with the taps and even the soap dispenser operated by hand movement. No towels, paper or fluffy, just one of those Dyson hand driers you put your hands in. So nothing to talk about really. In any case, she'd not seemed the sort of person you could have a girlie gossip with, heading with no more than a nod into one of the cubicles. I touched up my lippie, but since she didn't say anything, decided it was better manners just to slip back to the others.

I was just summarizing briefly – very briefly – to Harvey the conversation I'd had when she returned, looking thunderous for some reason. Should I have waited after all?

'It was my contact at the Met,' I repeated, so she couldn't complain she didn't know what I was talking about. 'He wanted to ask how today's operation went and to pass on his thanks to Harvey.'

'You told him how much he owes me?' It was hard to tell if he was serious or mocking.

'Yes. He says should the Met go bankrupt, you'd be able to claim it back from the stallholder if he's sold you a pup, which he obviously has.'

'Or claim a complementary repair from Tripp and Townend,' he suggested, raising an eyebrow at Griff, 'by way of compensation?'

By now his wife was furious, not sad. Naturally, she was far too polite to say anything, but she oozed cold anger, directed at me, of course. I was just the messenger, but that wouldn't stop me getting shot at if she had a chance.

Harvey didn't seem to have picked up her mood, turning to me with an ironic smile only a degree cooler than his usual flirtatious charm. 'I take it you'll take the damned thing back with you? I've photographed it and copied all the paperwork, just in case.' He handed over the sort of pretty card carrier-bag that usually comes with a present inside.

'Thank you kindly, sir. I think.' I wrinkled my nose. 'Thank you for disguising it so well. I'd seriously prefer no one to know I've got it.' I was going to witter on about being on local TV, but thought better of it. Whatever I said would be the wrong thing for poor Estelle. However, there was one question I must ask. 'Are you happy with the repair?'

'Perfectly. As I frequently tell Griff, you are a very talented woman.'

I didn't need Griff's glance to tell me the way to play this. 'He always makes sure I prioritize the work I do for you: he loves top-end china, you know. I think I understand why we only deal in middle-range – because he couldn't bear to sell the sort of stuff you presumably handle every day. On the other hand, I don't suppose he'd told you he walloped an intruder with a Moorcroft vase the other day – and intends to claim on our house insurance.'

'It was absolutely hideous,' Griff said, grinning. 'I shall buy an altogether more tasteful replacement.'

'Intruder?' Harvey repeated.

At last I could back out of the conversation, with the perfect excuse that I hadn't been there. But Griff recounted how I'd not dialled 999 but had summoned a police officer ex-boyfriend to his aid.

It was a pity for Estelle's sake he'd described Will as an ex. She'd have preferred me to be thoroughly engaged.

Declining an invitation to go back to their house with them – it was quite a schlep and we had to be ready for an early start tomorrow – we sipped a leisurely cup of coffee, though I knew Griff's beauty sleep would suffer, even with decaf.

I was half expecting Estelle to grab my arm and hiss a warning to stay away from Harvey. But I caught her face in repose. It was even unhappier. Trev might not like her, but, despite her wonderful outfit and her admittedly fading beauty, I surprised myself by managing to feel sorry for her.

Until she stopped, turned and asked, 'You may know a friend of mine, Arthur Habgood. He runs a pretty little shop down here. Devon Cottage Antiques.'

This was worse than grabbing my arm. It was grabbing my identity. Habgood had run a long campaign to persuade me to take a DNA test to prove I was his granddaughter. When I'd refused, for a variety of reasons, one of which was that in Griff I had a better grandfather than any biological one, he'd become very vengeful and had tried to do me a lot of harm. Damaging someone you claimed to want in the family didn't make sense to me.

On the other hand, Habgood had presumably given Estelle only one version of the story, the one that cast him in the light of a dear loving father seeking the only child of his late daughter. He'd probably made Griff the villain of the piece too. As for Devon Cottage Antiques, it could be as pretty as a picture, but it would never replace the equally picturesque Tripp and Townend in my affections. So did she believe Habgood, or, knowing that Harvey didn't like him much either, was she just being malicious?

There was only one person who could reply to her, and that, unfortunately, was me. It was a pity I was way out of my depth with all sorts of relationship undercurrents swirling around and carrying me away from the shore. Was this about Habgood and me, or really about me and Harvey? Or even her and Habgood? Whatever I said, I didn't want to give her any ammunition she could possibly use against Harvey, or against me for that matter.

'I've never seen his shop. Is it as sweet as it sounds?' I managed. I didn't add that he almost certainly sold dodgy china in it: he'd once tried to flog as perfect something I'd repaired, which was what had turned me against him. I knew Harvey didn't try that game, at least with stuff that had been through my hands. I'd checked his website several times, and anything I'd worked on always warned of some restoration.

'I'm sure he'd love you to go and see it. It'll be open tomorrow, of course.'

I shook my head with what I hoped looked like real regret. 'I'm afraid we've got to be on the road very early. Griff had to take time off to recover from being assaulted by that intruder – the one he socked with the ugly vase – and I'm way behind with the restoration work. I've got a courier collecting something I'm working on for a museum on Monday, and it's not quite ready.'

Her voice reduced me to something on the level of a worker ant. 'So you really do just the gluing and so on?'

Especially the so on. 'Of course.' I nearly spoilt it by pointing out that Habgood would confirm it, but managed to shut my mouth in time.

'So it's Griff who runs the company?'

He must have come back to look for me. 'It is indeed. You could say I'm the public face, doing the contracts, wining and dining clients, and so on. I don't quite lock Lina in an attic with only a candle to light her work, but she's very much a back-room person.' It must have been his acting past – he always lied beautifully. And I was happy for him to do so this time. There was only so much I wanted Estelle to know about me, and we were pretty near that point now.

Suddenly, we were past the point. 'So why was it you who were dealing with the Metropolitan Police back there? If you're just a back-room girl.'

Again I had a terrible sense that anything I might say would be taken down and used in evidence against me.

Griff jumped in. 'Oh, Estelle, didn't you notice the rosy

glow about her when she took that call? He's her boyfriend, of course. A very special one.'

'He's the one that asked Harvey to buy that snuffbox. He also wants him to look at some photos,' I said, since we'd reached Harvey himself by now. 'Did you recognize anyone?' How long was it since I'd sent the huge file through? Now I came to think of it, I felt a bit aggrieved he'd not got back to me, even to say no one rang any bells.

'Did you need to inflict so many on me? I've only just got through the first scan. Hell, such awful photos, Estelle – they'd have had you spitting tacks. Estelle's quite a dab with a camera, Griff – I often think she could have made a career out of photography.'

If he'd spoken about me like that I'd probably have slapped him. Patronizing bastard. And to think . . . No, it was she who'd married him.

'But there are a couple of faces . . . I didn't say anything because I wasn't sure. But I'll look tomorrow or Monday, if I have a moment, and get back to you – or direct to that inspector of yours, if you give me his email address.'

I printed Morris's details on the back of one of my cards. 'It really could be quite important, Harvey. You know how we prioritize your repairs: maybe you could return the favour,' I said, my face stern and unsmiling.

'Yes, ma'am.' He gave a mock salute.

Griff picked up the sudden tension. 'I hate to use the cliché, Harvey, but it really could be a matter of life and death.'

NINETEEN

After a long tussle with the M25 and a snazzy bit of parking on my part when we unhitched the caravan in the field a friendly farmer lets us use, we arrived home in Bredeham. I'd rather hoped to find Morris's Saab waiting for us. What I didn't expect was an ordinary car, with two uniformed women sitting in it. They looked very serious as they got out.

'Ms Townsend? We'd like a word, please.'

'Of course,' I said, smiling up at them from the driver's seat in what I hoped was a nice cooperative way. 'Can I just put the van in the yard? And then I'll let you in?'

'The old man can do that, can't he?'

I froze. My vibes were twanging alarmingly. Thoughts bombarded the inside of my skull like balls in a machine. If they'd come in logical order it would have helped, but they didn't. How dared they be so rude to Griff? Why were there two of them? Did it matter that they'd got my name wrong? Unmarked car? What about IDs? Why was one going round to Griff's side? So much make-up on duty?

The van was in reverse, and we were hurtling back up the village street before I knew what I was going to do. I pointed to the dashboard-mounted mobile. 'Speed-dial Freya Webb. I may be done for resisting arrest – I want to get my word in first.'

'My dear one!'

'Just in case. Tell her I'm coming straight over to Maidstone and she can arrest me there if necessary.'

'It's Sunday!'

'It's her personal mobile – she'll tell me what to do. For God's sake, Griff, do it.'

So why didn't the two women give chase? At least knowing they weren't on my tail I could dodge and dive through lanes only locals would know. But I could only do it slowly – you never knew when you might come nose to nose with a farm vehicle six times your size, not to mention the fact I still had a load of china aboard, and though it was well-packed, bubble wrap could only absorb so much shock.

I was concentrating so hard on not getting us squashed or even running into a road block they'd had time to set up that I didn't hear much of what Griff was saying. But I could hear that his voice was serious, and suddenly running didn't seem to have been the sensible option.

Maidstone seemed a most unattractive destination, even with Griff beside me. And it wasn't to Police HQ that Griff directed me, but to the police station. At least Freya was waiting for me, in what was clearly her gardening outfit.

'What the hell are you doing, giving my officers the slip, Lina? I thought you were a law-abiding type.'

'You know I am. But when two people turn up without giving names and without showing their ID, I'm bound to be suspicious. And – like Griff's assailant – they were wearing a lot of slap. I thought – who knows exactly what I thought? But here I am, as Griff told you I would be.'

'Good. Because I may just get you off the charge of resisting arrest. But you have to be questioned about something else, and it's serious. Do you have a solicitor?'

'Why ever should she need one?' Griff demanded. 'Leave it to me, angel heart – I shall get the best money can buy.'

I gripped his hand. 'Maybe that's a mistake. Maybe it'll antagonize people having some hotshot poking his expensive nose in.' But I held his glance and added quietly, 'But you know whom I'd like you to call.'

'I told you, it's serious,' Freya said. 'Everyone's entitled to legal support.'

'Am I under arrest?'

'Only by the fell sergeant, death, and we all hope he'll hang around a bit.' She paused to smile at Griff, who presumably appreciated her allusion. I didn't. 'As far as I can see, you came voluntarily. So I don't see why you should be under arrest at the moment. All the same, you'll be seen in an interview room – well, I'm sure you've watched enough TV to know the procedure.'

I looked her straight in the eye. 'I've never pretended that I don't know the procedure first-hand. I saw the inside of enough cop shops when I was a kid.' She handed me over to the women I'd escaped from.

I didn't even recognize them. Amazing! That must be what they mean by blind panic. They introduced themselves as Constables Smedley and Long. They were blonde, and from their scraped back hair to their bitten fingernails they were identical.

All the same, I gave my apology. Profusely. They seemed a bit bemused, but accepted it, raising identically plucked eyebrows when I explained why I'd been so afraid. In fact, Long seemed very interested in what she called the backstory. It was she who asked all the questions; Smedley might have been suffering from a severe attack of that itis thing that makes you lose your voice.

'So you didn't want to escape from the police, but from people you thought were criminals,' Long summed up.

I think she sounded more long-suffering than disbelieving, but I wouldn't have placed bets on it. I tried a smile. 'Exactly. So I'm sorry I nearly ran you over and – anyway, here I am, and I'll cooperate in any way I can.'

She changed the subject with a huge wrench. 'Tell us about St Jude's Church. That's in Kenninge.'

'I know where it is. I helped out at the fête there. Which is how all the drama of break-ins and the rest of it started.'

'Tell me about the church itself.'

'You'd need an architect to do that, wouldn't you? All I know is that it's very old, with a sagging roof and a slightly bulging wall. The porch is rotting. It needs a lot of money spending on it. More than a week of church fêtes would ever make.'

'Did you have any ideas how this money could be made?'

'I may have suggested to Robin Levitt, the vicar, that they should sell some of the family silver. The church plate, that is. But I don't know what they've got, and even if I saw it lined up in front of me I wouldn't be able to do more than date it. It's not my area at all. That's why I needed help with the silver snuffbox featured on TV the other day. Why I handed it over the Met for safe keeping.'

'We know about that, and very public spirited it was of you. But did you decide to recoup your losses, as it were?'

'I don't think . . . Recoup?' My dratted memory. 'You mean, get my money back? I only paid a few quid for it. You could say it was a charitable donation.'

'You could. But when you realized just how valuable it might be, weren't you tempted to claim some of the money?'

'I actually went with Robin to try to talk the donor into having it back! Look, if I've done something wrong, or someone says I have, could you spell it out? The A303's horrible, especially when you're towing a caravan, there are roadworks on the M3, and someone has sprinkled something highly flammable on the M25. I've been on the road some seven hours and I'm not at my brightest. Even apart from needing a pee.'

'Did you steal something else from the church to make up for the thousands of pounds you gave up when you surrendered the snuffbox?'

I tried not to laugh. 'A postcard? A guide book? What should I steal? I'm not sure where God is in my life, but I wouldn't push my luck nicking from His House, believe me. Especially when one of my best friends is the priest in charge.'

'Something more valuable than that, believe me,' Smedley said, making me jump.

'Look, I've not played games with you. Please, return the favour and just tell me what you think I've stolen.'

Smedley leaned forward menacingly 'We believe you broke into the safe and removed an item of communion plate with the approximate value of twenty-five thousand pounds.'

I gasped. 'Even if I knew where the safe was, I wouldn't know where to find the key or even if what was in there was worth stealing.'

'We think you did. Nothing else was nearly so valuable.'

'So there was other stuff?'

'Was it your own idea to rob the safe? Or was it anyone else's? The vicar's, perhaps?'

Maybe I shouldn't have turned down the idea of a nifty solicitor. 'Robin is the best, most decent man I know.'

'But he's been under a lot of strain. You might both have

seen stealing the plate as a way of easing his financial problems.'

'Stealing would make a priest feel better? Getting a friend to steal? From a church, of all places? Have I just stepped through the Looking Glass?'

Smedley took a deep breath, but Long continued. 'The thing is, Lina, as you know, your prints are on file. OK, it's been a long time since we took them, but they don't go off, you know. Which means we could identify the prints which we found all round the area of the safe.'

I pounced. And was really irritated when my brain chose that precise minute to remind me that in the period of the bloody snuffbox they used to call little boxes pouncet boxes. 'But not in or on the safe?' I managed at last.

'You'd wear gloves, no doubt,' Smedley sneered. There was a distinct suggestion of *even you* about her comment.

'But not in the area of the safe, wherever that might be. Where is it, incidentally? I wouldn't have thought leaving valuables in full view of a less reverent Joe Public than me was necessarily the best idea. I don't happen to have a JCB to hand, but I'm sure some people do. The people who drive them into rural post offices, for instance.'

They exchanged a quick glance. I had an idea I'd put my finger on something, but I'd no idea what.

'As a matter of interest, what were my dabs on?' I thought hard and had a sudden vision of myself crawling round. 'Hey, you didn't find any of my beads, did you?'

Got them! 'Why should we find beads?'

'Because I broke a string while I was in the choir. I was looking at those lovely misericords . . . Hey, Fi, the church warden would vouch for me! She found me in there on all fours! So you'll have knee prints as well as fingerprints. Are they admissible as evidence? I may even have left traces of blood. Hey, you wouldn't need a gob-swab to get hold of my DNA!'

There was a long silence. In a TV programme, someone would have knocked on the door at this point and brought in more evidence to scupper my whole story. They didn't now.

'Look, I really am desperate for the loo.'

'So you admit being in the area of the safe but nothing else?'

'If I knew where the safe was . . . Please? The loo?'

When I was brought back, the whole chara . . . charaba . . . the whole silly play got going all over again. Smedley fired a question about Robin and his mental state, but I told her that was his business, not mine. I just repeated that he was one of the best people I'd ever met. I was this close to asking Freya to give him a character reference but thought that that might do more harm than good. And then, this time, just like on TV, there was a knock on the door.

In my fantasy, in popped Morris, riding heroically to the rescue: 'She's my informant, my expert witness, my lover.' Any of those would have been nice. In reality it was another woman officer, clutching a DVD case. She inserted the disk into a player and left.

'We are now going to show you exhibit blah-blah-blah, Lina, and we would like you to look at it carefully before you say anything.'

The grainy, jerky footage showed the back of a young woman, who was arguing with a middle-aged man in a street somewhere that looked vaguely familiar. Neither meant anything to me, since they were well out of the camera's favoured range. The date and time ticked along underneath. Suspecting that these might be important, I tried till my brain squeaked to work out what I'd been doing and where I was when the footage was shot. It was only when the camera angle changed abruptly that I realized I did know one of them – the man was none other than Cashmere Roll-Neck, though on this occasion he sported an open shirt. Foolishly, I gave myself away by nodding. At least I suppose that must have been what I did: something made Smedley jot a hurried note. Then the camera cut again, managing to get a reasonable shot of the young woman.

It was like looking at myself from the other side of a mirror losing its silvering. Me, and yet not me. She was taller for a start, by about four inches, I'd judge. Griff wouldn't have passed the clothes as suitable to venture out in. And her face looked over made-up, even in the poor footage.

'What were you arguing about, Lina?'

Although I'd seen an attack coming, this particular line disconcerted me, probably because I was too busy wondering how to get in touch with this almost double of mine. I never did have much in the way of concentration, after all, except when it came to restoring china.

'I beg your pardon?' Then I remembered, with a blush, precisely what I'd been doing at the time and date shown on the screen – I'd been with Morris. In bed.

'I asked you what you'd been arguing about.'

From nowhere came the right response, even if Griff might not have approved of the grammar. Perhaps it was the thought of Morris, who was never lost for words, especially nice meaty ones. 'Telling you that would presuppose that one of the disputants was me.' Not so much as a stutter. I added firmly, 'I do recognize the man, but I don't know his name. I've met him precisely twice.' I gave them details. 'I've even got the Marks and Spencer till receipt, so you should be able to check – to verify what I've said,' I added helpfully.

Long gave a dry, not very pleasant, laugh. 'The fact that you can prove you were with him on one occasion hardly proves that you weren't on another.'

She was right, of course. Perhaps I did need a lawyer, to stop me saying silly things.

I waited for their next move.

'So what were you arguing about?'

'I don't know because I wasn't there. The woman he was talking to might resemble me but that's all.' She was my doppelgänger, of course. I cursed myself for not trying harder to find her, especially as Morris had said – with his copper's instinct, strong as my divvying – that it might be important. I took a breath. 'In fact, when I met the man, he looked shocked and horrified. He pretty well bolted. So when I met him by M and S's olive oil, I challenged him. He bolted again.' Their faces were imposs . . . impati . . . impassive. I continued, 'A dear friend of mine also mistook the woman for me. She's based in Hastings.'

They exchanged a look. 'How convenient for you.'

Raising my hands might have looked like a gesture of

surrender, but certainly wasn't. 'I have spoken to other people about the confusion. Look.' I pointed to the screen. 'She's taller than me for a start. And I do not do diamanté T-shirts. Ever.' I was getting silly now, not what I meant at all. What I really wanted to do, needed to do, was ask what I was supposed to have done, but I had an idea I'd soon be told.

'What we'd like you to do is agree to DNA testing. What this means—'

'Check those blood spots. If they don't help, I think I'm one of that generation of people who had their DNA routinely taken and stored, whether or not they were ever charged. So you don't need to repeat the gob-swab stuff. And while you're at it, you can tell me how to apply to have the sample destroyed.' It would have made a terrific exit line. But in such a situation you don't exactly get up and walk out. Not without risking arrest, which would be a problem. So I tried my hardest to morph back from the hard street-girl I'd been two minutes ago into the sweetly reasonable person I'd aimed at earlier.

'I don't think you appreciate how serious this is, Lina.'

'If I don't, perhaps it's because you still haven't told me why you've needed to question me for the last hour.' Calm down, calm down. No point in exaggerating: it couldn't have been more than twenty minutes' interrogation over Cashmere Roll-Neck.

'Suppose you look at this then.' She fast forwarded. She went through the rigmarole of identifying the disk again. The only words she didn't use were *showing the accused*, though her tone sure as hell implied them.

The argument was getting physical. At first, the woman got the worst of it, but then the man looked scared out of his wits and bolted.

'This is the last footage we have of our friend. Our late friend.'

'So what happened to him?' I asked. Just like that. I'd wanted to say all sorts of cool things: DNA at the crime scene, and the difference between mine and the killer's; my alibi. Instead I stared, probably insolently. At last, seeing the effect that my question and then my silence were having, I made my mouth move. 'I've already told you I've never met the woman, and I only spoke to the man once.'

'You said you'd met him twice.'

In my imagination, hearing the cell door close behind me, it was all I could do not to wilt. But I took a breath and squared my shoulders. 'Yes. Met him twice. Spoken once. When I met him in the Cathedral crypt, he bolted at the sight of me. I spoke to him in M and S. I told you. I've told you all I can. I don't even know his name.' When they didn't help out there, I added, 'Please may I go now?' After all that assertiveness, I ended up whining just like a school kid. Even though the alibi I could have given for my double's encounter with Cashmere Roll-Neck was certainly a pretty adult one.

As, grim-faced and reluctant, they ushered me back to the safer side of the police world, one where someone had found Griff a cup of tea and made sure the surveillance cameras kept an eye on our van, I asked myself a question this time. Just why hadn't I mentioned Morris?

TWENTY

Griff fussed and coddled me, chuntering away as we dealt with all the aftermath of the fair. I didn't know whether I was soothed and irritated – probably a lot of both. At last he picked up on my mood, and supper was a very quiet affair. Clearly, he knew I was holding something back, and since we'd not mentioned him telling Estelle Sanditon that I had a boyfriend in the Met, he'd probably got a pretty good idea of how relations between me and Morris stood. Or not. Morris hadn't been in touch today. Not at all.

As I sipped the tiny glass of port Griff insisted would settle what he called my nerves, and actually went straight to my head, a few ideas started to pop up. One was to contact Josie about sightings of my double; I nearly put it off, but hauling myself to the office I dialled her number. I held on forever. Nothing except her answerphone. I left a very short message, interrupted by a massive yawn. Another was to text Morris – nothing romantic in case he was spending time with Penny, but to ask him what to do with the fake snuffbox. I toyed with mentioning my encounter with Freya's colleagues, but thought face to face would be better for that. Face to face or at least ear to ear.

I was so tired – or so zapped by the port – I told Griff I needed an early night and was ready to head upstairs when I realized I hadn't checked our security footage. One of us always does this just in case anyone's chanced his or her luck, even if they'd find it next to impossible to penetrate our defences, so we could keep a particular eye open for them. We had a nice shot of the village postie, another of the woman who delivers the parish mag. So I could put it to bed. But I pressed the wrong button and found I was watching the shots from the camera watching the gates to the yard. I got a nice close up of myself, staring up at a policewoman looming over me. Something told me not to delete it. In fact, I rewound it a bit, to look at the pair of them, in their car. Why should they have come in an unmarked vehicle? That really worried me. And why should they look so very different from the blonde clones who interviewed me?

I could practically hear the cogs going round in my brain. I certainly felt them. Very carefully indeed, I saved the footage to disk. Then I called Griff.

He peered closely, with and without his reading glasses. His frown was puzzled, and eventually very relieved. 'No, I don't think you've gone crazy, loved one. The women are quite different from the ones I saw at the police station – though it was only a glimpse I had of all four, of course. But there is something very familiar indeed about this one.' He pointed at the one at the side of the van. 'Very familiar indeed.' This time it was Griff's brain cogs that worked overtime: he even held his head as if to steady it. 'No, it's gone. But I trust it will pop up at three this morning, as such things irritatingly do. No, I shan't summon you immediately – you need your slumber, sweet one. I shall write it down, so I still have it in the morning. By then everything will seem much clearer. It will for you too, you know,' he added ambi . . . ambid . . . ambiguously.

I was still in the shower next morning when Griff shouted that Morris wanted to speak to me. I yelled that I would phone back in five minutes. All the same, I speeded up; he had a career to worry about, not to mention a failing marriage and a baby.

What I didn't expect when I trotted downstairs, still in kimono and slippers, was to see his back view at the kitchen table. Should I bolt back upstairs and dress, not to mention doing something with my hair? It was too late. He'd turned with a smile that made my heart give a jolt that almost winded me.

'I'm on my way to Ashford to pick up Eurostar, but I thought I'd better collect that snuffbox and drop it into Maidstone for safe keeping.'

'Good idea,' I said matter-of-factly. Possibly. 'I'll go and get it.'

I probably established an Olympic record for throwing clothes on; I grabbed the box from my secret safe on the way back down again. By this time his face was very serious. No doubt Griff had been regaling him with the story of yesterday's encounter with the police.

'Obviously on a fishing expedition,' he said briskly, slipping the box into an evidence bag and scribbling a receipt. 'They haven't anything concrete against you – I assume! – and hoped you'd incriminate yourself.'

I could have wished Griff anywhere except in our kitchen, busying himself with the coffee pot. He might have had his back to us, but you could almost feel the draught as his ears flapped.

'You were right when you said we needed to find my double,' I said, which didn't seem to be an answer to anything. 'You see, they almost have a case against me for burgling the church – except I still don't know where the safe might be. But the footage of me arguing with the murder victim isn't of me at all – I was definitely at home at the times the screen showed.'

'The trouble is,' Griff chipped in, 'I was away with Aidan at the time, and can't give her an alibi. Whatever repair she was doing at the time could be at best a silent witness.' He sat down heavily and sipped his coffee in silence. 'However,' he said, perking up as the first drop of caffeine started its work, 'I did have a three o'clock moment, dear one, and I did write down the thought that had been so elusive. Morris, we have some curious footage of two women officers who came to arrest our lovely girl. They not only appear to be quite different from the ones who subsequently interviewed her, though presumably there could be an innocent explanation for that, but also one of them has a more than fleeting resemblance to the man whom I so foolishly admitted to our cottage and who tried to find the original snuffbox.' He beamed. 'As soon as we're all done here, I will phone Josie and ask for her immediate assistance with locating the double and you can show Morris our pretty photos, my chick.'

I was halfway to my feet when I heard myself say, 'No! Not Josie. If my double could kill Cashmere . . . No, not Josie!' Frail but as stubborn as they come. And more than

ready to fight my corner. 'In fact, tell her to stay at home until
– until Freya's colleagues have spoken to her, at least.'

Morris put his hand on my arm and forced me back on to
the chair. 'Are you having one of your divvy moments, Lina?
You are, aren't you?' He fished his phone out and dialled.
Sighing with frustration, he muttered, 'Best coverage by the
front door, yes?'

'Nice to know someone who trusts you implicitly,' Griff
said. He meant a lot more, didn't he?

Morris reappeared, closing his mobile. 'OK, someone's
going to talk to Josie. Maybe a call from you, Griff, to tell
her to sit tight till my colleagues turn up – but also to demand
ID before she takes her front door off the chain. Right?'

Griff scuttled off.

The moment he'd gone, Morris kissed me. 'You were very
quiet when Griff was talking about vases testifying you were
here. Do I gather this was because I'm your alibi?'

I nodded, swallowing hard. 'Just in case – you know, you
and Penny ever . . . They've no case, Morris, and I didn't want
to drag you into anything you didn't want to be dragged into,'
I ended lamely.

'You lovely girl. But if push comes to shove, name me and
be damned. They don't need to know what we were actually
doing, do they? Not every last detail?'

'They'll work it out, since I didn't say in the first place.
Are you OK with that?'

'I wouldn't be OK with you standing trial for something
you didn't do. Anything. But especially robbery or murder.'
He kissed me again.

'If you're sure . . . Anyway, look, these are the pics. I'll
burn them on to a disk for you.'

He peered at the screen, literally scratching his head. 'It's
a bit weird, two women officers coming to bring you in, and
another pair of women turning up at roughly the same time
to – well, we don't know what their intentions were, but I
bet they concerned the snuffbox or its fraudulent spawn.' He
cupped the side of my face, but didn't repeat the kiss, since
Griff bustled out of the office. 'Very weird, in fact,' he added,
as if he meant Griff to overhear.

'Now I am worried,' Griff said. 'Josie's always up with the lark, but there's still no response from her phone. Lina tried to contact her last night, Morris, but failed. No response from her mobile either. Before you say she's not the generation to take it with her everywhere, she was one of the very first of my friends to embrace the new technology – she had a website years before I recognized the benefits and succumbed to Lina's pleas to join the twenty-first century. Her phone had far more bells and whistles than mine. Which reminds me,' Griff rattled on, 'one day could you show dear Lina how to use one I gave her? It's like yours, I think, and makes no sense at all to me.'

I put an arm round his shoulders; even though he was pretending to be calm and efficient, I could tell from the way he gabbled on how stressed he was. His sentence length always went up with his blood pressure. I didn't point out I could have worked it out for myself, given a few hours, but just hadn't had a few hours to do it.

'Of course I will. As soon as I get back from Brussels.' He looked at his watch. 'I hate leaving you like this, Lina, but I have to catch that train, and I have to go to Ashford via Maidstone.' He patted his pocket.

'To save you time, I can pop it back into the secret safe.'

'It's tempting. But I've already marked it up as evidence, and – Hell, Lina, I'd like it well out of anyone's way. Take care of yourself, Griff,' he said, shaking hands in a curiously formal way. 'And of Lina, please.' This time he did kiss me in front of Griff – nothing Hollywood, but something for me to hug to me for the rest of the day.

I was trying to settle to work on a modern Doulton figure the owner was unaccountably fond of when the front doorbell rang. Griff would certainly check the camera before he opened the door. At least, I was fairly sure he would. All the same, I nipped into my bedroom and grabbed a can of hairspray, a crude but useful weapon.

It wasn't necessary. It was DC Steve White, to see Griff. Hiding the aerosol, I slid into the room and sat on the arm of the sofa.

Steve's face might have been designed to express maximum

grimness. He hardly needed to say, 'It's bad news, I'm afraid. Graham Parker's PM and toxicology tests do show he'd imbibed a fatal amount of alcohol. So at first sight it looked as if his death was self-inflicted. But the forensic pathologist was one of the best and spotted marks round his mouth and throat. As if someone had done this – if I may borrow you, Mr Tripp.' He pinched Griff's nose and tipped his head back. 'There, just like my mother used to do when I had to have nasty medicine. So it looks as if we're looking for a murderer.'

Griff was very quiet. At last he asked, 'Are Lina and I now at risk of the same fate?'

Steve looked quickly at me, as if registering my presence for the first time, flushed, and stared at the carpet. 'I couldn't really say.'

I got to my feet. 'It's OK, Steve. I'm sure all CID knows I was questioned in connection with an entirely different murder. Unless you think there's a connection, and that I could have held X just as you held Griff and poured whatever it was down his throat?'

'Different team,' he muttered, red chasing purple across his face. His phone rang.

'Best reception's by the door,' I said, watching him. It wasn't a good feeling – he might have been getting instructions to take me in again. I left him to it and went off to put the kettle on.

Griff joined me, putting his arms round me. 'My good brave child. Morris won't let his colleagues do anything foolish. I think we could show Steve the same photos without feeling disloyal. After all, he was in uniform till only recently – he'd surely be able to identify them as his colleagues.'

There was a knock on the door jamb. 'Excuse me, Mr Tripp,' Steve said, 'I gather you and Ms Townend were worried about a fellow antiques dealer, a Miss Honeycombe—'

'Josie!' we said as one.

'My colleagues called round there this morning, in response to a query by DI Morris – right?'

'Indeed. And Josie is—?'

'That was DCI Webb. She wants you to know that Miss Honeycombe is in the ICU at the Conquest Hospital.

She was found on the beach in the small hours this morning. Apparently, she'd fallen from the promenade.'

'As in "apparently" X drank himself to death?' I asked, gripping Griff's hand.

Steve's smile was swift and kind. 'The difference is that Ms Honeycombe is still alive. And may survive.'

'May?'

'That's what the medics are hoping. A night in the open air, particularly with a high tide to rock her to sleep, might not have been so good. The DCI wanted chapter and verse on Ms Honeycombe. Apparently, she met her once – liked her. Said she looked like a question mark?' Steve inserted one himself at the end of his sentence.

'Can we see her?' Griff asked.

Steve flushed. 'Not yet. And there's a particular reason why you can't, Ms Townend. There's some CCTV footage, it seems, with someone looking remarkably like you pushing her. The DCI would be grateful if you'd come along and talk to her.'

To Freya herself? I thought she was desk-bound these days, apart from when she thought she might catch a glimpse of Robin. I exchanged a look with Griff.

'Is now the time for a hotshot lawyer?' he murmured.

It was time for Morris, except he was under the Channel, and not a lot of use.

'Are you to drive me in, Steve?' I wanted Griff to be with me, but we had so much work piled up I didn't care to ask him.

'If you don't mind.'

'This is all very civilized considering I'm a murder suspect,' I said, kissing Griff. 'Time for me to put on some slap? If I'm going to have a mugshot taken, I want some lippie, don't I?'

TWENTY-ONE

Reminding Griff to lock himself in, and telling him to think about keeping the shop shut all day, Steve allowed me to sit in the passenger seat, and we talked – he talked – as if I was a casual acquaintance he was helping out. He yakked about tennis – his passion, it seemed – and how he'd won tickets for Wimbledon in his club ballot. I floated cricket as a topic, since when Griff watched it on TV I tended to watch too, especially when the players wore whites, not those silly paint by numbers pyjamas. But it came back to tennis, and I found myself saying I watched Wimbledon if I had the chance. Maybe *when I had the chance* would have been more tactful. So the journey passed quite pleasantly, considering the circumstances.

When we crossed the M20, you could see it was pretty clogged up, with a lorry dumping Portaloos at intervals along the hard shoulder.

'Operation Stack?' I asked.

'Didn't you catch the news last night? Nor this morning?'

I shook my head. How uncivilized was that? The *Ten O'clock News* and the *Today* programme were rituals Griff had always insisted on. Of course, this morning's listening had been rather disrupted by the arrival of Morris.

Sighing, he explained. 'The French are on strike yet again. Their civil servants, I think, this time. No customs officers, no passport control, so all these poor saps are stuck here for the duration! What other country would have to use a major motorway as a giant car park? So yes, it's Operation Stack!' Steve moaned, punctuating his comments with a lot of words Griff and I didn't use till later in the day. 'Seems they can't get planning permission to build proper car parks along the route.' He went off into a thoroughly un-PC, as in politically correct, rant that would have warmed Aidan's heart, but sounded odd from a young man once called to God.

Robin! Why hadn't I been in touch with Robin? I suppose
it might not have been good manners given the theory that I'd
robbed one of his churches, but that was only yesterday: you
should keep touching base with friends under stress, shouldn't
you? On the other hand the same applied to him. He
hadn't called me. Did that mean he thought I was guilty of
stealing his silver? I felt sick at the thought. I told myself he
was probably simply told not to contact me, lest it
prejudice whatever case they were building up. But the Robin
I knew and trusted would simply have lifted two clerical fingers
in the face of such an instruction.

I wiped my palms on my trousers, the navy linen ones I'd
grabbed first thing. I had a nasty feeling I had a divvy moment
coming on.

In 'fact, tact or not, the first thing I blurted out to Freya
Webb when I was ushered into her office was, 'Is Robin OK?'

She managed to ask coolly, since the constable who'd taken
me up hadn't quite shut the door, 'The clergyman?'

'Robin Levitt. I haven't heard from him, and the rate my
friends and acquaintances are dropping I'm . . .' I stopped –
my wretched lip was quivering.

Closing the door firmly on my escort, she pressed me down
on to a chair. 'Lina, the man takes half a dozen services on a
Sunday, more or less. And that means sermons to prepare and
what not. So I wouldn't be surprised if he was incommunicado
yesterday, or even Saturday, which I believe is his day off,
isn't it? Or is that today?' Her cool facade melted. 'Would it
make you happier to phone and check? Or,' she added casually,
'I could try? His number's in my phone. At least,' she added
with a brave attempt at a smile, 'we know he's not *much
bemus'd in beer.*'

Did we indeed? What was she waiting for? After all, I wasn't
the one with the hots for him.

She turned her back, walking towards an impressive notice
board, the information in frighteningly tidy columns. She left
a message and turned back to me, no longer quite so serene
and in control. 'Of course, he could be with a parishioner.'

'Of course. And I think he does assembly at a couple of
schools in the benefice – only I can't remember which days.'

'Lina, even if I had the manpower, I couldn't send someone hurtling down to his rectory just on the off-chance. It would demean him. And,' she added with a grim smile, 'it would take forever to get through, the roads being what they are today.'

'If you want me to go – when you've finished with me, that is – I will.' Lack of car apart, of course.

She snorted. 'This is all highly irregular, and we're being complete idiots. Lina, there's a lot going on at the moment, all apparently circling round you. I've checked the CCTV images of a woman who could be you arguing with a man we believe has been murdered, and I'm happy to believe you when you say it's not you. For the time being. And I'm happy to believe that you didn't try to tip poor Josie Honeycombe into the sea. For the time being. But I need the person who did – and that someone clearly looks like you. Where do I start looking?'

I must have gaped.

'Look, we have procedures for murders – the case isn't even in my hands any more, but being run by an MIT.'

I nodded. 'That's a specialist murder team?'

'Yes. Pros to their fingertips, every gizmo going. But sometimes it's nice to prove my team aren't complete hicks, only capable of parking Euro lorries on a motorway. Not to mention saving you an awful lot more hassle, only at their hands this time. Let me put this bluntly: do you have any relatives who look sufficiently like you to fool our facial recognition programs into thinking they're you?'

'I may.'

She slapped the desk. 'Come on, Lina, what sort of answer is that?'

'A truthful one,' I bridled. I took a deep breath. 'You'll know from Robin that my father, Lord Elham, is eccentric. He may not have told you that Pa had an . . . an unorthodox sex life. None of his children is legitimate. None, as far as I know, knows any of the others. He kept a list, in a tatty French vocab exercise book, of his lovers and his offspring. As it happens, it's in my keeping, not at Bossingham Hall,' I said airily.

'Why?'

'People think he owns the hall.

'He doesn't?'

'No. Trustees. He's confined to one wing. But that didn't stop a very dodgy claimant turning up and trying to destroy the record that would have proved he was a fake.' The little book meant more to me than I could possibly have explained to a comparative stranger, so without my father's knowledge and against Morris's advice I'd removed it. It was still lurking in my special safe.

'And does this vocab book list the gender of the lovers?'

Playing for time, as much as anything else, I managed a grim laugh. 'My father might be the most amoral person I know, but he was outraged at the thought that one of his neighbours might want to bugger me.'

'I'm not surprised.'

'I mean, he's deeply conventional in many ways,' I said slowly. I didn't want to lie, but I did need to think. 'He liked women, pretty women, and kept a list of the outcome of their affair. Sometimes it was an STD, sometimes an abortion, sometimes a baby, the gender of which he'd note. No addresses, unfortunately – not even the towns they came from.'

'OK, we'll question your father,' she said briskly, as if that would solve everything. 'Would you want to be there?'

I thought about other people's conversations with my father – Morris's, for instance, when he'd perceived my father as a dippy old soak, and also Harvey's, during which Pa had proved himself as fly as they come. 'It's not easy questioning an alcoholic . . . Morris tried once—'

'Ah! Morris! I wondered how long it would take you to drag his name into the conversation! Oh, Lina – get a grip. I can see you've got a mega-crush on him, but the guy's married. And no matter what they say, married men always go back to their wives. Actually,' she added, with a kindish smile, 'he's got an even bigger crush on you, hasn't he? But he's old enough to be your father. Twenty years older than you at least. Not so bad now, but in twenty years' time? And even if he doesn't have the same problems as your dad, you know what the police are like for lasting personal relationships. I'm sorry, but someone had to say it.'

I could hardly speak for the blood pounding my ears and flooding my face. I was off my chair, ready to grab something – anything – heavy and smash it into her face. She wasn't hanging around: she was on her feet, retreating behind her chair.

I think what made me sit down again was the thought of what being the subject of a catfight might do for Morris's career. Even more than what being in said catfight would do for mine – spell in the nick, at very least . . .

'OK, let's leave Morris out of this for a bit except as far as your case is concerned,' I said slowly, sitting down and crossing my legs. 'And putting my father on one side – and yes, I'm happy to be with him when you interview him – Morris took a disk from our cottage and promised to show it to you. Have you seen it yet?'

Returning warily to her own seat, she patted her desk top papers, and, burrowing under a pile of files, produced the disk. 'Seen as in having it here, but not as in having looked at it,' she said. 'Sorry, Lina – I was out of order there.'

Somehow I felt myself in a much stronger position.

She said, almost humbly, 'OK, let's look at it.'

We watched in silence.

'Shit,' she concluded. 'Though such language is strictly off the record, eh? How did someone know two genuine police officers were heading your way? A mole in the control room? Bugger!'

'Or just coincidence?' I said, trying to cheer her up. 'After all, if the so-called woman and Griff's assailant are one and the same, they might just have been chancing their arms. Though it was exceptionally good luck on their part arriving just as we got back from our travels,' I added, raising an eyebrow at her. 'Assuming they hadn't been parked there all day on the off-chance.'

'I don't like that sort of good luck,' she said. 'Mind you, you do make it easier for people to track you with that highly-visible van of yours.'

'I hired a car for a bit, but Griff insisted that we were letting the bad boys win the psychological battles.'

'He would.' She scowled at her mobile, as if willing Robin to ring. 'But sometimes it's better to win the war, even if that means becoming White Van Man – or in your case, Woman.'

I was worrying too much about something else to argue. 'What if this man/woman fake police officer finds out you mean to send someone to interview my father? You know, that mole you mentioned,' I added, seeing her face tighten.

'Easy: I'll go with you myself. Except there's this bloody conference in half an hour about Operation Stack.'

'How long is it likely to last?'

A little delay suited me – or it would have done if only I'd had some wheels. I certainly needed to warn my father in advance, as I always did. Then there was the matter of retrieving the exercise book from its hiding place. And for all Freya's bravado, I wanted to know Robin was safe and sound.

'Piece of string. Look, I'll see you out, and – problem?

'Steve White ferried me over. And he's a bit senior to ferry me back. Tell you what, I'll take your advice – at least some of it,' I conceded with a grin to show that there weren't too many hard feelings, 'and phone the hire car people. They can bring the Micra or whatever over here.'

TWENTY-TWO

A part from St Jude's, which I really couldn't face seeing again for a bit, I looked in at every single church in Robin's benefice. I was amazed that they were all still open to the public, collection boxes and silver plate temptingly within reach of any potential thief. In one there was even what looked like Georgian silver gilt candlesticks. I'd have checked the hallmark, only I didn't want to be accused of casing the joint. Presumably, they relied on the fear of God – literally – as a deterrent. Being struck down by a thunderbolt as you made away with it, or paying for a good haul with eternal damnation were not good prospects.

But there was no sign of Robin. Logically, I supposed I should have called at the rectory first, so I headed back through the narrow lanes, once almost being run off the road by a yummy mummy in a huge 4x4 bearing the legend TWINS ABOARD, for a reason I couldn't work out.

Despite the summer warmth, every rectory window was shut. There was no sign of Robin's car on the weed-ridden gravel, with or without its brand-new tyre. Come to think of it, no one had mentioned anything about the tyres Trev and Robin had had to replace: perhaps there was a queue for any sort of forensic examination that wasn't top priority.

At least there was enough mobile coverage here – sometimes I wondered what it would be like to live in a real town, where you took such a thing for granted – for me to text my father, warning him I was on my way. One came back straightaway. 'No SHAMPOO Urgent Running OUT fancy lunch pa.' He didn't need to sign that one, did he?

A delaying tactic or real need? It suited me anyway, buying me enough time to get home and dig out the exercise book, though what excuse I could give Griff for having hung on to it I'd no idea. In any case, he'd see through it, since it involved my father, of whom he was still deeply suspicious.

As it happened, he was more interested in the rented Fiesta than any reason for my sudden reappearance, accepting with only a shrewd glance that I was acting on Freya's advice. 'If you're going to Bossingham Hall, I should change those nice trousers,' he said. 'Unless your father's suddenly evinced an interest in spring-cleaning.'

Easy-peasy to get the exercise book, then. Except I felt a total worm for hiding the truth from him.

What I did tell him was that I couldn't raise Robin. He said much the same as Freya. 'A priest's public property, my child. He could need to switch his phone off – what if he's at someone's deathbed?'

'So long as it's not his own,' I said, dourly.

'I wondered where that had gone,' my father said, eyeing the exercise book. 'Thought you must have it. Quite glad really. In fact, calls for a drop of fizz. No, not that stuff – not after it's been shaken to death over that bloody track. Can't understand those motor-racing chappies wasting it like that when they win – good stuff, too, unless they put fake in posh bottles.'

I didn't refuse the glass he handed me. Sometimes my father really mystifies me, and this was one of them. 'And you're happy to talk to DCI Webb?'

'Have him to lunch if you've got your eye on him. Not too old for you, is he?'

'It's a she, and you're more likely to have your eye on her. Trouble is, the top she's wearing today clashes something shocking with her hair – she's got a wonderful red-gold mop.'

'Like that Lizzie Siddal?'

I took another very careful sip: that observation was much more likely to have come from Griff's lips than my father's. 'Exactly. I think she and Robin are fond of each other, by the way.'

'Robin the Cava? Oh, dear – church and state. There'll be tears before breakfast. Anyway,' he said, rubbing his hands, 'give her a bell.'

I didn't point out that he'd changed the usual cliché, presumably in the light of his own experience.

*　　*　　*

Lunch, which we had late, was an interesting meal. Freya all too clearly didn't take to my father, who was doing his best to charm her – as he must have charmed my mother and every other woman in the book – and refused to talk business, as he quaintly termed it, till we had finished. At last, she actually removed her glass from the table to prevent him quietly topping it up.

'As I said, Pa, Freya needs information – and I have to say she needs it now. Let me make us all a cup of green tea – unless you'd prefer coffee, Freya? – while Freya explains the problem.'

Whatever reaction either of us might have expected when Freya had finished speaking, I doubt if it was the one we got. 'My precious child's life is at risk because of some evil woman who bears a passing resemblance! Lina, you and Griff will move in here tonight and remain under this roof until the danger is past.'

Freya held up a hand. 'I just need to ask, My Lord, if you might have a daughter roughly Freya's age who could be living in Kent.'

'It's all in the book.' He pointed. 'Why didn't you look and tell her straightaway, Lina? Save your skin?'

'Because this is yours, not mine, Pa. I couldn't give away your secrets.'

'That must be that Griff Tripp's mealy-mouthed middle-class influence. I've never made any secret of my doings. Pass it over. Let's look.'

The three of us scanned the columns. Suddenly, my father jabbed with an index finger still, to my horror, stained with ink. As far as I knew, Freya hadn't the faintest idea of what he was involved with, so perhaps she'd not register it. 'See. Eileen. Lovely woman. At least, I thought she was until she tried a spot of the old blackmail. Not like Lina's mama. She was a lady. Even brought Lina to come and see me a couple of times, eh, Lina?' He squeezed my hand. First time ever. I nearly died. 'No, can't be Irene. She had a son, look. Marigold? Strange how they've named rubber gloves after her – she had this fetish . . . No, another son. There's your mother, Lina. And you, of course. Now, who's this up here? Olivia.

Olivia Petham. A real lady. County set. Lived in Sussex. And in Scotland, of course. Her brother was a real bad egg. Now, *she* had a daughter. See? About four years older than you.'

Freya, who'd been sitting with her mouth agape, started scribbling. 'Sussex? Any idea which part?'

'Check your *Burke's Peerage*, dear lady – everything's in there. Or here – now this woman did not turn out well. Pauline Webster. Gave me the clap for a start.' He pointed at the column in which he recorded results. 'The clap and another daughter. Frances. Would call her Frankie. She went back to Brighton, as far as I know.'

'*Burke's Peerage* again?' Freya gasped.

'Good God, no – father ran a chip shop. Jolly good one too. That's how I met her,' he added helpfully.

None of the other women seemed to have local connections, so Freya snapped her notepad shut. 'Do you mind if I take this?' she said, reaching for the exercise book.

'Up to Lina. I know she treasures it – she doesn't have many relics of her ma, you know. Tell you what, Lina, would your phone take photos of it? Just the pages this good lady wants, of course. And then – well, I think it should go back in the hidey-hole where you found it. Safer than with you at the moment. And I meant what I said about you and old Tripp coming to stay. Plenty of bedrooms. No one'll notice.'

In other words, in the main part of the building. The part open to the visitors who paid a tenner a time. The idea appealed – or appalled, in equal measure.

Neither Freya nor I had heard from Robin by the time my father ushered us out. I led the way past the worst of the potholes, seeing her grimace as she steered her Audi in my tracks.

At the bottom I stopped. 'Anything you wanted to say you couldn't say in front of my father?'

She got out and leaned against the bonnet. 'Bloody hell, I could do with a fag. All I can say, Lina, is that you're a credit – to yourself. How weird is that, to talk in front of your daughter about the sexual tastes of other women?'

'Could have been worse – could have been my mother's sexual tastes.'

'All the same . . . Look, thanks for the info from that book. I think. I'll get on to it the moment I can get bloody mobile coverage.'

'And Robin?'

'Quite. Maybe it's some church thing. Why did I give up smoking?' she added, frantically patting her trousers in case one last gasper remained.

'You know Robin's started to smoke again recently,' I said. 'Do you know why? He really is incredibly stressed, you know. Before you came on the scene, if that's any help,' I added drily.

'I thought it was the usual, overwork and underpay. But it shouldn't be like that for vicars, should it?' She looked at me earnestly. 'Look, you two were never an item, were you?'

'For five minutes, a long time ago. Friends ever since. No pangs.'

''Cos I'm going to do something in even worse taste than your Pa. When – when we were . . . you know . . . I've never known a man so driven.' Hell, was she talking about sex with him? She was, wasn't she! She must be desperate with worry, poor woman. 'So compelled . . . I shouldn't have said anything – forget it.'

I don't often squeeze a woman's shoulders, but I did this time. 'Let's just assume there's some big problem he can't talk about. He's a good man.'

'*He that doeth good is of God,*' she murmured, though I wasn't sure if I was meant to hear.

'We must help him,' I urged her.

She blinked hard and straightened her shoulders. 'And that means finding him.'

I reported my morning's travels.

'Shit. OK, I'll see what official strings I can pull, in a highly unofficial way.'

'I don't see why it shouldn't be entirely official,' I said. 'X is dead, almost certainly murdered. You think Cashmere Roll-Neck is dead – the one I'm supposed to have done in,' I explained. 'I never knew his proper name, and for some reason no one filled me in with all the details the other day.'

'Ah. Simon Bonnaventure.'

'Wow. A name like that, I'm surprised he ever lived. What did he do – was he an explorer or something?'

'An architect, apparently – specialized in disabled access to public buildings. He popped his clogs in Hythe, near Waitrose. Which I happen to know is one of your haunts.' She pulled a face.

'Griff. End-dated goodies,' I explained.

'There's one slight problem, though, that I don't think you'll have learned when you were interviewed – you were commendably poised, by the way, as I should have said before. We do have a crime scene. But we don't have a body yet.'

'Whoops. Who is he? Was he really on the Cathedral guest list or did he gatecrash, like me?'

'I understood you were a genuine guest,' she said, her mouth tight, as if she was recalling that but for a perverse twist of fate, not to mention the fact that she and Robin weren't then an item, even if they were now, she'd have been there instead.

'Strange music, vicious seats, Bonnaventure being dead rude. Not the best function to be a guest at. So was he? A guest?'

'You're very tenacious, aren't you?'

Tenacious sounded a really good word, though from the way she used it I wasn't sure if she was paying me a compliment or the reverse. I pulled an *if you say so* sort of face.

She continued, 'Some poor sap is probably going through every single guest to check if he or she brought him in at the last minute – you know, *ran into him at the concert and thought it would be OK.*'

'And why have you got a fully-fledged murder team on to it if you've not got a body?'

'You don't want to know.' She shuddered as if she hadn't seen all sorts of stomach-churning sights.

Didn't I? Well, maybe I didn't. 'This Bonnaventure guy missing, presumed dead. My lovely old friend Josie in an ICU. You know, I'd worry about Robin very officially indeed, if I were you.'

It seemed a good line to part company on, and we both

turned back to our cars. But then I remembered there was one church I hadn't checked out, and I ran towards her yelling, 'What about St Jude's?'

'Lead the way,' she snapped.

I did.

TWENTY-THREE

I f Freya'd been an ordinary vulnerable woman five minutes ago, by the time we'd thrown our cars on to the lay-by beside the church she was a cool professional again.

'Back in your car, please, Lina. We don't want any more of your DNA around the place confusing the issue. No. I'm telling you officially. Get in and stay put.' She was already hurtling towards the church, where police tape still fluttered. Snatching at it, she disappeared from view.

She reappeared immediately. 'Where can I get a key? I've broken down enough doors in my life, but not one like this.'

'Fiona Pargetter's the churchwarden. But I've no idea where she lives. I'm nothing to do with this parish, Freya!' I said sharply as she raised furious hands to heaven. 'Is there anything on the noticeboard?' I pointed. I could see the peeling wooden structure but not read anything on it, not from the car.

She came back with a torn sheet of paper, which she thrust at me. 'Can you make anything of these? I shall be needing fucking reading glasses next.'

The sheet with the Churchwarden's number was bleached by sun and washed by rain. 'I can guess . . .'

'Call them out – I'll dial. If I can get sodding coverage.'

It took three attempts to get the numbers right, and then Freya only located the last warden but one. She snapped a great deal, and eventually must have got a result.

'Why can't these people keep things up to date, for God's sake?'

'All volunteers,' I ventured.

'If a job's worth doing it's worth doing well,' she snarled. Was this yet another of her quotations? At least it sounded homely enough. How a woman under pressure could come out with bits from the Bible or Shakespeare or whoever as if it was as normal as breathing defeated me. Meanwhile she was dialling a number as if she was jabbing her finger into inefficient eyes. At least she could demand to speak to Ms Pargetter.

'Away!' she repeated. 'But she's the keyholder.'

There was a pause. I presume whoever she was yelling at tried a gentle answer.

'So why wasn't that on the noticeboard in the first place? Thank you,' she added, as if at last remembering her manners – which Griff had dinned into me made the man. Or at least the woman.

But I wouldn't point that out.

'Apparently, some yokel in a cottage near the church holds a spare. No, I told you to stay there.'

I stayed. She went. She came back tailed by a man in his slippers carrying a huge key. They headed off to the church. He returned, muttering and looking at me with a mixture of anger and pity. She didn't.

What was keeping her? I imagined all sorts of things, from first aid to prayers. I tried adding a few of my own. Maybe a hired Fiesta wasn't the best place to concentrate, but I still had my eyes tight shut when she came back.

'Not a sign,' she said. 'I'll get this back to that hayseed and head back to Maidstone.'

I nodded. 'Sorry to have wasted your time.'

'These things happen.' She stomped off.

She was just starting her car when something struck me. Waving wildly, I ran towards her.

'For God's sake—!'

'Did you try the loo? It's in the old stable block, right at the far end of the churchyard. And there's probably some of my DNA left in it: it was where I applied plasters and bandages when someone had tripped me up.' I tried to explain as she galloped ahead of me, but it was clear she'd rather hear any explanation later.

The door was locked, of course. But we exchanged a glance and as one rushed at it. She was a good deal more scientific than I – I suppose they teach door-busting at police academy. And soon we were in.

'Christ.' She stopped dead and pointed at the drops on the tiled floor. 'Did you lose that much blood?' She must have been listening after all.

'I don't think so . . .' And surely someone – some volunteer

– would have cleaned it up by now. Then I got a grip and looked properly. 'I certainly didn't leave those splashes on the wall there.'

'So whose is it? Please God, don't let it be Robin's.'

My route back to Bredeham took me – near enough – past Bugger Bridger's and the convenient lay-by. Fi had been sure the boxes had come from him. He was emphatic they hadn't. What if they'd come from one of those tatty outbuildings that stood cheek by jowl with his? It was time someone had a look – why not me?

One very good reason not to was a couple of healthy-lunged dogs, running loose behind what seemed a brand-new fence. It didn't look very substantial, however, and I didn't want to test it or the padlocked gates for dog-proofness. The outbuildings were as unpromising as the colonel's – worse, in some cases. Griff used to chunter from time to time about the decline in vernacular farm buildings for which no one had any use these days: did he mean that, like these, they were literally falling down? The house itself was set almost a hundred yards from the road and the flimsy fence. There wasn't any sign of an entryphone, but perhaps, after all, they had a canine one – in which case I'd better scarper.

Once I'd got my breath back I called Griff to say I was returning to Bredeham. 'As there's nothing I can do, she's sent me home,' I said, really pissed off, if the truth be told.

'I'm very pleased she did. Frustrating though it must be not to be in the thick of things, you have to remember that they're not necessarily your things to be in the thick of. Now, I wonder if you'd do me a little favour – make a pilgrimage to Canterbury Marks and Spencer to buy some of their wonderful balsamic vinegar . . .'

Yes, that was Griff for you. Anyway, there was plenty of space in the multi-storey car park when I got there, and a girl does like to see a few shops from time to time. Any other day, that is. My heart felt swollen with anxiety for Robin: it's one thing being awash with adrenalin when there's lots of action, quite another when you have time to reflect on the possible fate of a dear friend.

I was so dazed I forgot the upper exit from M and S direct

to the car park and headed out to the main entrance, where I found myself stunned and confused in the bright sun. Confused as in *in tears.*

'My dear, are you all right?' a concerned voice asked – a vaguely familiar voice.

Blinking a couple of times, and eventually giving up and wiping mascara all over my face with a soggy tissue, I managed to place the speaker. It was the lilac-shirted clergyman who'd spoken to me the night of the Cathedral nibbles. Today his shirt was midnight blue.

'You're young Robin Levitt's friend, aren't you?' He put a hand on my arm.

It felt – what was the word Griff had taught me? – avuncular. 'Would you like to talk? There's nowhere very private round here, I'm afraid.'

The words came tumbling out. 'It's not you I need to talk to so much as God. I'm so worried something dreadful's happened to Robin, and—'

'I know just the place.' His grip tightened.

For a bulky man, he was surprisingly swift on his feet. He propelled me through the gaggles of Japanese photographers, guiding my steps as Griff did when he taught me to dance the waltz. I was ready to panic, we were moving so fast. Where was he taking me? Was he trying to kidnap me in broad daylight? Was he part of the whole evil plot? Why didn't I call out, or try to break away? Our progress away from the shops and the tourists was breathless and inexorable.

At last I realized that we were heading towards the Cathedral itself, via the clergy steps, not the tourist queues, and started to relax. I'm sure I'd have been turned back, but he said something inaudible to the gatekeeper and sped me on my way across the green towards the Cathedral itself. It was all beginning to make sense. Possibly.

My feet stopped of their own accord as we went inside. 'It's one thing talking to God,' I hissed, 'quite another doing it in front of all these people. It'd be like praying in a museum. Too . . . too ostentatious.' Actually, with the noise a bunch of French school kids were making, alongside even more Japanese photographers, it would have been like praying in Disneyland.

'So it would. Rather like that complacent Pharisee. But come into this chapel, Our Lady Martyrdom – it's set aside for people like you. Take no notice of Dean Boys and his bones – in those days they were into gruesome reminders of our last end.'

They were as well. All those skulls, with an old guy sitting on them looking as if he'd got toothache.

He smiled and gave my shoulders a little pat. 'Take as long as you want.' And he was gone, before I could even thank him.

'Robin's on *what*?' Freya squeaked down the phone.

'Retreat. According to this clergyman I met this afternoon,' I explained. He'd been waiting for me when I emerged blinking into the sunshine, basking, as he'd put it, like an elderly seal, on a convenient bench.

'And who is this guy?'

'He said his name was Tom – he's a rural dean, apparently. And he nipped into the diocesan office and asked.'

'Are you sure he's kosher?' Freya sounded terribly suspicious.

'I'm sure you could check. There can't be all that many rural deans, can there? The thing is, we can't get to talk to Robin, because retreat's a time when he's deliberately excluding the pressures of the outside world.'

'That's a lot of fucking use!'

'But he – Tom – will get a message to him asking him to let us know he's OK.'

'And pigs may take to the air. Let me know if you get any hard news, will you? And when you stop believing in Father Christmas.' She cut the call.

Griff was a little more encouraging, but not much, not even breaking off as he chopped onions. 'You can see why she'd rather have had a more comprehensive identification of your new friend. After all, she's paid to be suspicious. And you must admit it's very strange that Robin's not allowed to take calls or even letters.'

'Tom said that that's what a retreat's all about. And the state he's been in, Robin needs time to contemplate and do whatever you do on retreat. And give up smoking,' I added, less idealistically and probably less realistically.

'True. Now, you've just got time to shower and change before our supper guest arrives. Shoo, dear one, shoo.' He touched an oniony finger to my lips.

So it must be someone I'd want to see. I'd no idea who. Morris was in Belgium by now, and Harvey, who'd always been a fairly welcome and very charming guest in the past, had really annoyed me, both by his attitude to his wife and by shoving my urgent request for help to the bottom of his in-tray. Aidan?

Funny, I reflected as I tried to scrub away the memory of the blood-smeared tiles, how many of our friends were male. Josie had been right when she said I needed a woman friend to talk lippie and shoes with. Not that Griff wasn't an expert in both, of course. Would Freya and I ever be mates? As she hadn't pointed out, she was almost old enough to be my mother, but when she wasn't treating me as a village idiot – and she obviously made a habit of that – she might be at least becoming a friend. No, perhaps not. But we were closer than just acquaintances. I think. All the same, she didn't strike me as the sort of woman I could share lipstick secrets with. And I would like to know one of those.

As I dressed and applied slap, I made a To Do list:

- *Ask after Josie*
- *Nag Harvey*
- *Ask Freya about the tyres still in custody*
- *Ask Freya about the buildings behind Bugger Bridger's place* (I'd have liked to find another word beginning with B, but couldn't)
- *Repair a few vases, even if it means working later than Griff likes*
- *Not think about Morris too much*
- *Do something about that poor folio*

There. That felt a lot better. As if I was taking control of my life again.

As if.

I heard Griff greeting someone and the sound of a reply.

There was only one man with a voice like that. I was halfway down the stairs before I realized I'd only got one sandal on. Kicking it off, I ran barefoot.

'I thought you were in Brussels!' I said, flinging my arms round his neck regardless of Griff's interested smile.

'I've been stuck under the bloody Channel for more hours than I care to remember. The French strikers. They usually let Eurostar through, but not today. And I thought of Griff's cooking and the way you've always got some white wine chilling and here I am.'

So how would Griff react to knowing that Tim the Bear would be ousted tonight?

As if he read my mind, he added, 'Only one problem: I can't drink too much of the wine. I've got to get back to London tonight. Leda's babysitter's just phoned to say she needs to get home tonight – some sort of family emergency. So she can't stay over as she usually does when the orchestra's working away from London. How's Josie?'

'I was just about to phone,' Griff said, obligingly disappearing into the office.

Perhaps he approved of Morris all the more since he wouldn't be under our roof tonight.

But he emerged tight-faced with fury. 'It seems old friends aren't entitled to ask about the health of people they love and respect.'

'Not when the old friend's business partner is suspected of putting the patient in the ICU in the first place,' I sighed.

'Leave it to me,' Morris said, heading towards the front door.

'Use the landline, for goodness' sake, and press redial,' Griff snapped, heading for the kitchen, where he clashed his beloved saucepans with fury.

I'll swear he even gave them an apologetic pat when Morris rejoined us in the kitchen with his news. 'She's still very ill. Still touch and go. But the officer guarding her – hell, the police budget won't like that – swears she kept muttering, "It wasn't Lina."'

'Wow! Really?' I sat down hard.

Griff stroked my hair. 'She loves you a great deal, my child. The granddaughter she never had.'

I was up as if he'd stuck a pin in me. 'Granddaughter! Who wants me as a granddaughter? Bloody Arthur Habgood. Who's a friend of his? Wanted me to go and see his shop? Estelle Sanditon. Harvey's wife,' I explained.

'I gathered. And this would be the Harvey Sanditon who bought the dodgy snuffbox on my behalf?'

'Exactly. The Harvey Sanditon who couldn't be arsed – sorry, Griff – to look at the photos I'd sent him to see if he could recognize anyone at the fête where the first one turned up and was nearly stolen.' I subsided. 'But Harvey doesn't like Habgood one scrap, and relations between him and his wife looked pretty fraught, so maybe I'm seeing things I shouldn't.'

'And you've already drained your first glass, without it even touching the sides, I'd say,' Griff said. 'Come, my child, the news of Josie isn't all that bad – and she's certainly helped you a great deal. I think we should calm down and raise a glass to the dear lady, don't you?'

'Not to mention Robin,' I added grimly.

'Tell Morris about it while you lay the table in the garden, sweet one,' Griff said, and he thrust a fistful of cutlery at me.

TWENTY-FOUR

'You can't expect my colleagues to report everything back to you, Lina,' Morris said, adding with an ironic smile, 'they don't even tell *me* what's going on. And that's my own team. Joking. I think. Freya took a huge risk this afternoon consorting with someone else's suspect – I just hope the MIT find an alternative suspect pretty soon, or, mark my words, they'll haul you in and talk to you in a fairly unpleasant way, despite what Josie said. At which point you produce your alibi, like the proverbial white rabbit.'

I nodded, leaning back to savour the last of the evening sun, the good wine and Morris's company, in whichever order, while Griff made coffee. Then I sat up. 'There is someone who should be reporting back, though. Harvey Sanditon. Hell's bells, the number of times I've put his work top of the list because it was urgent. You'd think he might look at a few photos for me. Well, sixty pretty bad ones,' I conceded.

'Maybe he's sent the information to me.' He sounded, as he stroked my hair, as if he couldn't care less abut Harvey. 'After all,' he added, 'knowing you, he might be afraid of your going haring round the countryside chasing wild geese. Whoops, I've just mixed my metaphors.'

'Something I can hardly forgive,' Griff declared, making us jump as he placed the tray on the table. He lit a couple of those candles supposed to drive away midges. 'Morris, you will ensure our dear child doesn't do anything foolish, won't you?'

Morris removed his hand, flushing slightly, possibly because of the word *our*, which made him sound like a co-guardian. 'Ensure? I can only add my pleas to yours, Griff. And I know which one of us she'll take more notice of.' His voice sounded a good deal more regretful than the words deserved.

Deep breath time. 'I had a closer look at the farm buildings that back on to Colonel Bridger's place. Tumbledown old wrecks, most of them. And no, I didn't get any further than the verge outside, not with two hounds from hell on border patrol. But if you wanted to conceal something or someone there, I'd have thought it was ideal.'

'Why didn't I meet the dogs when I had a look? And funnily enough I don't remember a fence.' He fished out his phone. 'I don't like wasting time with you making phone calls, but—'

'Go ahead,' Griff said. 'The best signal's by the washing-line whirligig.' He made a rotary gesture until Morris twigged. He added, when Morris was possibly out of earshot, 'He's doing the right thing, my child. As I said earlier, this is work for experts. You wouldn't want Freya tackling one of your repairs, now, would you?'

From inside the house, we heard a phone. Griff preferred his old-fashioned phone, complete with fax, answerphone and firmly attached handset, to all the more modern and user-friendly phones I'd tried to push on him. So one of us would just have to go and pick up said handset – or, of course, leave the work to the answerphone. Knowing he simply couldn't do that, and knowing he shouldn't scuttle after a big meal, I ran inside myself.

I came back feeling sick. I said to Griff and Morris equally, 'That was Aidan. He reckons someone's been hanging round his place all afternoon. Tenterden,' I reminded Morris.

'He uses the same top-grade security system as us,' Griff said, a bit pettishly.

'I think there's more to the story, isn't there, Lina?' Morris said, taking my hand.

'The someone looks like me.' I sank weakly on to the chair next to Griff.

'Excellent,' said Morris, rubbing his hands. 'Nice touristy place. CCTV coming out of its ears. And you, Lina, with a pretty well watertight alibi; I can't imagine prosecuting counsel trying to tell Freya Webb that you weren't together, can you? No, with luck, we'll pick up not just your lookalike, but also her car and its lovely all-revealing registration plates.' He fished out his mobile and, retreating to the whirligig, apparently left a message. 'Freya's got her phone switched off, and who can blame her at this hour? Look, I'm so sorry, but I really must go. Use every security device at your disposal. Tell your friend to do the same, Griff.' They shook hands. I followed him into the house, where he kissed me pretty thoroughly and then pushed me away. 'No, Lina, don't even think of seeing me to my car.'

'I'm not thinking, I'm doing.' But I stopped dead by the front door. 'Wait there. Just wait.' I turned and hurtled.

He didn't wait. He followed me to the security console and watched me bring up footage of the past hour. As he did, he let fly as comprehensive range of swear words as I'd heard in a long time. 'So what did he attach to my car?' he asked at last. With a few extra words in-between.

'A tracking device, I suppose. Why on earth didn't you park in our yard? Anyway, take the hire car. I'll go online and sort out the insurance. Morris, you know that's what you have to do. Just give me your keys and your licence details and push off. Before I change my mind.'

'What an ignominious way for such a nice car to depart,' Griff observed early next morning, as Morris's Saab was waiting to be hauled off on a tow truck to have what Freya called a complete forensic examination. 'But your quixotic gesture last night has left you without transport, I'm afraid, unless you care to use our van. And I'll tell you straight, I don't care for you to use it.'

'And I don't care to use it. I don't even care to open the yard gates. I don't care to let Mrs Walker, with or without her poet, risk working in the shop. Look, we've got enough food to hunker down for the day. We've got a backlog of Internet enquiries and sales to deal with. And I've got a very sad row of pots just crying out for my attention. Let's – what do you call it? – make virtue of necessity.'

He hugged me. 'Let us indeed. We'll have a nice quiet day.'

We had about a minute's worth of quiet.

It was broken as one of the Saab's tyres exploded.

Actually, that's an exaggeration. It just sounded bad in the quiet street. But, as Freya phoned to explain later, if you'd been driving, you'd have called it a blowout. If you'd been driving at thirty, it would have been inconvenient. If you'd been passing someone in the outside lane of the M20, it might have been a bit more than inconvenient.

'Thank God Morris took the hired Fiesta,' I breathed.

'Thank God indeed. Next time you're in the Cathedral, you might light a candle on his behalf. At least it's done one good thing. It's stepped up police interest – we don't like it when one of our own is involved,' Freya said.

'Involved?'

'I think the blowout was meant to happen later; that it was planned and someone's plans misfired, if you'll forgive the pun.'

'Someone sab—'

I think she took my hesitation as disbelief, not a sign that I'd forgotten the word. 'Quite. Someone sabotaged the tyre.'

'Those other tyres – the ones from Trev and Robin's cars—'

'Quite. Now I feel entitled to push the forensic tests on those tyres further up the list. Budgets and prioritization, Lina – a major juggling act, believe me.'

I knew all about that from the business Griff and I were trying to run. 'Griff, who used to be an actor, remember, is convinced that all the people we've been threatened by have been made-up: the guy who got into the cottage, the so-called policewomen who got to me before the real officers, the old man planting tracking devices and thingies to blow up tyres. Is there any make-up artist living in the area? Or an ex-actor?'

'As I'm sure Griff would say, tap on the woodwork and you'll get an army of ex-actors. We can't interrogate all of them: think what Equity would say,' she added with a laugh that sounded a bit hollow. 'The same with make-up artists – take a look round House of Fraser or Fenwick's.'

'I didn't mean the ones who try to sell you wrinkle products when you're not yet twenty-five,' I said. 'I mean those with serious skills in latex and stuff. Think *The Elephant Man.*'

'I'd rather not. OK, I know what you mean. I'll get someone on to it,' she said, sounding as if she'd much rather not. 'Now, I must fly – we've got a briefing two minutes ago.'

'I don't see why I shouldn't scrape round the recesses of my memory,' Griff said, when I reported the conversation. 'Before you so much as squeak, all my investigations will be done online. While you toil in the heat of the workroom, I shall exert myself in the office.' He added, 'Have you heard from Morris yet? He's intimately concerned, after all.'

'It's a bit early for a man caring for a baby, isn't it?' I hoped my voice didn't give too much away.

'What did you say when you phoned?'

'That there was a bit of a problem and that he might want to call me or Freya. Maybe he chose the second option, to get the facts.'

'A veritable Gradgrind! No, I suspect there's a feeding or a nappy problem, my love. And let us not forget that it's barely nine. It's going to be a glorious day, too, far too good for incarceration indoors,' he added wistfully.

'Lunch in the garden,' I said briskly, heading off upstairs so I didn't have time to think about Morris.

We'd both earned mid-morning coffee in the garden. Griff had dealt with half our Internet orders, and the parcels, plump with bubble wrap, sat in the living room. When and how they'd get to the post office neither of us cared to ask. I'd made some progress with a very tricky piece of Meissen, but my hands weren't as steady as I really liked, so I'd turned to another wretched Toby jug, one with a particularly idiotic expression on its face, although it was Royal Worcester. As soon as I'd managed to match the sides of his broken hat I could sign him off the sick list; with luck he'd be the last for a while.

As soon as we sat down to bask, of course, the phone rang. So I trotted back inside, blinking at what seemed near darkness. The mouse, the modem and the screen standby lights glowed eerily. No wonder people worried about global warming and light pollution.

'Lina, my darling,' came familiar plummy tones.

However did I once think I fancied him? 'Hi, Harvey. How are you?'

'All the better for hearing your voice. And you?'

'It depends what I hear your voice say.' Was I being gracious or taking the piss? I wasn't sure myself.

'It's going to tell you that I may have placed a face in one of those appalling photographs. I'm only halfway through, but I thought you should know. What I've done is email the image and indicate who it is – oh, some clever program Estelle uses to separate the foreground from the background. You'll see.'

'I'm picking up the emails now,' I said, clicking away. 'Yes, here we are. It's just going through the Digital Image thingy now. Wow, that's clever.' Harvey had managed to cloak everything in a sort of grey screen except the face of one man. 'Who is it?'

'Darling Lina, before I tell you, you must promise me absolutely not to go haring after him yourself. As far as I know, he's an ordinary decent man, but I do not want you putting yourself at risk. Promise?'

'I suppose so. An ordinary decent man?' I prompted.

'He had a most respectable career when I knew him. He was a junior science teacher at my public school. Burgess Rushton.'

'That's the school or the teacher?' I asked, deliberately pert.

'The teacher,' he said tartly. 'But he left, as I recall, rather precipitately, as if under a cloud. Lots of rumours why – he was only a year or so out of university. So you can tell your policeman boyfriend that. Now, I have another call coming in—'

Whoops, I really had offended him, hadn't I? I said humbly, 'Thank you, Harvey. I'm really grateful. And if you recognize anyone else you'll promise to come straight back to me?'

'Darling, of course. Now, you will take care, won't you? Just in case he's turned out badly. Promise?'

I promised. And this time I didn't have my fingers crossed behind my back.

TWENTY-FIVE

I sent the JPEG to both Freya and Morris, plus Harvey's identification of the man as Burgess Rushton.

Morris phoned back immediately. 'I'm sorry – I've had baby crisis here. But it's all cleaned up now, and the nanny's arrived and calm prevails. Every time I picked up the phone, there's been another squall. What didn't come out one end came out the other. I don't know if it's a bug or something she's eaten. Sorry, too much information!'

It was, definitely. But maybe that's what parenthood did to people.

'Anyway, here I am, looking at Burgess Rushton and ready to run every check going. I'll be back to you the moment I have.'

It wasn't long before Griff wandered in. Hand on hips, he peered at the screen. 'Why is it that every undistinguished face seems vaguely familiar? Even more than vaguely, perhaps . . . But with a name like Burgess Rushton, he ought to stand out.'

'Why not look at the rest, with him in mind?' I suggested, pushing him into the chair and producing his reading glasses. If I hassled him, he'd remember something just to please me, so I went back to the Toby jug.

Not for long. The phone rang again, and Griff summoned me down to talk to Freya.

'Have you heard from Robin yet?' she asked, almost breathlessly. Just as I'd ask about Morris.

'Not yet. But the post comes at all hours.'

'You're expecting a bloody postcard with a second-class stamp? Can't the bugger use the fucking phone?' I heard her draw breath. 'Sorry, Lina. The whole situation's getting to me. And now I've got Morris to worry about too – though I shouldn't have said that, should I?'

'I think I'd gathered already,' I said mildly. 'I suppose there's no sign of Cashmere Roll-Neck, the guy you assume's a corpse?'

'Simon Bonnaventure,' she said sharply. 'No. Nor of Ms Pargetter.'

'Tell me,' I interrupted her, 'do you want Fi as a possible victim or as a likely criminal?'

'No comment. No sighting of your putative siblings either. They've vanished into thin air. Why can't the bloody countryside have CCTV?'

'What about the sighting of my double in Tenterden that Morris phoned you about? Last night, outside Griff's partner's house,' I prompted, giving his address.

She whistled. 'That must be must be worth an arm and a leg.'

I didn't have time to discuss real estate. 'Lots of CCTV coverage round there, he said.'

'Shit, it's still on my To Do list. I'll get on to it. Now.' She cut the call.

It was a good job she did. It was nearly midday, for goodness' sake, and she still hadn't checked. I was so furious that I had a pick at the last few scabs from the gravel rash from my fall at St Jude's and made my knee bleed.

Cross with a lot of people, including myself, I still managed to work. I'd just signed off the Toby jug when Griff called. I went down expecting lunch; what I got was a printout.

'Make-up artists in the Kent area,' he declared with a flourish. He picked up the sheets. 'One or two of them known to me personally. I thought I might make a phone call or two. No, goodness me, not to interrogate them, but to ask if they had any dodgy colleagues.'

'What if they turned out to be the dodgy one?' I asked. 'Oh, Griff, you're as bad as I am for sticking your nose in. Leave it to Freya's team.' He was silent. 'Oh, Griff, you already have, haven't you? OK, what did you discover?'

'I only phoned my oldest contacts. And they knew nothing. I swore them to secrecy, incidentally – but then, you know what gossips all theatrical folk are. So I also made them swear to keep my name out of it. All the same, you might prefer not to mention me when you send the details to Freya?'

I hugged him. 'I might indeed.' I didn't point out that even if Freya didn't have the time to delegate googling to one of her team, the MIT was supposed to be awash with people and technology. But she was in some strange competition with them, wasn't she, and might welcome Griff's bit of homework.

Lazing in the sun with an occasional bit of gardening would have been the best option for this afternoon, but now the Meissen called, and even when that was finished there was plenty waiting in the queue. I was just about to allow myself a stretch and a break for some of Griff's home-made lemonade when the office phone rang. Since I suspected Griff was asleep under that straw hat of his, I nipped down myself.

'Darling Lina, I think I may have recognized another face in your rogue's gallery. A woman's, this time. The trouble is, I can't remember her name, not all of it. She married an actor and rather dropped out of the antiques scene. I'll send her photo through anyway. And to that copper of yours?'

'Please.' The fact that he'd mentioned Morris gave me the right to mention his wife, didn't it? 'Harvey, this is really awkward. Your wife—'

'What about her?'

'It's just that she knows Arthur Habgood.'

'She has bad taste in friends as well as husbands, I'm afraid. I thought you handled the suggested visit to his twee little shop with great dignity, Lina. She knows I loathe the man, I think I may have mentioned to her the harm he's tried to do you. She was just being malicious, something she does very well. I think – please, never allude to this – I think losing . . . She had several miscarriages, and we never had the large family we both wanted. She's become more and more bitter. Perverse. And sometimes it's infectious. We both do things to annoy the other.'

'So when we all ate together, Griff and I were pawns in your private chess game? Thanks a bunch, Harvey.'

'I thought I'd be on my own when I invited you. She found out and insisted on coming. I'm sorry. Anyway, as far as I know, your possible grandfather has expanded his business by

opening a cafe and local produce shop. I think he's too busy
to be involved in any more malevolence against you. But
my ear will be constantly to the ground.'

Did I recognize the woman in the JPEG? Maybe I did; perhaps
she'd bought some paperbacks from me. But I couldn't swear
to it. Griff squinted at the screen too, but eventually shook his
head. He jabbed a finger at her eyes and temples. 'A face job,
and not a good one, I'd say. So she may be older than she
wishes us to think. If only we could see her hands: always a
giveaway. Was she with the other man – the one with the name
like a firm of gentleman's outfitters or some Leicestershire
village?'

'Burgess Rushton. Not in any of the photos, not as far as I
can see. But that doesn't mean anything either way.'

'Thieves are like wolves, aren't they? They hunt in packs.
And don't forget that there were three people involved when
you first came across the snuffbox. One to make off with the
box; a second to promise to dial nine nine nine; a third to trip
you up. Maybe a fourth, to jemmy the van. Or one of the
others could have done that, of course.'

'A jemmy's not the sort of thing the average punter takes
to a church fête, though. And in my day you could get arrested
even for carrying one round, on the grounds you were going
to use it for something.'

He looked at me sideways, as he always did when I referred
to my teen years, the ones before he came on the scene. 'They
couldn't have known they might need to use it on your van,
angel heart. But it does seem to me they must have known
the box was going to be at the fête. Didn't you and Robin act
on that principle when you went to see Colonel Bridger?'

I nodded. 'Robin said they'd only have had to ask him and
provide reasonable proof of ownership and he'd have handed
it back. He might have asked them to reimburse me, but that's
all.'

'All the stuff on sale was brought along or collected from
local people. No, bear with my poor slow brain for a moment.
Someone sees you handling it; takes it; has to get rid of it –
the sort of person who wouldn't want his or her reputation

soiled by an accusation of theft. It's also someone who lives close enough to slip back home and return to the fête before you decamp in the van. Please don't frown – you'll end up with wrinkles.'

'What about all the other odds and ends? The church itself being robbed? The double of mine going round assaulting people?'

'I wish I had the answers. Meanwhile, perhaps some lunch in the garden – I've prepared a Salade Niçoise – might help you think.'

It did. But not the sort of thought he wanted.

'Go down to the coast and flush her out? Are you out of your mind? What would dear Morris say?'

'I didn't say I'd do it on my own. But if she is my half-sister, she may share my dislike of people muscling in on her territory. Dislike! I hate it, Griff. I don't care about Bonnaventure, apart from the crime scene being at your favourite haunt—' Hell, I'd not meant him to know that. 'Near Hythe Waitrose,' I explained, quickly adding: 'Then there's Josie down in Hastings, and Aidan in Tenterden. Poor X – Graham Parker – in Kenninge. Not to mention the attack on you in Bredeham. I want her out of here. Now.'

He grabbed my wrist and pulled me gently down beside him. 'Striding round in this heat's going to get you hot and bothered and not much else. You're making too many assumptions, loved one. You're confusing actual crimes and the sightings of a woman who looks like you. She may have nothing to do with them, though I concede that things look bad for her in connection with that man Bonnaventure's disappearance. If she is involved with any or all of the others, look at it from another viewpoint – she wanted, and in this she's partially succeeded, to implicate you in her crimes. I know nothing about the ins and outs of DNA, but I do get the general idea that there are family similarities.' He coughed gently. 'Have you discussed all this with Freya?'

'No. But I'm sure if they'd found an exact match at any of the crime scenes she wouldn't be hobnobbing with me. And neither would Morris.' I suddenly heard Freya's voice, observing that I dragged his name into the conversation whenever I could. 'I wonder if she's heard from Robin yet,' I said quickly, trying to change the conversation in my head as much as with Griff. 'Oh, Griff, what if Tom, the rural dean, is part of it? He saw me with Cashmere Roll-Neck, after all, which means, looking at it another way, I saw Tom with Cashmere Roll-Neck, doesn't it? Simon Bonnaventure,' I added, cross with myself for forgetting his name.

'Not quite. You saw them near each other, but not in conversation. And taking you to pray, slice it how one may, doesn't sound like the work of a bad man. Trust your instincts, sweet one. Just as your friends trust your instincts about you. Even Harvey, whose treatment of you wasn't particularly admirable, still cares enough about you to try to identify strangers in bad photographs, not to mention sending work your way.'

I snorted. 'I sometimes wonder if he only cares for me because he knows I shall bring his precious china and porcelain back from the dead.' I got to my feet. 'I'd better go and do a bit more res . . . resuc . . . Oh, Griff, these words are so difficult and I try so hard. Resuscitation!' I grinned. 'It sounds as if I've got bad hay fever, doesn't it?'

The computer was still purring away in the office. Remembering that I ought to be green, I reached to switch it off. The mouse movement brought up the email in-box, complete with the photo Harvey had sent. I looked at the JPEG, again doctored so that the woman's face was brighter than everyone else's. No, I didn't recognize it. But I did recognize the woman she was talking to: Fi Pargetter. And then I remembered that Robin and Simon Bonaventure weren't the only people to have gone walkabout. I emailed the photo to Freya. Her problem.

TWENTY-SIX

'Lock me safely in, if you want, but for goodness' sake free my poor child from what has become her cage and take her on a lovely walk. She's been cooped up in her workroom all day and needs to stride out and get some air in her lungs.'

I looked from Griff to Morris and back again. I ought to insist that Morris take Griff too, but my mouth wouldn't quite manage it.

'I might take a taxi over to Tenterden and let Aidan babysit me: surely that would be safe enough?'

'I'm sure it would,' Morris said. 'Especially if you were driven over and then collected by a police officer.' A policeman, giving up his evening so two old men could enjoy each other's company? It seemed a bit extravagant. Or did I smell a rat? The two of them had been talking for several minutes before I could let go the piece I was working on and run down to join them. But then, as Morris smiled at me, the penny dropped. 'Besides which, we need to change the hire car, and you have to do that in person, Lina. Then we can drop you in Tenterden, Griff. I don't know if there are any exciting walks near there, but I'm sure we'll find one.'

At first I thought it was strange that Morris kept Griff and me talking outside Aidan's house, when the two old ducks were plainly ready to go and eat whatever feast Aidan had bought. It was only after he took my hand and led me away, promising to return in a couple of hours, that it dawned on me that he'd kept me within sight of the nearest CCTV camera, probably facing it most of the time.

'All this stuff about a brisk walk,' Morris began.

'Don't know where that came from. Unless,' I added slowly, thinking of the plan I'd let slip to Griff, 'you'd fancy a trip down to Hastings, to see—'

He looked at me closely. 'To see what, Lina? The sea? Or
to see if you could see your double? Because you know what,
a nice summer evening like this speaks to me more of romantic
meals for two than anything else. In fact, while you were
sorting out the hire car, I booked a table at Number 75. Al
fresco, I thought. And – just for this evening – no mention of
crime at all.'

Ashford isn't the most sympathetic place to say goodbye,
especially when the lovers go their separate ways in individual
hire cars, he off to London and Leda, me with a very relaxed
Griff beside me. Aidan was no cook, but he knew his wines
inside out and he'd been happy to indulge Griff in his new
favourites from the Chapel Down vineyard just outside
Tenterden. Griff clutched a bottle of white so that I could have
a taste when we got home.

Some idiot had parked so close to our yard gates that it was
going to be a struggle to get in. Normally, I'd have sworn;
this time I squeaked with fear – who was after us this time?
Then I recognized the driver. Freya Webb.

Nonetheless, I stowed the car, and Griff, and zapped the
gates closed, before walking round to the driver's door. It was
certainly Freya, but I'd never seen her like this before, her
face blotched with tears.

I zapped the gates again. 'Better park safely,' I said, almost
tempted, watching her amateurish attempts to reverse inside,
to offer to take the wheel myself. At last, however, she was
inside, horribly close to the hire car, and I locked us in.

Griff took one look and herded her into the living room.
Within moments he appeared with red and white wine, not
the expensive one he'd brought home, incidentally, and a couple
of bottles of whisky, complete with crystal water jug, and,
being Griff, an assortment of appropriate glasses, plus some
nibbles and a box of tissues. Then he withdrew, as silently as
he'd waited on us, with hardly an enquiring glance at me.

'Robin?' I prompted at last, passing the tissues.

'Dumped me. Fucking dumped me by fucking text.' She
helped herself to a glass of sauvignon blanc and downed it as
if it were water.

Never having needed to do it, I wasn't sure of the etiquette of dumping by text. It didn't seem the kindest thing to do. But then, dumping never was – and dumping in front of someone else, as I had once done, was a bit low too. I wasn't keen on being dumped by posh dinner and even posher teddy bear either. So I made a few sympathetic noises, which seemed enough. I made sure the next glass she sank really was water. She didn't seem to notice.

Another problem, of course, was that I'd never had a close woman friend, as dear Josie had pointed out. I did realize that it wasn't the moment to ask after Josie, though I'd dearly have liked to know how she was. What could I say to comfort her?

'What did he say?' I ventured.

'Oh, just a lot of crap about his vocation and a time of uncertainty. Isn't that what *people* are for, to be there in times of uncertainty?' she added, in a parody of the sort of vicar-ly tones Robin never, ever used.

'Very long words to text,' I mused. 'Where was he when he texted you?'

'I don't know. How should I know? Bloody text.'

'I was just wondering . . . Did you get it at work? 'Cos you might have been able to put a trace on the phone.'

'Why should I want to do that?'

'Because he's disappeared off the face of the earth. And we only have the rural dean's word for it.' Maybe in her situation I'd have been so shocked that I couldn't think straight. And the more I thought of it, the more I wondered if she should have been suspicious about Robin texting such intimate stuff in the first place. The Robin I knew and loved – as a friend – would surely have phoned at the very least. Wouldn't he? Except that he'd not been himself at all recently: the bad temper, the smoking – heavens, the state of his kitchen should have rung enough alarm bells. Not to mention nearly forgetting a wedding.

'Have you tried contacting him?'

'The shit doesn't deserve me.' That might have been her second large glass of wine speaking.

'The thing is, Freya, he's not usually a shit. Why not text him back and say you want to talk?'

Because she was so drunk that she couldn't make her fingers and thumbs work, that was why. She must have started before we arrived, which would explain the rotten job she did of parking. She was nearly asleep now. Actually, she was probably knackered after all the hours she'd been working.

'Too late now. He'll be asleep,' she said at last, as if from the bottom of a deep pond.

'We'll do it in the morning then – right? I'll just get a pillow for you.' Should I give up my own bed for her? I really ought. But I doubted whether she'd make the stairs. So a pillow, a sheet and a lightweight duvet were all she'd get. She certainly didn't demand more. She was fast asleep by the time I returned.

We woke her at about seven, with a mixture of the smell of bacon – the sort of fry-up I'd fed an equally hung over Robin – and the sound of Radio 4. It didn't work on her. Green, she demanded dry toast, which I suspected she dashed off to throw up. Conversation was clearly not on her agenda.

It wasn't until I unlocked the yard gates for her that I said, 'You will phone Robin, won't you? In front of your colleagues, so they can locate where he is. After all,' I said slowly, as she stared at me as if I was talking Chinese, 'anyone could send a text. It doesn't have to be Robin.' Which meant, of course, that I was admitting that my avuncular guardian angel (thank goodness Griff had taught me that useful word) hadn't necessarily been on the side of the angels after all. What did that make him? It was a bit early in the day for theology, wasn't it? I just told her the facts. And she didn't like it at all that Simon Bonnaventure had been in his company. She hardly waved as she drove off.

As I looked up after her, I heard my mobile ring. I took the call, pleased that Griff was cleaning his teeth and wouldn't know to whom I was talking.

'Long time no hear, Titus,' I said.

'Been watching your back, like I said?'

'You know I got hauled in for questioning?'

'Fair do's to the filth: someone looks like you, talks like you, might well be you. One of his lordship's by-blows they're looking for, I hear.'

Was there any point in asking how he knew? None, really. 'Getting tired of all this business, Titus.'

'Not too tired of it to be shagging coppers.'

'Just the one,' I said tartly, giving myself away nicely. 'Look, I want my life back. Any advice?'

'Why d'you think I phoned? Has that Fi Pargetter turned up yet?'

'Not that I know of.'

'Funny friends some folk have,' he said.

'I need a favour. Other people's friends. Photos. If I leave them at Pa's, will you look at them and see if you recognize anyone?'

'Fucking hell!'

'I'll take that as a yes.'

Those parcels had sat in the living room quite long enough. So we planned an expedition to the post office. I was to carry the large canvas bags we'd stowed them in. Griff, having checked first that the street was empty, via the street cameras and using his own eyes, would wave me on my way. Then I was to leg it as fast as I could. Meanwhile he'd lock up as carefully as if we were off to the North Pole and follow at his own pace, armed with the illegal spray and the equally illegal swagger stick that my father had once pressed on him to protect me. It would all have been ludicrous if it hadn't been so deadly serious.

It was even more serious when, well clear of the comparative safety of the post office, where we'd completed what must have amounted to a week's worth of business for them, and still fifty metres from the safety of the yard gates, we saw a strange car draw up outside our front door. An anonymous Focus. I had Griff by the arm, ready to drag him back some-where. Anywhere. The pharmacy, maybe.

Then we breathed again.

The man getting out of it, arms outstretched, was familiar enough. 'I thought we'd go in this,' he said. 'Maidstone, of course. To talk to Freya. She wants us to pool our ideas before the MIT, which has been a pain in the butt, from what I can gather, trampling all over our own delicate enquiries.'

'Time for a coffee while I put on some slap?' I asked, returning his hug with interest. 'And even if we're not going to be long, you'd best park in the yard. No point in putting temptation in people's way.'

Despite my earlier wise words, Griff insisted on opening the shop, with Mrs Walker and her fiancé, Paul Banner, in attendance. Mary was better than any of us at wrapping parcels and, with the wedding coming up, was glad of any extra cash. Paul seemed impervious to anything as he tapped out his poetry on his laptop, but stationed himself strategically close to the panic button. The day's repair list, headed by a hideous epergne of very doubtful provenance, could wait.

Freya looked a different person altogether from the one we'd waved off an hour or so ago. Changed into a shirt and a straight skirt, and newly-made up, she looked ready for anything. She raised an ironic eyebrow when Morris followed me into her office, to which I responded with a mouthed enquiry: 'Robin?'

She shrugged the shrug of a woman who didn't care if her man was in outer space without life support. Her shirt rose with the shrug but didn't fall again: it was too tight across the bust.

I took a breath, then shoved Morris outside. 'You have to phone. You have to find out where he is.'

She opened a file, turning it so I could see the photo. 'Is this your Tom the Rural Dean?'

'Yes.'

'In that case he is who he says he is. And the diocesan office confirmed Robin was indeed on retreat. Please can I have my colleague back so we can discuss the somewhat more important problems that remain to be dealt with.'

'So long as you phone. And make sure he is where he's supposed to be. Please. He's my friend too, Freya.'

'Afterwards. OK?' She moved behind me to open the door for Morris, who stepped in, innocent as if he hadn't been eavesdropping on every word.

'No. Not OK. Apart from anything else, as parish priest he might even recognize some of the people we're interested in.

Sure, it was he who brought me the photos of the folk at the fête in the first place, but, given the state he was in, if he'd given them more than the quickest of glances, I'd be surprised. The other person you could ask,' I added with as much irony as I could manage, 'is Fi Pargetter, the churchwarden, who, if you recall, has vanished off the face of the earth. We need IDs, Freya, so Griff and I can live normal lives again, the snuffbox that started all this mayhem can be sold and St Jude's rescued before it falls down.'

She held up a hand. 'Enough. This is supposed to be a civilized meeting, not a chance for you to grandstand.'

Morris sat down, crossing his legs and smoothing his chinos reflectively over his knee. 'She's not put it very tactfully, Freya, but I think she might have something. Robin's input would be very useful. However, if the situation is what I deduce it is, I'm happy to phone him simply about the photos. Then you've got a reason for all the listening in and triangulation palaver. Hey, give me his numbers, fix me up with a couple of your team and I'll go and do the deed now.'

I don't suppose Freya knew whom she hated more, and we couldn't tell, because the looks she gave us were equally poisonous. But she led Morris off, leaving me on my own, which was probably illegal in itself. However, she was back before I could hack into the whole of the Kent Police network – joking. She looked like thunder. Yes, I think it was with me, not Morris.

'Just don't say anything about last night,' she hissed. 'Ever.' But she was more upset than angry, I was sure of it. Considering they'd only been an item for a couple of weeks, she was amazingly distressed. And the vibes I was getting were dead interesting.

TWENTY-SEVEN

'No reply from his landline, and his mobile's switched off,' Morris announced. 'I presume he's still at the retreat. Freya, on a professional, not a personal note, I want him found. The diocesan office will tell you where he is.'

She looked icily down her nose. 'And are you my superintendent? Or are you plain DI Morris?'

'About to become a DCI myself, ma'am,' he said, clicking his heels ironically. Or even offensively. This was a side of him I'd never seen before. 'At the moment, I'm just a human being whose girlfriend is in all sorts of schtuck. I'm supposed to be investigating forged snuffboxes, but I'm being side-tracked into all sorts of highways and byways I don't honestly have the time for. It's not just Robin's health I'm interested in – it's what he can tell me about the other people who may be involved in the attempted theft of the original snuffbox, current estimated value in excess of a million.' My whistle interrupted his flow long enough for him to say, as an aside, 'A Fabergé one sold at auction for six-hundred thousand pounds recently. This one doesn't have the intrinsic value, but as a rarity . . .' He turned back to Freya. 'I would like formally to ask you, ma'am, for your cooperation in organizing a raid on the premises next to Colonel Bridger's property. MIT might want to be involved too, but I've not asked them to the party yet.'

'Anything else?' she asked, in a tone I couldn't quite place.

He sat down. 'I bet Lina's got some questions. About her potential half-sisters, for instance. So she can speak to someone in the street without being accused of their murder.'

'As it happens, we have made some progress there – thanks to your father, Lina.'

'Jesus, you needed help from that old soak? Sorry, Lina. Out of order there.'

I said nothing, largely of course because I'd done my best to convince Morris that Pa was a sozzled halfwit.

Freya's chin went up. 'When I met him he seemed fly enough.'

To stave off another spat, I muttered, 'He was having a good day. He has bad days too. Very bad.'

She shook her head as if at a midge. 'Whatever. Thanks to the documentation Lord Elham provided, we are aware of two young women much the same age as Lina, and looking very similar. Frances or Frankie Cartwright, daughter of Pauline Webster, is a teacher working in Canterbury.'

'Canterbury! So I could—'

'Canterbury, New Zealand, Lina. She hasn't left the place in five years.'

'So she's completely eliminated from your enquiries,' I said bitterly. 'And not likely to want a touching reunion with Pa.'

'Or you. Sorry.'

'What about Olivia Thingy? The one whose brother was a bad egg, according to my father?'

'The Honourable Olivia Petham married Lord Allonby. God, the inbreeding of all these aristos!'

'One risk my father never took,' I said dryly.

'Their daughter, Florence, was registered as Lord Allonby's daughter. She went to Benenden School, started a degree in natural sciences at Cambridge and then dropped out big time. Worked her way round the world, with special emphasis on places where drugs were the norm. She used to work at a betting shop in Hastings. At one time she seems to have been what they loosely call an escort. Now she's involved in what are even more loosely described as "promotional activities".'

'I suppose she couldn't have what you might call a professional association with Cashmere Roll-Neck? In any of these jobs?'

'For God's sake, Lina, the man's called Simon Bonnaventure!'

I had an idea that Morris was about to ride to my rescue. So I got in first. 'I can't remember names. Or words. Whereas my father had a French vocab book, I had an ordinary English vocab book. So I could write new words down and learn them. Haven't quite got there with names yet. OK? Could she have been blackmailing this Bonnaventure guy, who seemed to pride himself on being respectable?'

'In which case it was probably more likely that *he* would assault *her*,' Morris objected.

'Whatever,' Freya chipped in. 'This Florence Allonby is almost certainly the person recorded having an altercation with Bonnaventure; there is DNA at what we are still preserving as a crime scene and we would like to establish that it's hers. Before that, of course, they have to locate her and pick her up. All that's the MIT's baby now, however. We don't even have to think about that any more.' She reached for and unscrewed a bottle of water, finishing it in two long gulps.

'And how long have they known this?' Morris asked quietly.

She felt around on the chaos of her desk, went green, and dashed from the room.

'I presume for some time,' he said. 'Why the hell didn't she tell you? Spare you a lot of grief?'

'And you a lot of CCTV coverage,' I added, squeezing his hand. I'd promised not to talk about Freya's visit last night, or I might have poured a little fuel on his obvious anger. 'She's got a lot on her plate.'

'She's got quite a large team to help her eat it, to extend your image. What a silly expression that is,' he said suddenly, sounding amazingly like Griff in one of his outbursts of pedantry. 'A lot on your plate's almost always better than not enough.' He touched my face. 'Do you want to meet these half-sisters of yours?'

'One day. When I've got less to worry about.' I grinned. 'Neither Pa nor Griff would regard Florence as a *suitable acquaintance*, would they? Not, before you ask, that that would bother me. I wonder what happened to the silver spoon she was born with? Sounds as if it got horribly tarnished. Perhaps she got to know her father wasn't her biological one and—'

'That's pure speculation, Lina.'

'So it is. What I'd really like to know, and I'm not sure Freya would have the answer to, is why this Fl . . . Fl—'

'Florence,' he mouthed.

'Thanks. Why Florence should be bombing around in my

haunts. Seems to me there's still a lot unexplained here.' Then I thought of something of more immediate interest. Though my face felt stiff as I spoke, I managed to smile. 'Hey, what's that about your getting a promotion? Well done you.'

'It may be a poisoned chalice, Lina. We'll talk later, OK?' This time he squeezed my hand.

Freya erupted back into the room, juggling two paper cups of coffee and another bottle of water. 'MIT say they're up for a raid, provided, of course, that there are sufficient grounds for applying for a search warrant, which means they want surveillance and all the rest, which they want us to organize. Hunting for old silver isn't their remit, and there's no reason to suppose that your sister's lurking there or that she's concealed a body there.'

'Half-sister,' Morris and I corrected her, as one. 'And I'm not her keeper,' I added, feeling suddenly Biblical and pleased to get a quotation in before Freya did. 'But I'd like to know if either of them knows anything about me,' I added, quietly. That wasn't a police matter, after all.

Ignoring us both, Freya continued, 'Someone's on to the diocesan office, too, telling them to cough up the details of Robin's retreat.' She flushed and then went pale.

'Excellent, ma'am,' Morris said, neutrally. 'Would you prefer me to go and talk to him, or would you prefer to delegate that to one of your team?'

'I've got a prioritization meeting in an hour. And it really is your case, isn't it?'

'No problem. I'd welcome some help with the surveillance, if you've got some bodies to spare.'

'Be my guest.'

All so very polite and so very far from cordial. What was going on?

Morris and Freya got to their feet to shake hands. The meeting, it seemed, was over. Not in my book it wasn't.

'You remember the fake policewomen turning up just before the real ones came to take me in for questioning? Did you ever discover if it was more than a coincidence? You thought it was a serious enough possibility to keep our visit to my father secret.'

'Procedures are in place to check the situation. I'm going for coincidence, just at the moment, but we'll see what turns up. But I'd expect you to contact me direct, as you always seem to, and not deal with the control room. Just in case,' she added, with a pale smile.

'And – I'm sorry, but things are buzzing round my head in no particular order – did you ever find who'd robbed poor St Jude's safe?'

'Now that's interesting: several of the missing communion chalice's cousins have turned up. Sotheby's suspected their provenance and contacted my office,' Morris said. 'Sorry – I should have told you both before. It's major.'

'You'd have had to get a word in edgeways first,' Freya said, not quite joking.

I wasn't going to apologize. 'And did you manage to run make-up artists to earth? If not, here's a list from Griff of people operating locally.'

'Thank you kindly. Now, anything else, Ms Townend?' she asked sarcastically. 'Or are you a lady or an honourable?' she added, hand across her mouth as if pretending to have been caught out in a gaffe.

So many people had asked me this when they discovered my ancestry that I had an answer pat: 'Neither. But always both, I hope.'

'I'd have expected something a bit more impressive than this,' I said as Morris pulled up outside what seemed to be an ordinary Victorian country house north of Canterbury. 'A bit more churchy.'

'A few cloisters, a mad monk or two?'

'Preferably. I take it it's too much to hope that you'll let me in on the interview with Robin?'

'Initially. I'll mention you're around and would like to talk to him if he feels like it, but this really is a police matter, you know.'

'No problem,' I said, looking wistfully at the pretty garden glowing in the sun. 'I'll try and make this radio work. When are you getting your Saab back, by the way?'

'About the same time as you feel free to use your van.'

*   *   *

I didn't have long to wait. Morris appeared from the side of the house, chatting to Robin as if they were old friends. There was no doubting the way Robin tensed as he saw me, however, although he gave me an air kiss and a tiny hug.

I found myself walking round the garden with him, Morris taking his turn on radio duty. I hoped he'd have more success than I'd had.

'I'm sorry I just disappeared like that,' Robin said at last. 'But I needed space.'

I nodded: space from overwork, when he'd totally lacked support, including from friends like me who should have taken more interest after I'd seen the state of his home.

'The thing is, I'm also having a different calling from the one I had in the past,' he said. 'An inner city parish, perhaps. And I may – I may be moving over to Rome.'

'You mean bells and smells, and vows of poverty, obedience and celibacy?' I squeaked.

'Why not?' he countered.

'And have you consulted Freya about these plans?'

'Why should I?'

'You know why.'

'This is none of your business, Lina. Though,' he added with a grin, to show there were no ill feelings, 'that's never stopped you yet.' He hugged me, more convincingly this time.

Stepping away, I said, 'Imagine texting a woman to chuck her – that was rank bad manners, Robin. Inexcusable. You owe her an apology for that, apart from anything else.'

'But—'

'Face to face. Not a sorry letter or phone call. And certainly not a text. No, don't argue. You have to talk to Freya. Have to, must, need to. Understand?' And deciding that discretion was definitely called for, not just as the better part of valour, I turned tail and marched away. I stopped four or five metres away. 'And you know that whatever you do, you're still my best friend and I love you,' I added, running back for another hug.

'Bit of a waste of time as far as identifying the people in the pics, though,' Morris said as he started the car.

'Morris, do you trust me?'

He cut the engine. 'With my life. But,' he added, narrowing his eyes, 'not necessarily when you use that tone of voice. It means you're up to something.'

'I need to see my father and leave something for a friend. I could dress it up and tell you Pa wants more fizz and some food. He probably does, and I shall take him both. But there is another reason, and you may not approve.'

He took a deep breath. 'In my job I have to deal with dodgy characters to get results. I'd rather you didn't. I don't want to know any details of your doings. But I respect you for telling me what you have, Lina. Hell, more than respect. Why isn't there more room in this bloody vehicle?' he demanded as the gear stick got in the way of his attempts to kiss me.

We'd agreed that he should ask for the loo so I could hand over the photos for Titus.

'Look at them yourself, Pa,' I whispered. 'And remember, I don't want to know how either of you knows anyone. Just names. Text me. OK?'

'I don't want my little girl putting herself in danger,' he said.

'More info, less danger,' I said, falling into Titus-speak again. 'Meanwhile,' I added out loud, 'You might want to sit down. Freya Webb's colleagues have located two more of your daughters.'

He pulled a face. 'Did they care enough to find me? Don't know if I care enough to find them.'

'For heaven's sake, Pa!'

He shuffled into hangdog mode. 'It's not as if they definitely know about me, is it? Their mothers might simply have passed them off as their husbands'.'

'Lord and Lady Allonby registered Florence as their joint daughter,' I acknowledged. This wasn't the time to tell him what else I knew about Florence.'

'Married well, did she? Well, she would. *Noblesse oblige*,' he snorted. 'One thing at a time, Lina. One thing at a time.' He patted the envelope of photos, as if they were about to become his life's work. 'And we don't want to rock any boats, do we? Now, tell me when the charming Freya will be round again. Lovely hair, with that beautiful pale skin.'

'Don't you be getting ideas, Pa. I've an idea she's got the hots for someone else.'

'What a dreadful expression that is. And how's young Robin?' he asked, as if by association, though I couldn't recall ever linking their names.

'Not good.' I was explaining as Morris joined us.

'Tell him to come and see me and drink some proper shampoo. I'm sure that gassy stuff he brings me doesn't do his brain any good. Now, what are you going to find to sell today?'

'That didn't take long,' Morris observed as I stowed a couple of pearlware jugs in the rear footwell.

'I always keep a stash of stuff handy for when I need a quick getaway. He prefers me to divvy, but sometimes that takes time, and I don't necessarily come up with anything special.'

'He seems a lot better than when I last saw him. Sorry!' He pulled over to take a phone call.

I looked for something else to talk about while he finished his conversation. All in all, the less he knew about Pa the better, for all concerned.

'My stomach says it's time for lunch,' I announced. 'And there's quite a good pub not that far from Bugger Bridger's. You wanted surveillance,' I added. 'The best place would be from his house, wouldn't it? No other cover nearby, after all. I'm quite happy to wait in the car while you go and talk to him. In fact, I'd really welcome your take on him and his house. Mind that pothole! Now, right at the bottom of this track.'

'I can't just march in and commandeer a room, you know. Hell's bells! This would tax a four-by-four.'

'Griff always gets out and walks. I think Bridger would respond to estr . . . espr . . . Something to do with a corpse.'

'*Esprit de corps?*'

'Right. A colonel, after all, of what Griff calls the old school. He knows my father, remember, though I'm not sure that's a good thing.'

*   *   *

The weather was so perfect that I wanted to grab Morris and run away with him, not sit in a stuffy car while he smooth-talked the colonel. At least I could do something about the sitting. A little stroll was surely OK? In the bright sun, under those little white puffy clouds, a lark singing in the distance? If it took me in the direction of the farmyard Morris wanted to watch, all the better.

This time the dogs were chained. But they could still see and hear me, so I gave the gates a very wide berth, using my eyes, all the same. There'd been a good deal of activity since my last visit, with a couple of large horseboxes in one corner, and a trailer or two. The track through the gates was much more worn: if the weather had been bad, it would have been rutted.

Maybe it was time to drift back to the car. Morris was waiting, arms akimbo.

I waved and speeded up a little. As I did so, an Audi came along the lane. The driver slowed right down as he approached me, a frown visible from where I was. Turning my face, I zapped the car and got straight in, taking the driver's side.

'Just get in,' I yelled, starting and reversing as fast as I could. 'We have to get out of here. Now.'

'What the hell? I thought you'd been kidnapped. And here you are, driving like a wild thing.'

I found a wider bit of verge and did a quick three pointer. The sooner I was on a main road the better.

'Actually, are you insured to drive this?' Morris asked gently as I forced the car round bends.

'Shit, so I'm not.' Pulling over, I leapt out and ran round to his side. 'Take over and just drive. Fast.'

He drove. Fast. 'Would you like to tell me why?'

'Because the guy in the Audi thought he recognized me. And he was surprised to see me with you. Well, with anyone, I'd say.'

'*Thought* he recognized you?'

'I didn't recognize him. Not from real life. But his face is in one of those photos. Robin's fête photos. Right?'

'Right. I think. Let me get this straight. You go for a walk. Fine. Don't blame you, even though you lock me out of the car. You come back towards me, leaving Flimstead Farm – yes, according to Colonel Bridger, that's what it's called – and this Audi driver thinks you're someone else leaving the farm. And you don't think he's very pleased?'

'Surprised rather than displeased. Like I said. I think by now he's gone back into the farm and found whoever I look like is still safe and sound there. But,' I added, with a grin, 'I've no idea what his emotions are now. Or hers. Because although I know I've got half-sisters, she may not.'

'And you think Florence Allonby is the woman he thought was going walkabout?'

'Lot of speculation,' I admitted.

'Surely she'd have a different surname,' he mused. 'Allonby's the title, not the name, isn't it? What about your father's family name – what's that?'

'No idea. Never even thought to ask,' I said truthfully. 'Hell, I'm starving.

TWENTY-EIGHT

'I don't suppose,' Morris said, turning south, 'that Ashford is the gastronomic capital of Kent, but at least there's a motorway heading that way, with the car hire place just by a junction. So we'll change this car and grab a snack and then report to Freya.'

There was a tiny edge to his voice; he really hadn't enjoyed her pulling rank, had he? And what was that about his promotion? Why hadn't he shouted it from the housetops? Now didn't seem to be the time to ask, however. His face was very grim, and not just because of the chaos as we approached Junction 11, where he'd hoped to get access. For some reason we were being diverted via all sorts of highways and byways.

'Last time they had Operation Stack the police allowed heavy lorries to park right across the roundabout, so you couldn't get on or off Stone Street,' I said. 'Sorry, I should have thought of that. Back up the hill again and I'll navigate you across country, via Wye. A couple of nice pubs there, too,' I said.

'Ashford first,' he said. 'Just to please me. Ah, you were right. Look who's coming towards us. Your friend in the Audi, I fancy. Head down now, Lina. And brace. I may have to risk the insurance excess.'

Head down, I braced. Apart from as hard an acceleration as the Fiesta permitted, nothing happened.

'Stay down. I think he's trying to turn. Is there a left turn I can risk?'

'Stowting. Brabourne. Then look out for Hastingleigh and Wye. Tell me when I can come up.'

The car lurched – by the feel of it he'd almost lost it on a hard left turn, but he righted it and pressed on. He slowed.

'Tractor ahead. I wonder . . .'

Only one side of the car could have been on the road. We bucked all over the place. Finally, we lurched back left, to the sound of someone's horn.

'Poor bugger. Bad enough having a tractor that size coming towards you, let alone a car overtaking it, not just on your bit of road but on your bit of greensward too. OK, Lina, you can come up now. I don't think the Audi will manage that. What worries me, though,' he mused, 'is how he managed to discover our route.'

'From there you've pretty well got to head north or south. Maybe he tried north and gave up, knowing you'd be delayed if you headed south. Satnav or local knowledge,' I added with a shrug. 'Unless you think—?'

He didn't seem to think anything, at least not aloud, but that might have been because he needed a lot of concentration to pick his way through the lanes.

'How did you get on with the colonel?' I asked at last.

He threw his head back and laughed. 'Not as well as someone else was getting on. The poor man appeared at his front door in the shortest silk bathrobe I've ever seen. Pink, embroidered with roses. You could actually see –' He choked. 'The thing is,' he managed round his giggles, 'he was carrying the biggest vibrator I've ever seen. And a woman, no doubt the owner of the robe, was calling from upstairs. So I muttered something about it obviously not being convenient and backed away. And do you know what he did? He asked for my card and tried to tuck it . . . And then he went off and got his own card and handed it to me just as if . . . Anyway, I'm supposed to call him this evening. Oh, Lina!'

Thank goodness the road was clear. At last he had to pull over to mop his eyes. 'The trouble is, we're no further forward with the surveillance issue. But I tell you, organizing it is definitely one job I shall delegate.'

The car hire people were inclined to be sniffy about the dust all over the car, and they didn't appreciate my quip that it could have been mud. Anyway, we were soon equipped with yet another set of wheels, and we found a pub on the edge of what seemed to be car-showroom city.

'Council of war,' Morris said as we ate chicken salad. 'I could do with making a lot of phone calls and sending a lot of emails. There are other investigations in progress I need to keep an eye on. It won't be very exciting.'

'I'm not a kid, Morris. In fact, I'm so behind with my work, if you could use our cottage as your temporary office, it'd help me. Unless you want to beg a room from Freya?'

'I'll call her – see if there've been any developments. Hmm. Her mobile's off, and just in case there *is* a mole problem, I won't risk the main phone line.' He left a message to call him. 'Your cottage as office sounds very good. Will Griff be there?' he asked, not quite casually. 'By the way, I'm afraid I've got to dash back this evening. The nanny's still got problems. Sorry, Lina.' He kissed my hands. 'We'll get this sorted, won't we?'

'We will.' I kissed his in return.

I'd much rather not have spent the afternoon toiling in the stillness of my workroom, but there was something very nice about knowing that Morris was working in our office, just below my feet. Griff had been all too glad of an excuse to get out into the garden, bringing death to weeds and the wrong sort of insect. Eventually, knowing that Morris had resolved to be home by seven, Griff summoned us for late afternoon tea, complete with his home-made lemonade – well, home-made everything.

Goodness knows what we all talked about. I think Griff reported on a test match, but none of us wanted to go inside and watch it, or the tennis that would no doubt have fascinated Steve White. Griff mentioned the Proms, too, but then realized he hadn't been entirely tactful.

'So long as it's a different orchestra,' Morris said with a grin, 'that'd be a great idea. You could stay over and meet Leda again. But check with me before you book anything; I may have to go abroad again, but not for too long, with luck.'

'You youngsters and your peripatetic amours,' Griff sighed, smiling benignly, leaning back, eyes closed.

It was all too tempting to do the same, my hand safe in Morris's.

A mobile burst into Beethoven. Morris's. He hauled himself to his feet and, with a quizzical smile, headed in the direction of the rotary washing-line that Griff pointed to without bothering to open his eyes. Morris muttered a bit and cut the call, coming back to me and dabbing a kiss on my forehead before settling beside me again.

I didn't move. Not until my phone sounded too. Just an ordinary ringtone.

'Go on, take the call. I've got to be on the move any moment now anyway,' Morris sighed, getting to his feet.

Pulling a face, I drifted to the spot by the washing-line whirligig that Morris had vacated. 'Pa?'

'You got that police chappie of yours there, Lina?'

'Yes.'

'Put me on to him, would you?'

'He's just on his way back to London.'

'Won't take a second. Put him on anyway. I want to talk to him about the snuffbox.'

Summoning Morris, I passed him over to my father.

At first he looked amused, even resigned. But then he looked increasingly serious and fished out his own mobile to make one-thumbed notes. When he cut the call, frowning, he used his own phone to make another call. That done, he came back to the table and sat heavily. 'Just how compos mentis is he, Lina?'

Griff surfaced. 'Since my darling girl took him in hand he's improved a great deal. He'll never be anything but an old soak, but he's coherent enough. Does Sudoku like shelling peas. Always beats the contestants on quiz shows.'

'So we can trust his memory?'

'Yes,' I said.

'Good. He's just remembered who he saw use the original snuffbox. A neighbour, whose son became an actor. There is just one other thing, though. He says he phoned Freya Webb and was told she wasn't there. I guess he misdialled and got put through to the main switchboard. Apparently, he told the person at the other end what the problem was – and was told they'd send a couple of officers over as and when.'

Griff and I exchanged a glance. 'Pa doesn't really do as and when, does he?'

'So I gather. Hence he's summoned me. We have a problem,

Griff,' he added, glancing at me. 'There might just be a mole in the control room. I think Lina's father has just invited the wrong people to visit him.'

I started to run, God knows where.

'Hang on! Where are you going?' Morris grabbed my arm. 'Riding to the rescue's one thing. Making a phone call is easier.' He passed me my mobile. 'Tell him to let no one in. No one at all.'

'And then what? Just sit it out?' Griff, rarely on my father's side, demanded.

'Yes – but not in his wing,' I said, thinking again. 'He can let himself through the security door into the main building. All those lockable rooms . . .' I yelled instructions down the phone to my father, who was now thoroughly confused, and who could blame him? 'Pa, just do as you're told – OK? I'm on my way.' I looked at Morris, trying not to let my lip tremble. 'And you must be on your way too. Leda can't babysit herself.'

He shook his head. 'Plan C. I'll phone my mother. I know it means I'm a bad father, but she gets to be a good granny. Griff, will you call Freya's private number from your landline? She needs to know what's going on, quite clearly, and I don't want to risk poor mobile coverage. Here, take Lina's phone.'

Griff grabbed it, trotting into the house after us. 'Hang on – I'll just jot it down.'

'Lina, you drive till I've spoken to Mum – OK?'

I did as I was told. Thrusting my phone back to me, Griff did the business with the gates, I shot out, and we were on our way. No, I didn't try to listen in on Morris's call. I was too busy wondering about reinforcements and making a decision.

'Now call Robin,' I said, as soon as he'd finished his call. 'Pa trusts him. He'll do what he says. And maybe Robin needs to be needed,' I added, nipping round a heavy lorry, but only just making it. Dared I stop to let Morris take over? The road ahead was empty. My foot went down and stayed down.

'Why this way?' Morris asked as we sped up the main drive to the front of Bossingham Hall.

'Better than the track. Safer than all those pot holes. We

park and shin over the wall. Trellis – lovely foot holds. And a mounting block to land on. What are you waiting for? Hell, we're not the first here.'

A familiar Audi sat in my usual space.

'I'll get armed backup. Direct number, of course. And you – you stay here.' He held me, but not tenderly, while he made his call. 'OK. Now what are you up to?'

'Heading for the coal hole next to Pa's kitchen. You and I secured all the other exits and entrances last time you were down, didn't we? But not this. OK?'

It took two of us to drag away the huge metal sheet covering a chute. There was still some coal at the bottom. Morris went down first, crabwise, raising a hand to help me to do the same. Both using the torches in our mobiles, we picked our way through a maze of cellars.

'We put locks on Pa's cellar doors, remember, so I need to find a way up into the main house. Then it's easy-peasy. Unless they've got Pa and he's been forced to talk.'

We came up in the servants' corridor behind the library. 'We have to go through that door.' I pointed. 'The CCTV camera does a regular pan. I'll wait till it looks up there, and then hare across. You wait till it does it again and do the same – right?'

The library door opened easily. But inside I stopped dead. It was either that or have my father smash a cast-iron poker over my head.

'But you're both black!' he said, when I told him off roundly for using the N word. 'How was I to know it was you?'

'All the more reason not to use it,' I said firmly. 'Absolutely never these days – OK? So you did as Griff told you? Excellent.'

'Except I think someone's broken in. I didn't have time to set the alarm, you see. Heavens, Morris, take your shoes off, man. And you, Lina. This carpet's three hundred years old, or near enough.'

'Lina, what are you doing?' Morris hissed. 'Come back here!'

'I've not spent all that time sorting out Pa's stuff only to have someone steal it! It's his pension fund.'

'Stay where you are,' Pa snapped. 'Let the man do his job. Are you going to arrest him, Morris? Take care, he may be armed.'

'Correction,' Morris said. '*They* may be armed. We've no idea how many we're dealing with. That's why we have to wait for back-up.' He looked at me sternly, and then glanced out of the window. 'Hell, now someone else's arrived! Robin Levitt. And he's just the sort to dash in where angels fear to tread. Damn. No bloody coverage!' Then he saw me. 'Stay where you bloody are, woman! What's that?'

'Pepper spray. Don't ask. But if whoever's in there tries anything nasty with Robin, he's going to get an eyeful. *They'll* get an eyeful. Whatever. OK, Robin will too, and he won't like it. But it'll give us a chance to disarm Chummie.'

'For us read me. Put it down.'

I'd not seen him in policeman mode for ages. To my surprise, I did as I was told, plonking it on a side table. 'Pa, stay here and try to get mobile coverage. There'll probably be an almighty racket as we set off the alarms. That's fine. Because I can pick my way round the rooms and end up near your front door. Via the link door, of course. Coming?' I asked Morris.

He pointed at Pa. 'Stay here. Right?' And, like me, leaving his shoes behind, followed me out to the corridor leading to Pa's wing.

TWENTY-NINE

There were two intruders, one male, one female, in Pa's living room, tearing it apart. Both had their backs to us. Since we were unarmed, with not so much a pair of handcuffs between us, I could think of only thing to do. All the locks in the house were the same – presumably the eighteenth-century servants were too scared even to think of stealing from their masters. So, touching my lips to keep Morris quiet, I padded from room to room till I found a key. It was the work of seconds to close the huge mahogany door on them – it swung and closed as silently as the original craftsman intended – and lock it.

With luck, no one would know till they tried to open it, which might be any moment now. There was a terrific peal on the bell, and knocking on the door as well. Peering through the spyhole I'd installed years back, I found myself eyeball to eyeball with a policeman – possibly. What if he was one of the mole's mates, ready to cart us off God knew where?

I was halfway down the corridor before I knew it, pointing in terror at the door, unable to speak a word. Morris pushed me behind him and strode the door himself, making sure the thick security chain was in place before he opened it. Whatever he said produced results. A black-clad arm appeared, pushing an ID.

Meanwhile, Pa's uninvited guests must have realized what was happening to them: the noise they made possibly exceeded that made by the police as they thundered in, all yelling what seemed to be quite contradictory orders. It was only Morris's firm clasp on my hand that stopped me bolting.

Trying not to scream and make things even worse, I pointed. Outside Robin was flat on the gravel, two policemen pointing guns at his head.

Morris didn't yell, but he got silence, at least from the officers inside. Those pinning down Robin continued to yell,

God knows why. Perhaps just because they could. Before
Morris could act, more vehicles arrived, including one I
recognized. If ever there was a good time for Freya to turn
up, at least this was it. Here she came, doing a very good
impression of leading a cavalry charge.

And then, just to add to the chaos, no doubt in response to
the alarm still ringing through the main house, the fire
brigade turned up too.

The police, in their wisdom, wanted to make the whole of
Pa's wing a crime scene. That was standard procedure,
according to Mandy, the crime scene investigator I'd met
before.

'After all,' she said, waving me away, 'all the rooms are
sufficiently messy to suggest they've had a good going over.'
She blinked behind those killer spectacles, as if she was
weighing up the next salmon leap. Or was it seals polar
bears hunted?

'Give me a suit,' I sighed wearily, 'and the moment I've
phoned home to say I'm all right I'll tell you which have been
trashed and which are just in their usual state. Lord Elham
doesn't do spring-cleaning . . .'

'So you're sure it's just the hall and that room they were locked
in that I need to examine,' Mandy said at last, sounding
relieved.

'Positive. Now, have you seen DCI Webb or DI Morris
anywhere? 'Cos I need a few answers. Not least for my father.'
I pointed, as he wandered round haphazardly, denied the security
of his den. At last, raising his clenched fists to the heavens, as
if he were Griff playing King Lear, he suddenly yelled, 'For
God's sake, can't someone turn off that damned alarm?'

It seemed the fire service had procedures too. The alarm
must be allowed to ring on.

Poor Pa probably wouldn't have recognized a procedure if
it bit him. Never having seen him as distressed as that, I did
the obvious thing. I nipped illicitly into the main house
and flicked the switch myself.

By the time I got back, a policewoman had settled him into

the kitchen and was looking bemusedly in all the cupboards. Every time he got to his feet, he was pushed gently down again, as if he was a child.

I hugged him. 'It's OK, Pa. I'm here now. Cup of tea?'

'Shampoo, Lina. The good stuff. That's the thing for the shakes.' He lifted a trembling hand.

'That's what I'm looking for,' the harassed policewoman said. 'But why does he want to wash his hair?'

'I'll sort him out,' I said. 'But I really, really need to talk to DI Morris. As does Lord Elham here.'

'Lord Elham?' She embarked on a horribly predictable kowtowing and gibbering apology that my father waved away, not very graciously; after all, he was still waiting for his champagne.

One good swig, and he was ready to be charming to Morris, still without his shoes, who appeared almost at once.

'Pa,' he said, really disconcerting me with its intimate tone until it occurred to me that the police probably had procedures for speaking to the old and doddery, 'this isn't going to be very comfortable for you. When we've taken you to the police station to make a statement, would you like us to book you into a hotel?'

'Statement? I've nothing to say. You and my daughter seemed to be in control, until all those heavies turned up. What were those Hell's Angels doing in my house?'

Hell's Angels?

'Ah, the black gear,' Morris said. 'Actually, sir, they were the armed response unit, come to deal with the intruders.'

'And did you get them?'

'Too right we did. Thanks to your phone call about the snuffbox.'

'So it was that man who used to take snuff? No, dead years back, surely.' He looked totally confused.

'His son, actually. He had a son who became an actor. This son and his daughter Marietta, otherwise known as Mrs Burgess Rushton.'

I sat down hard next to my father. 'So if the box was his father's why didn't he simply ask for it back? Doesn't make sense.'

'It does if it was left to the Victoria and Albert Museum in your father's will and you nicked it. And if you used it to make very high quality copies which you discreetly sell to enthusiasts, all of whom want to lay their sticky mitts on what they think is a priceless item going cheap – like the one your friend Harvey bought for us.'

'Just two people! I thought we were fighting a whole gang.'

'I'm sure they weren't acting alone. Lina, love, I'm going to have to go now to begin interviewing them, or the MIT will muscle in and claim the collar as theirs. After all, it very much looks as if they were the ones who at very least instigated the killing of our friend X.'

'And the murder of Cashmere Roll-Neck? Simon Thingy?'

He kissed my hair. 'Simon Bonnaventure. That may tie in with the CCTV photos,' he said cautiously, raising an eyebrow to shut me up. In other words, now wasn't the best time to break it to Pa that one of his offspring might be a killer. 'Or it might not. I dare say we'll be questioning them till late, Lina, and the forensic team will be poking round here – so you might want to take your father home to Griff's.'

Pa, outside his third glass of bubbly, got to his feet. 'Morris, my dear chap, this is my home. These meagre quarters may be uninhabitable, but there are plenty of bedrooms at my disposal. Sleeping under a tester again will no doubt revive a few happy memories.' He smiled. Correction: he leered. 'I don't suppose that that lovely redhead is anywhere around?'

Morris walked me to the front door, so that I could be registered as having been in and having left – another procedure.

'So where is Freya?' I asked, once we were out of range of interested ears. 'It must have been quite a shock for her to see Robin pinned down like that.'

'Enough to make her go bright green? Police officers are usually stronger stomached than that.'

'I don't doubt it. Usually. Did someone tell him how upset she was?'

He grimaced. 'We've all been a bit busy.'

'Someone's got to. And someone's got to make him ask

her. All this stuff about being a celibate priest – huh, and double huh!'

Before he could ask me what I was on about, his phone played Beethoven again. He took the call, his eyes rounding and his mouth desperate not to quiver with the sort of hysterical giggles he'd been struck with earlier. I turned away so as not to distract him. At last he cut the call and collapsed shaking into my arms.

'Bugger Bridger. Wanted to know . . . Wanted to tell me the farm next door was swarming with people. He liked their boots. Wanted to know where he could get some. Oh, Lina.'

At last he said, 'I should have left ten minutes ago. Are you going back to Griff's?'

'Wouldn't want to spoil my father's chances of filling his tester bed,' I said. 'If not with Freya, obviously. And Griff'll be waiting for all the news. What about you? Do you have to drive back to London tonight?'

He shook his head. 'Not necessarily. But don't wait up.'

'Why not? I'll want to hear the latest news. And you deserve some shampoo too. Especially if you wear some of those sexy black boots.'

If Griff was disconcerted by two people descending for a very late breakfast in the garden, he didn't say so. However, he was just as keen to hear what Morris said as I – well, nearly – as we all tucked in to croissants and apricot preserve.

'So you have a husband and wife team working on these fake snuffboxes?' Griff asked.

'More of a family venture, actually. They have a son who does some of what you might call the heavy work, such as forcing his way into your house, and a daughter who took a course in film make-up but did a bit of lucrative part-time work while she was waiting for her media breakthrough. This is the scary part, Lina: in her workroom – oh, yes, there was plenty of space for everyone to have their little area in the farm buildings, in addition to the silversmith's workshop, of course – on her wall were a couple of dozen photos of you. The real you, as opposed to the one she faked. Herself. When you'd foiled their attempt to nick the proper snuffbox, they decided to wreak their revenge and set you up for things. So your sister isn't involved at all. Just another unfortunate lookalike. Half-sister,' he corrected himself. 'Are you going to get in touch with either of them? Florence, at least?'

'I might. But I can't just turn up and introduce myself. There must be agencies . . . and it might be something to talk to Robin about, or even Tom. My father's not keen on waking sleeping dogs. Looks as if I might have to let the whole thing go.' I straightened my shoulders and made a rewinding gesture. 'This here snuffbox. Why should it appear in Bridger's box?'

'He's consistently denied it, remember. The theory is that the Rushtons – who were to all intents and purposes decent members of the community – simply handed over a box of stuff to the fête, and that Pargetter woman forgot it was theirs.'

'It was Marjorie, the lady in charge of the bric-a-brac, who told me, actually. Fi Pargetter wouldn't make a mistake like that. Anyway, it was total rubbish – they should have been ashamed of themselves,' I chipped in. 'So why store something as precious as the snuffbox there?'

'They didn't want to keep it in the house – just in case. Put it in a safe, it's an obvious target. But then Fi comes bustling along and takes a box of books – bingo. And from what I hear, Fi's not the sort of person you ask for your goodies back from – if that makes sense.'

Griff pulled a pedantic face and poured more coffee.

'But the box of fête junk wasn't the only thing stored in the outhouses,' Morris continued more soberly. 'The search uncovered a body.'

'Not Fi! I didn't terribly like her, but she was devoted to the church.'

'Not Fi. We still don't know where she is, which is worrying. But the MIT are happy. Simon Bonnaventure. It was his blood in St Jude's loo. More in a lock-up they rented in Hythe till they'd fortified their farm.'

'Why him?' I squeaked. 'Wasn't he just an architect?'

'People are rarely "just" anything, my love,' Griff said, passing me the last croissant.

'Bonnaventure was an architect, and his work took him into all sorts of public buildings, including, of course, churches.

Freya's team are still trying to find who he tagged along with to that party you went to. He used to do an extra line in checking foundations and so on – a nice kind freebie, no fee, just advice. So legitimately he could get into all sorts of nooks and crannies.'

'And safes? He's not the man Sotheby's put you on to?'

'Almost certainly. When he nicked the silverware from their home church, our friends got cross, in case it would draw attention to their profitable little sideline.'

'So that footage that seems to show me arguing with him actually showed the deliberate lookalike of me arguing with him. Ah.'

'Exactly. They forgot about DNA testing, maybe – just because you can dress up to look like someone doesn't mean you take on their genes. Bad mistake.'

'I can see why they needed to increase security round their farm,' I said. 'The dogs and the fencing . . . But why all the horseboxes? Were they planning a flit?'

'You bet. You can get a lot in a horsebox, as well as a horse – which they'd need for cover, of course. There was a lot of equine documentation – the sort you'd need if you were moving it to France, for instance. Had it not been for your Pa's sudden brainwave, they'd probably have got away with it.'

'Or he might have been lying alongside Bonnaventure. Have they found the control-room mole yet?'

'Yes, I'm glad to say. She'll get a good long stretch, I hope. We don't like it when coppers or anyone associated with us are bent. Which brings me on to my next job, Lina.'

Griff fussed with a couple of wasps and decided to remove temptation from their way, gathering all the jammy plates and disappearing into the house.

Morris took my hand. 'That promotion I flung at Freya – a very unprofessional thing to do, by the way, and very unfair to you – it's in Lyon. There's a problem in Interpol. Information about stolen art works isn't being shared, and we don't think it's just Euro-inefficiency. So when things between Penny and me went pear-shaped, I applied for secondment. And I've just heard I've got it. It's only temporary, though I probably get to keep my rank at the end of it.'

I tried to keep my voice steady. 'What about Leda? Does that mean you're giving up on her?'

'Actually, quite the reverse. Penny and her horn player decided – just to place her out of my reach, I suspect – to apply for jobs with l'Orchestre de Paris. He's at the final audition stage, and Penny's ready to take up her post in a couple of weeks' time. So I shall probably see more of Leda. But less of you, Lina. One word from you and I'll turn it down. I promise. Otherwise, I shall be hopping on trains and planes whenever I can. And, as I said, it's only a short-term contract. Six months, probably – a year maximum.'

'It's better than New York,' I managed.

'It is. And with flights really getting going from Manston Airport . . .'

'And it'll be better for Leda. The thing is, Morris, she's more important than any of us. She didn't ask to be born into a mess.'

'It might be better for Leda if I simply bow out of her life except as a nice kind uncle who drops by from time to time. I haven't proved a specially good dad when she needed me. Police officers aren't good at relationships, I'm afraid. Even those that really matter put a strain on the loved ones. Hell, I want to spend the rest of today with you – the rest of my life with you, if it comes to that – but do you know what? I've got to leg it into Maidstone and help sort out all last night's arrests.'

I took his hand. 'And then it's back to London for Leda?'

'Uh, uh. The orchestra's back in town. Tonight it's back here to you – if you and Griff will have me.'

'We might. So long as you promise to come back for Freya and Robin's wedding.'

'What wedding?' he squeaked.

'Wait and see.'

THIRTY

I've never regarded myself as hot on morality, so it was a bit of a surprise when Robin called me and asked me for advice. As Griff was tiptoeing round me as if I was an invalid, I welcomed the chance to get out – particularly as I could now drive our van without fear of being run off the road. Since I'd be going past Pa's, I loaded it with food and drink, to be delivered not to the main house – from which he'd been expelled, after his night of glory in his favourite four-poster – but to his usual quarters, now mercifully free of police activity.

We were stowing stuff in his fridge and freezer when he turned to me.

'This Morris chappie: are you going to marry him?'

It was one question Griff hadn't dared put. 'Why do you ask, Pa?' I busied myself reorganizing the freezer.

'I like to keep my eye on you, that's all. I prefer him to young Robin – he's got better taste in booze. Nice shampoo he sent to apologize for all that mess. Mind you, I hoped that that gorgeous Lizzie Siddal woman would bring it.'

'Freya's been busy, I dare say, tying up all the loose ends.'

'I suppose in her condition she shouldn't be carrying heavy weights,' he mused, putting the kettle on.

'Her condition?' I asked carefully.

'Anyone could tell she was preggers. Who's the father? Not that Morris of yours, I hope to God!'

I shook my head. 'But I think God's going to be involved before long. Sorry, Pa – I must fly. I'm late for lunch already.' To my surprise, I dotted a kiss on his forehead.

There was no way I was going to eat in the rectory kitchen, not if it was in the state it was when Griff and I had had to sort it out. It'd be the Rose and Crown for me, tactful or not. However, the whole place gleamed. Surely not Freya's work!

'When you phoned you said I should start making small changes and the big ones would look after themselves,' Robin said. 'So I started in the kitchen. Just putting things away. And then I could clean. And – you see, I mowed the lawn, too. Actually, I borrowed a couple of sheep from a guy who keeps his flock on the Minnis. And I'm beginning to feel better. So thank you.' His eyes rounded when I started to unpack the goodies Griff had sent. 'Proper lemonade – let's drink it in the garden. Don't worry: the sheep have gone and I've got rid of the poo.'

He had, more or less. We sat under an apple tree and I prepared to listen.

'I know I said I might move to Rome. Would it seem dreadfully inconsistent if I said I didn't feel I could?'

'No one else knows, do they? OK, you may have talked to someone while you were on retreat, but surely any conversations you have with them are confidential. And I shan't tell. But why the change of heart?' As if I didn't know.

'I want to save St Jude's first.'

That was one answer I wasn't expecting.

'You don't think I should?'

'Of course you should. But isn't there something else you should save first?'

'Is there?'

Despite the heat, I shivered. 'Have you spoken to Freya? You know I said you should.'

'I've phoned – she's always been busy. Hey, what are you doing?' he demanded as I took the glass from his hand.

'Telling you to do what you ought to have done when I first told you to do it, you idiot. Go and see her. Now. Tell her you love her and have done from the moment you first saw her and how you want her to have your babies. Especially the last bit. Practise saying it in the car as you go over. If she's in a meeting, burst in. If she's interviewing a suspect, get them to confess. Just bloody go.'

He went.

If he got there in time, Freya might not have the abortion I was sure she'd be considering. A single woman, a job like hers, even worse for childcare than being in an orchestra, I'd

have thought: a baby wasn't an easy option. But when the
father was a clergyman . . .

Just to help things along a bit, I stopped off at St Jude's on
the way home to have a word with God. The police tape had
disappeared at last, and the door was open. The flowers weren't
in the same league as those on the day of the fête, but they
still brightened the place up. I sat for a long time in a quiet
corner, thinking not just about Freya and Robin, but about
poor X, killed so he wouldn't steal any more fakes, according
to Freya, and about Josie, now moved from the ICU to a high
dependency ward, whatever that meant. I thought about Morris
and me, too, and little Leda.

It was time to go. First I'd pay my respects to the misericords.
Squatting to look at them, I felt a sudden pang of guilt. Shouldn't
I have been kneeling in a church? I grabbed a kneeler donated
by the Mothers' Union.

At last, as I got up, ready to leave, a familiar outline appeared
in the doorway. Fi Pargetter.

I braced myself. As far as I knew, the police no longer
wished to question her, but I wasn't sure I'd forgiven her for
dobbing me in as a possible thief when all I'd done was grub
round for my beads.

Her wave was friendly enough, however, and, since I'd
finished trying to tell God how to run His universe, I strolled
over to join her. She was grovelling with apologies before I
could speak.

'At least you have your silverware back,' I said, putting up
a hand to cut her short. I wished I could tell her she'd have
the profits on the sale of the snuffbox, but since it had been
left to the V and A, it wasn't mine to sell. They didn't seem
likely to offer me a reward, either, or St Jude's could have
had that.

'It's a terrible thing to say, but the insurance money would
have been more welcome.'

'Sell it. Get a faculty and sell it. The market's really good
for silver at the moment. In fact, you may find it's underinsured,'
I told her.

'If it's so precious, do we have a right to sell? I couldn't
live with myself if I made the wrong call.'

'From what the rural dean told me, it's all done by prayer and committee, in whichever order, so it wouldn't be your personal decision. The money could save the church. And think: a buyer might put it on public display, so hundreds of people could enjoy it, rather than no one, while it's locked away where it is now.'

She smiled. 'Perhaps you're right.'

'I may be. Tell me, did you have a good holiday?' It was a safe question. She was very brown. But why had she kept it all so secret?

'Lovely, thanks.' She smiled again. Her mouth was full of wonderful, even, white gnashers.

'Good,' I smiled back. Dared I exploit her good humour? 'I hate to ask, but something's worried me ever since – since the police spoke to me about your safe. You know now that I didn't touch it, and for one very good reason. I don't know where on earth it is!'

Another smile. 'Not so much on earth as *in* earth. When I found you on your knees in the choir, I was sure you'd found it. Follow me. It's where no JCB will ever reach it, not unless they knock the church down first.'

And there it was, under the choir carpet. I'd been kneeling on it all the time.

Some of my kneeling seemed to have worked. The news of Josie was good. She was at last moved into an ordinary ward. Now I was no longer suspected of assaulting her, Griff and I were finally allowed to visit her.

She looked desperately frail, but brushed aside all our sympathy. 'They say I shall get a lot of compensation for this,' she announced gleefully. 'So I shall have a big party. Well, not too big. Not when you think of the size of my house. But I want all my friends there.' Her smile faded. She took my hand and held it. 'I just wish I knew why someone should attack me. I've only ever tried to do good.'

'Of course you have. I wish I knew, Josie. I know someone was trying to get me into trouble. Maybe they did it to frame me.'

'I didn't believe for one second it was you. And to think

they wouldn't let you even speak to me, let alone come and see me! I don't understand people these days.'

Was she talking about the attacker or the police? I wasn't sure, so I said, 'It'll all come out at the trial; at least, I hope so.'

She smiled again and rubbed her hands together. 'Bring it on, that's what I say. Now, how's that handsome man I said was too old for you?'

'Still with his wife,' I said firmly.

'He never! Oh, sweetheart, what a shame. When will you get a nice young man you can call your own?'

'All in good time,' Griff said helpfully. 'And you know I can't spare her yet.'

She looked him in the eye. 'You'll have to let her go one day, Griff. Tell you what, you and I can move in together. You, me and Aidan. How about that?' she cackled.

Although it was two weeks since Morris had left for Lyon, Griff still treated me as an invalid. Today he had decided we were having a treat. We'd packed up our stall after a quite profitable fair in Beaconsfield and by rights should have headed for home. But he'd booked us into an hotel – 'I hate the M25 on Sundays,' he said, by way of an excuse – and promised that we'd travel slowly on Monday, after the beginning of the week rush had died down.

By now I was smelling a rat, but I'd always indulged Griff, so why change? I was a bit surprised, however, when he navigated us in the opposite direction from home north west, to Aylesbury, and then a bit further.

'Claydon House?'

'Why not? You've never been there, and it must be twenty years since I last came.'

I thought of the lengthy queue of repairs and said nothing. I didn't even say anything when he burrowed in the back of the van and produced a large carrier bag, which he parked on the front step while he produced a chiffon scarf to tie over my eyes. We were to play Blind Man's Buff, were we?

But once inside, suddenly able to see again, I could see why we were here. Whoever had designed the items in that poor, tatty folio, had designed everything here.

'Here you are. Luke Lightfoot heaven,' Griff said, as if he'd done all the wonderful carving, all the exquisite plasterwork himself.

So it was. We wandered round laughing like kids.

I found we were to have lunch with the regional administrator, all very formal, with excellent food and wine. Then there were photos for their national magazine. Why not? The folio had come home, and here it would stay.

We toasted it with champagne at home that evening. We toasted Luke Lightfoot and his weird ideas. We toasted Freya and Robin and their wedding by special licence the next weekend. Talk about marrying in haste! All his friends must have prayed that neither would ever have cause to repent at leisure. But Robin had got it into his head that the baby must be born in wedlock, and Freya was equally insistent that she wouldn't walk down the aisle or even into a registry office with a visible bulge. Tom, the rural dean who'd been so kind to me, would officiate. Half of me was almost surprised he was a real person, not some sort of guardian angel. Although they wanted a small, private ceremony, I couldn't see them getting away with that, not with Fi to organize all the parishioners in the benefice.

We didn't so much toast as raise a glass to poor X, as I still thought and spoke of Graham Parker. As soon as the coroner released his body, he would be buried yards from where he'd been killed. Robin would take the service, of course. While Griff insisted he would keep his promise and pay for the funeral itself, a number of other dealers he'd provided with car-boot bargains had chipped in for a memorial stone.

Then, as if to shake off our sudden gloom, we toasted the snuffbox, and anything else we could think of. Eventually, with a cautious eye in my direction, Griff toasted Morris and me. There wasn't very much champagne left in my glass, but I lifted it anyway.